The dragon ~~~~~ skin. Then, slow~~~~~ ~~~~~ Profion . . . and stopped.

Its ruby eyes glowed with a hellish fire. It stared at Profion with a hatred as old as the age of Man, perhaps older still. Profion returned its glare with a small, triumphant smile.

"I told you, Damodar. I *told* you it could be done."

DUNGEONS & DRAGONS
THE MOVIE

LOOK FOR THESE EXCITING TITLES!

DUNGEONS & DRAGONS
THE MOVIE

Neal Barrett, Jr.

THE MAKING OF
DUNGEONS & DRAGONS
THE MOVIE

John Baxter

DUNGEONS & DRAGONS
THE MOVIE
(YOUNG ADULT NOVELIZATION)

Steve Atley

DUNGEONS & DRAGONS

THE MOVIE

NEAL BARRET JR.

DUNGEONS & DRAGONS®
THE MOVIE

©2000 Wizards of the Coast, Inc.

Cartography by Dennis Kauth
First Printing: November 2000
Library of Congress Catalog Card Number: 00-101970

9 8 7 6 5 4 3 2 1

US ISBN: 0-7869-1493-4
UK ISBN: 0-7869-2605-8
620-T21439

U.S., CANADA,
ASIA, PACIFIC, & LATIN AMERICA
Wizards of the Coast, Inc.
P.O. Box 707
Renton, WA 98057-0707
+1-800-324-6496

EUROPEAN HEADQUARTERS
Wizards of the Coast, Belgium
P.B. 2031
2600 Berchem
Belgium
+32-70-23-32-77

Visit our web site at **www.wizards.com**

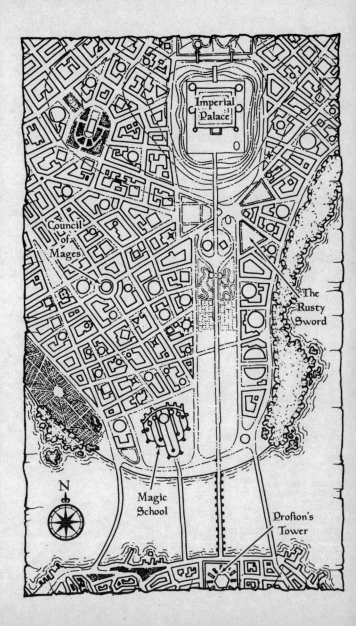

Imperial Palace

Council of Mages

The Rusty Sword

N

Magic School

Profion's Tower

She woke up dying, woke from the cold eternal night, woke strangling on the dark and viscous bile, on the vile, odorous corruption that coursed through her veins, through the wings pressed tight against her sides, through her head and her heart, through her thick and scaly hide. The deadly fluids filled her throat, filled her lungs, spilled from razored jaws, coursed down her breast, bathed her talons and her claws.

She ripped and she tore, thrashing frantically about, struggling through the fleshy shell that held her back. She had lived a thousand lives and died a thousand deaths. She knew this horror was the way of all her race, that she was born with a rage, cold, pure, and undiluted by the small, pitiful emotions of men and creatures of lesser kind.

Blood was made to kill her. Rage kept her alive. If rage was too weak to conquer blood, then she would die. Thus it had ever been, and thus it would ever be. For only a dragon whose anger is afire could come into the world and live again. . . .

CHAPTER 1

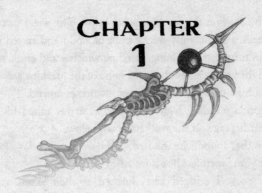

In a place far below the deep and stony roots of the city, in a darkness darker than night, a thousand ancient tunnels, shafts, and murky passageways cut a tortured, twisted maze. Here lay the bowels of mighty Sumdall, greatest city of the Empire of Izmer. Most of these ways were long forgotten, like the trail of some massive, blind, and pallid worm. Many were clogged with the mud, silt, and secrets of centuries past—traitors, lovers, counts who laughed at kings, kings who drank a cup of poisoned wine, bits of offal, slops and mire, and over all the waste of some magician's gross miscarried spell. Some of these forgotten ways carried sluggish waters through the depths of stone and out again, finally emptying into the river that crossed Oldtown below the city walls. Other tunnels led into the unknown dark, and where they went, none but those dark things that dwelled there knew, and no one from the world of light had been so foolish as to brave their depths in generations.

In one small part of this subterranean dark, torches shed a pale, unhealthy light on the brackish water below. The water turned a waterwheel, a big, clumsy device built of wood and rusted iron, which, in turn, drove whining, grinding winches and crude metal gears. In the hollow cavern here, the noise of the machine was bone jarring, a high-pitched shriek that set the nerves on end.

The man standing high above the waterway raised his fists and spent his rage on the workers down below.

"Stop that sound!" he shouted. "I'll have it stopped—*now*, or I'll have your worthless heads for it!"

The workers cringed and clutched at their skulls as the terrible pain of the spell turned their heads to molten lead. Quickly, they stumbled over the waterwheel with buckets of oil, swabs of heavy grease, rags, wedges, and wooden pegs, anything that came to mind, anything to avoid the wrath of the man again.

Profion muttered under his breath. The noise didn't stop. It never did, but it softened for a moment to a less annoying pitch. He hated—no, *loathed*—the miserable workers, the half-men he'd created with tiny brains and massive legs and arms. They were ugly and vulgar, and daily they tended to fall in the fast-moving rods and gears. Still, when they didn't kill themselves, they managed to do a halfway decent job.

"You won't have to look at them after today," said the man at his side, seeming to read his thoughts. "I'll have them removed."

Profion showed the man a cutting smile. "Don't be in such a hurry to perform your *duties*, Damodar. I shall let you know in good time."

"Of course," Damodar said, lowering his eyes. "You must know, sire, I would never act without your word."

"No, of course you wouldn't, dear friend."

Profion looked away, knowing the greed, the hatred in Damodar's eyes, feeling the murder in the man's heart.

He was no longer interested in Damodar. His eyes, his every thought was on the sight below. At the heart of the strange device, a cylindrical rod somewhat longer than Profion's forearm was spinning at breakneck speed. The foreman of the work crew, a human, glanced up at Profion. Profion nodded. The foreman shouted commands, and the machine began to howl, shrieking up to high-pitched whine. The spinning rod was now no more that a blur.

Profion watched it, his eyes black as stone, his hands clutched tightly around the railing, every bone, every atom in his body vibrating with the intensity of his power, of his need.

Behind him, Damodar waited. No expression crossed his features, but Profion knew his feelings well. Damodar's eyes, his mouth, no part of his body would betray him. He had not gained his high position by letting a weakness such as emotion give him away.

A stranger seeing the two together might think he had come upon two fearsome night creatures of the air, creatures with darkness in their hearts and black murder in their eyes. Indeed, both of the men were predators.

Profion, the eagle, would, to fill his needs, tear at his kill without mercy in the sight of other men. His clothing mirrored his manner and his soul. He wore a blood-red cowl that swept like wings past his shoulders. Under that flowed a purple robe of spider silk cut into intricate patterns, squares, angles, and twists, a pattern near dizzying to the eyes for those who did not know what they meant. Finally, and perhaps most frightening of all, were the two mantles of runics that trailed from his chest to his knees. If anyone was fool enough to doubt the power of the most feared mage in the land, the runes would tell the tale.

And Damodar? If Profion was an eagle, then Damodar, with his lean and angular face, his haughty manner and his quiet and deadly grace, was a predator of a different kind. Men like Profion, who sought power and honor for themselves, were very good at that. Damodar was a raptor who flies in shadow, in the dusk and in the dawn, a scavenger, cunning and sly, who feeds on the kill of his betters and has no heart for meeting those foes who might deign to strike back.

Profion watched the spinning rod, his eyes bright with fascination at the energy, the force, locked in that rippling blur of motion. He waited for the moment and cursed the seconds that held him from his prize.

Too long. It has been too long.

Taking one deep breath and then another, he threw back his head and slowly raised his arms, the long magician's robe filling with the rush of heated air from the humming, high undulation of the machine. His lips scarcely moved as he chanted a toneless spell, words nearly lost in the countless ages of time.

Behind him, braced against the shadowy walls, soldiers of Damodar's Crimson Brigade shifted uneasily and muttered among themselves. Without looking at them, Damodar moved his head a bare quarter inch. At once, every warrior there went silent as the dead.

The spinning rod began to glow, pulsing like a living thing and shifting from one brilliant color to the next. Profion's arms began to tremble. His hands began to shake. Dim auras of power danced like tiny veins of lightning about his fingers and his wrists. The lightning brightened and expanded to a nebula of energy, a swirling, angry mass of atoms set afire, a cloud of tiny stars.

With a sudden, blinding flare, a jagged beam of blue light exploded from Profion's fingers and struck the spinning rod. Profion shuddered, closed his eyes, and opened them again. The rod began to glow, throbbing first a thousand, then a million times a second, so fast it appeared to no longer have motion at all, but Profion felt every pulse like a hammering in his soul.

Sweat darkened Profion's brow, stinging the sunken hollows of his face.

The rod, now bright and searing as a captured sun, rose slowly from its nest among the cogs, gears, and singing wires of Profion's device. At once, the machine gave a final, clattering sigh and hummed down the scale to a stop.

Profion stepped forward, and the rod dimmed to a pale red glow, the color of embers in a late evening fire. He stopped, hesitated an instant, then grasped the rod in his hand. The stunned, wide-eyed workers shrank back in shadow, nearly mad with fear.

Profion smiled and let his hands run over the surface of the rod, a surface smoother than the rarest eastern silks, slick and polished as any glass.

"At last, it's done. It is done!"

His words struck the cavern walls and came back.

"It's done . . .

" . . . done . . .

" . . . DONE!"

He looked for Damodar and nodded in grudging satisfaction. Damodar and his Crimson Brigade were gone, as Profion had willed them to be.

Someday pride will prove too great a temptation, Profion

thought, and then he'll disobey, and I will find great joy in that.

Holding the precious rod against his chest, Profion climbed the steep stairway from the now silent machine, from the dank and sluggish river. The stairwell circled up to a high, weathered stone tower that loomed above the heights of the city. Even before he entered the large room, the terrible odor reached out and drew him in, held him, and smothered him in its loathsome shroud. It was the smell of rotting flesh, the stench of offal, the heavy, cloying smell of smoke and fire. Most unnerving of all was the stink of anger, unremitting rage, and hatred of every living thing in the universe.

Three of Damodar's guards stood at rigid attention on each side of a high, rough-hewn arch. Profion loathed the creatures of the Crimson Brigade. Damodar chose only the most debased, ruthless men in the Empire for this corps of villains, men whose only virtue was their blind obedience to Damodar. He dressed them in outlandish uniforms of brilliant scarlet, garish armor, and spiked iron helms. As a final stroke of irony—to amuse Damodar himself, Profion guessed—he adorned these brutes with the hideous half-masks of horned and snouted beasts, creatures both real and imagined, whose very visage struck terror in all who faced their wrath.

"Serves a purpose," Profion muttered to himself, as he passed the ugly louts and marched into the great room. But they move at Damodar's will, he thought, and there's danger there.

Past the high arch, Profion turned down a narrow corridor to his left and into the vast central hall, a large, stone-walled room that stretched up into the dark.

He stopped and let his glance sweep the great room. Massive iron doors stood at the far end of the chamber, a door lined with broad bands of hammered metal, pounded into greater strength, and finally pierced with iron bolts the size of a man's head.

On each side of the door stood seven half-naked workers, each grasping lengths of an enormous chain connected to a derrick that held a massive winch. The workers were larger than those who worked Profion's device down below. These fellows were broad of chest and back, bred for strength alone, with scarcely any wit at all.

Profion glanced at Damodar, who stood before a full troop of Crimson Guards, long lances and cleaving axes at the ready.

"Ah, Damodar, nicely done," Profion said, with only a touch of acid in his voice. "However, there will be no need for weapons. We will not be assaulted here."

Only Damodar's eyes betrayed the slightest hint of displeasure, and only one such as Profion could have read what was there.

"They only salute your success," Damodar said. "They would beg me to tell you they are honored to be present at such a wondrous occasion."

"Are they, indeed?" Profion relished the moment, for there was half a truth in Damodar's words. Even those ugly masks could not hide the guards' awe of the mage's power and the moment that was to come. Every one of the overdressed brutes was as frightened as the poor devils hunched by the iron door. Only Damodar himself showed no trace of fear, but Damodar, Profion knew, had barely enough warmth in his heart to feel anything at all.

With a last glance about the room, Profion faced the great door.

"Now," he said, his voice scarcely rising above a whisper, "now we begin. Release him."

The workers stared, dull eyes wide with fear. Near witless they might be, but they knew what lay beyond the door.

"Do you hear me?" Profion's form seemed to grow and swell with sudden rage. "I said release him. *Obey me now!*"

The workers whimpered, sweat coursing down their backs, their limbs quivering with fright, but they did as they were told, for their fear of the terror Profion could bring down upon them was beyond anything that lurked behind the door.

Grasping the bars of the great winch, the workers strained against the weight of the chains. With a deep, metallic rumble that shook the very floor, the heavy iron door began to rise.

At once, a black plume of smoke billowed from under the door, curled like a creature alive, blossomed into a greasy cloud, and choked the vast chamber with the foul odor of gastric vapors, putrid flesh, sulfur, and pitch.

The workers cried out and began to flee. Profion stopped them with a single gesture, a motion of the hand that clutched their hearts and left them gasping for breath.

Something massive threw its weight against the iron door, slamming against the heavy portal until the stones that held it in began to shake. Something beyond the door bellowed with a roar from the deepest pits of hell.

"Yes!" Profion shouted. "Come out and show me your strength! Come out and face me with all your fury!"

Profion glanced at Damodar. Damodar hadn't wavered. The line of Crimson Guards was not as straight as it had appeared a moment before, but to their credit, not a man of them broke and ran.

The iron door clanged open. A deafening roar of rage echoed through the room. The dragon's massive head appeared through a veil of smoke, then a ponderous foot slammed against the floor. The thing was a beautiful nightmare, every man's horror and hope, a great and writhing beast with a hide of gleaming golden scales. Standing solidly on its taloned feet, it arched its furrowed back and lashed its tail about like a cutting whip.

It stood, then, in all its height, leathery wings outstretched. Lowering its monstrous, serpentine head, it looked directly into Profion's eyes.

Profion was close enough to smell its choking breath and count every tooth in its cruel jaws. The dragon rumbled deep within its throat, stretched its neck, and brought its snout within an inch of the mage's chest.

Profion stood his ground. He didn't move and didn't blink. To move, to show fear now . . .

A terrified yell broke the near silence of the room. The dragon jerked straight up at once. One of the workers, blind with fear, had bolted across the room.

The dragon seemed to move in a blur. A searing blast of white-hot fire exploded from the creature's jaws, reached out, and caught the fleeing man. He shrieked and burst into flame, flailing his arms about as he stumbled down the stairs. In three heartbeats, the screams had weakened, and then died.

The dragon twisted its long neck and faced Profion again. It breathed slowly, and with each breath came a small burst of flame.

Fire left from its wrath, Profion wondered, or what it has in store for me?

As if in answer, the dragon dug its great talons into the floor, grinding mortar and crushing stone. It threw back its massive head and loosed a frightening roar. With uncanny speed, its jaws snapped open, and it came at Profion . . .

. . . Came at the mage and stopped, stunned and bewildered by the small, insignificant human in its path.

Profion stood rigid, unmoving, the rod extended straight at the dragon's open jaws. A low, menacing rumble came from the creature's chest. The rod began to glow, pulsing in Profion's grasp. The steady, measured oscillation seemed to hold the dragon transfixed. Profion never looked away from the beast, answering its malevolent stare with a force that came from deep within, a mage's practiced power and the strength of the magic rod, an instrument forged in fire that now belonged to him.

"Come. Come to me," Profion whispered. "Come to me . . . *now.*"

The dragon hesitated, muscles tensing beneath its leathery skin. Then, slowly, it took three steps toward Profion . . . and stopped.

Its ruby eyes glowed with a hellish fire. It stared at Profion with a hatred as old as the age of Man, perhaps older still. Profion returned its glare with a small, triumphant smile.

"I told you, Damodar. I *told* you it could be done."

"Great mage," Damodar said softly, "never did I doubt your power."

"Hah!" Profion turned on Damodar with a scornful burst of laughter. "You thought that brute would roast me for supper. A little tough and stringy, perhaps, but a mage all the same." Profion brought a finger to his chin. "It is said, and I doubt not it's true, that next to virgins, a dragon prefers the flavor of an experienced, mature mage. We're full of tasty spells, you know."

Damodar didn't answer. He watched Profion as he strutted about the room, now and then glaring at his newly captured dragon in disdain.

12

"You'll stand there and starve to death if I will it," Profion boasted from across the floor. He reached out and touched the dragon on its nose, turned, and loosed a great roar of laughter at what he'd done.

"I've tamed it! You were there. You saw it happen, my friend."

"You have the power of the Immortals," Damodar said, awestruck. "You can control a dragon."

"No, not 'a dragon.' " Profion turned his dark eyes on Damodar again. "*Dragons.* An army of dragons at my command. An army that will crush everything in its path once that prancing fool of an emperor is dead. Maybe I'll feed his flesh to this fellow right here. You'd like that, wouldn't you, beast? A little bite of royalty for a snack?" Profion tapped the dragon on the nose and glanced at Damodar. "That little matter of the emperor's imminent demise. There will be no problem there, I trust?"

"Even as we speak," Damodar said.

"Ah, good, good." Profion leaned down, as if to whisper in the dragon's flaring ear. "Go on, hate me, despise me for what I've done to you. I want you filled with every bit of your terrible anger, every ounce of your rage."

Damodar held his silence and watched the great mage drink his full measure of glory.

CHAPTER 2

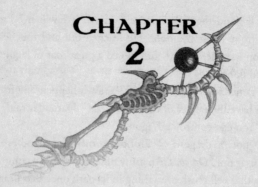

Ridley watched the girl squeeze her way through the noisy crowd. He admired her courage and prayed she'd make it all in one piece. Braving the wall-to-wall mob at the Ferret and Fox was no easy task. Nigh impossible, Ridley thought, and risky at that, if you happened to be incredibly tall, lean, and blessed with good looks. If, on top of that, you were holding six heavy clay mugs above your head . . .

Now that was something else again.

When she finally broke through to Ridley's table, he saw she was well worth the wait—silver-green eyes and tiny, golden spiders in her raven-black hair. Her shoulders were bare, and her skin was the color and scent of spice.

"I'm glad you made it," Ridley said. "Now that you're here, you shouldn't try to get back. It's a whole lot safer if you'll sit down here with me."

"Is it now? I'd not be certain of that." The girl laughed and set a mug of ale on the scarred table top. When she moved, the golden spiders danced and made a crownlet in her hair.

"What's your name, then?" Ridley asked. "I haven't seen you here before. I'd remember if I had."

"Alycia. And you haven't seen me, sir, as I started only tonight."

"I'm Ridley, and I swear on all the gods that I have never met such a beautiful lady in my life."

"You're just saying that now, but I'm right pleased you did."

"Tell me, Alycia, how do you keep those spiders in your hair? I'd think they'd get away or bite."

"It's a small spell is all." She lightly patted her hair. "I wanted eight, but they only had six."

"Only six?"

"You're very nice, Ridley, but I can't sit around drinking ale like some I could name. I have work to do."

"Well, of course you do. I only—"

Alycia was gone, swept up in the crowd. Ridley sipped his ale, made a sour face, sniffed at the mug, and set it down.

"If you're not going to drink that, I will."

Snails suddenly appeared across the table. He carried a nicely carved chair in one hand and a dirty cotton sack in the other. Setting down the chair, he perched on the edge and, without waiting for an answer, finished off Ridley's ale.

"Good," he said, wiping a line of foam off his lips. "Best ale in town. Who's the lovely lass? I confess I've not seen her before."

"She's too tall for you."

"Oh? But just right for you?"

"We talked. She has spiders in her hair. What's in the sack?"

"A lady's mirror—partially intact—two fresh apples, a twist of yellow cheese, and brand new barber's shears. I doubt they've trimmed half a dozen heads."

"And the chair?"

Snails looked blank. "What chair? This chair?"

"That chair. They don't have chairs in the Ferret and Fox. They have benches—like the one I'm sitting on—not chairs."

Ridley stared at Snails a long moment, rolled his eyes, and looked at the sooty ceiling.

"You stole it. You stole a chair."

"What's the matter with that? There's never any place to sit in here."

"Get up. Leave the chair here."

"What for? I just got here. I haven't finished your ale."

"Yes you have," Ridley said, standing and glaring at his friend. "Get up, Snails. We're leaving right now."

Snails stood and followed. He knew Ridley well. When he got some fool idea in his head, the best thing to do was listen and let him talk it out. After a while, he'd go back to being the same old Ridley again.

*   *   *   *   *

The air outside was heavy with the smells of the city—garbage smells, food smells, smells from the people passing by. Now and then, the familiar odor of a corpse wafted up on the hot evening breeze—some poor soul murdered and tossed in the river for half a copper.

Still, Ridley told himself, a breath outside was almost refreshing after the Ferret and Fox, and that was a most depressing thought.

He leaned against the stony tavern wall, slapped at a giant mosquito on his neck, and brought his palm away red. He sniffed the air again and decided he was wrong. The smells were very little better outside. The foul odors of the river were particularly strong in the lower, older part of the city. The Ferret and Fox was only a short spit away from the damp stone quay where every sort of unseemly dreg washed up on the shore.

From the front of the tavern, he could see one of the heavy stone bridges that linked Oldtown with the opulent domes and towers of Sumdall City—or, he thought, cut off the very rich from the multitude of poor. On the far side of the river, behind the high walls, secure from the swarming masses below, lived the wealthy merchants and traders, high lords of the land, powerful mages, and the royals themselves.

Ridley let his gaze wander up the dark, massive walls, the battlements ridged with sharp crenellations like the jaws of some enormous beast. The capital of the empire was ageless, stretching back to a time when short, bronze-armored warriors had come down from the north to conquer. The riders themselves were still in the blood of the people, descendants of spoilers who'd tired of pillaging far from home and settled down themselves.

Through the long years, through wars and plagues, through fire and flood, one city was built on the ruins of the next. Now, it was a maze of dark and narrow streets, grand avenues, and frail, twisted stairways that wound like serpents through the jumble of twisted keeps, golden spires and gilded domes, great vaulted halls of emperors, and shadowy tombs of careless kings. Parapets, palaces, and castles of marble and ancient stone perched on precarious heights as if they'd simply sprouted there. In the last faint moments of the day, a thick and ominous haze turned the towers of Sumdall a grim and ominous shade of red.

While Oldtown was nearly dark at this hour, the portals of the denizens of power were still ablaze. What was it like to live there, Ridley wondered, to drink fine wine from crystal instead of sour ale from clay, to eat all the succulent, crispy pig you could hold, all the fruit pies with syrupy juices bubbling up through the crust? Would he ever tire of that, become bored with silken underclothes and warm fur jackets made to fit his form alone?

"No, by damn, I would not," Ridley said, certain he could smell a berry pie, instead of rotting vegetables floating by.

"What's the matter with you?" Snails asked. "What are you muttering about?"

"I'm not muttering," Ridley said. "I'm thinking is all."

Snails let out a breath. "That's what I was afraid of. Ridley, I'm asking you nicely, please don't do this again."

"Do what?"

"You know. *Think* about things, things that I don't want to do. Nothing good ever comes of this, and usually something very bad."

Ridley turned to his friend, his eyes reflecting the light from the portals above.

"You know what we are, Snails? We're thieves. Great dragon dung, Snails, we steal *chairs*. Chairs, apples, broken clocks, jewels made of glass, old men's purses, which, by the way, are empty most of the time."

"Barber shears," Snails reminded him, "and cheese. Good shears and very recent cheese!"

"Exactly. That's what I'm talking about."

Ridley reached out and got a firm grip on Snails's arms. "We're through, Snails. We are not going to waste the rest of our lives. We're not going to do this anymore."

Snails stared. "We're not?"

"No. We most certainly are not."

Snails was horrified. His features seemed to collapse. He looked as if some terrible pain had just struck him in the heart, which, indeed, it had.

"Ridley, don't say that, please. I'm a thief, that's all I am. That's all I know how to do. My old dad was a thief, and mama was too. If I can't steal anymore . . ."

"Hey, old friend." Ridley released Snails's arms and gave him a playful slap on the cheek. "You're not listening, or I'm not talking straight. I didn't say we weren't going to steal anymore. I said we're not going to do what we *did*."

"No?" Snails was more confused than ever now.

"No. We are not going to be common thieves, stealing trash from people who own little more than we do. That's a disreputable— a *despicable*—thing to do, and we're not going to shame ourselves again."

Ridley paused and glanced up once again at the dark and lofty heights, at the pure yellow light, light as bright as gold, winking from the crimson-tainted towers far above.

"We're going to steal from them," he said, "from those fat and lazy louts eating pork and pies up there."

Snails grabbed at his chest. For a moment, his heart seemed to stop.

"Up there? Oh, no, Ridley! I don't want to go up there. I'm perfectly happy down here. I like stealing apples. I *like* stealing chairs—"

"Stop! Stop it, now." Ridley draped his arm over Snails's shoulder and walked him farther from the tavern door. "There're riches up there simply lying about, waiting to be taken. Rings, gems, silver plates, goblets of gold . . ."

". . .Thieves like us, hanging in the streets," Snails finished.

"Not thieves like us. Thieves who are ignorant, dense, thieves who don't have a plan."

Snails felt his heart stop again. "Gods protect me, you don't have another *plan*. Please say you don't have a plan."

"Ah, but I do, and it's one you'll thank me for, Snails, when you're wearing velvet trousers and silver buckles on your shoes."

"I don't want silver buckles on my shoes."

"How do you know? You never tried 'em before." He slapped his companion heartily on the back. "I'll see you later on. I've got a matter of importance to attend."

"Like what?"

"Like a lady named Alycia, who serves the worst ale in town."

Snails opened his mouth to speak, but Ridley was already gone.

"It's always that way," he muttered to himself. "If I got a word in, we wouldn't be in trouble all the time."

A sudden burst of laughter reached him from the Ferret and Fox. Snails looked up at the high battlements of Sumdall City, and in that instant, something cold touched the back of his neck and crawled all the way down his spine. This time, he would not let Ridley talk him into some hapless venture, some hopeless scheme.

There was nothing he wanted in Sumdall City. Nothing waited there for a snatcher of cheeses, a stealer of chairs, nothing but a dark and untimely end. . . .

CHAPTER 3

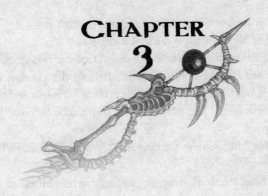

Damodar was bored but didn't dare show it. Taming the dragon wasn't enough for Profion. He had to humble the creature, humiliate it, drain it of all its majesty and strength. He would stalk around the monster, first one way and then the next, taunting it, cursing it under his breath. Now and then he would pause, inches from the dragon's great nose, and stab at the air with his staff, lunging back and forth, as if the two were engaged in a courtly duel.

The dragon, frozen in the mage's spell, scarcely moved except to breathe, its massive sides heaving like a bellows feeding a flaming forge. Its blood-red eyes, though, followed its tormentor's every move, and the cold, unrelenting hatred in those eyes gave even Damodar pause.

No man could say what thoughts coursed through a dragon's brain. Did they truly think like men, or merely with the cold, calculating cunning of a cat—an alien, unreasoning creature with little more than murder on its mind?

The latter, most likely, Damodar thought, though there were

tales from ancient times, true or not, one couldn't say—

God of Night! What is the fool doing now?

In spite of his awesome powers, Damodar wondered if Profion was addled or simply mad. Raising the glowing rod above his head, the mage spread his arms as he might embrace the universe itself. The purple sleeves of his robe billowed like silken wings.

"Come," he spoke to the dragon. "Come, I tell you. Follow. Follow me."

The beast trembled, struggling mightily to resist. It raised one taloned claw, moved it slowly forward at Profion's command . . .

"Yes, follow!" Profion demanded, his voice as harsh as a rasp on iron, "Do as I tell you. You have no will now, dragon. Your will is mine!"

Its claws mere inches from the ground, the dragon fought to ward off the mage's power. Every muscle and leathery tendon strained to break free. Its jaws opened wide, and a viscous green fluid dripped from its mouth. One claw, touching the stone floor now, bowed to Profion's will.

The mage roared in triumph, sweeping his glowing rod in a circle about his head. The dragon was his! He had broken its spirit, shattered its power with his spell!

At that precise moment, the creature suddenly stopped and balked, as if the magician's victory cry had brought it to life again.

"Follow!" Profion shouted, his eyes ablaze with anger. "You . . . will . . . follow . . . *me!*"

Once again, he whipped the bright rod above his head and thrust it like a lance directly at the dragon's red eyes.

The dragon quivered, fighting the rod's spell, and from deep within its fiery soul, it summoned a magic of its own. Its ruby eyes faded then glowed with a pale, unearthly green, a green as cold as glacial ice, cold and deadly as the space between the stars.

Profion drew in a breath and quickly stepped back from the creature, its body now webbed in a shimmering azure veil. Profion stared in disbelief at the rod in his hand. Its glow suddenly vanished, all its power gone. Now he held nothing but a dull gray bar of iron.

The dragon shook its great head in fury, spread its great wings, and stretched its scaly form above its small tormentor.

Furious, Profion lashed out with his hand, and unseen magic lashed out. Wood splintered with a shriek, and the winch gave way. The loose chains lashed at the air, and the massive gate thundered down. The dragon bellowed in pain as tons of weighted iron crushed its skull. The fire of the dragon's eyes faded, flickered, and died.

Profion stared at the useless rod, then tossed it to the floor in disgust. The terrified workers fled in panic, spilling over one another to get away from the site. The monster seemed somehow more frightening dead than alive.

"Clearly, the metal was impure," Profion scowled. "If it had been tempered as I instructed . . . There's another, better avenue. Another way."

Suddenly aware of the howling mob behind him, he turned and glared at Damodar. "Get those fools back here. And get that stinking carcass out of here!"

Damodar had anticipated his command. One pair of guards and then another pounded after the workers. Some were running in circles, some had simply collapsed on the stone floor, too frightened to move.

"I'm not finished with this," Profion said, glaring at the enormous, fetid corpse. "No one has truly seen the powers I can bring to bear."

"Of course," Damodar said, with a slight bow of his head. "I'm sure it won't cause us great delay."

"I assure you it will not." Profion paused to make sure he had Damodar's full attention. "Make certain that anyone who played a part in this . . . *unfortunate experiment* does not live out the day. I do not want this business to reach those chattering jays at court." Profion caught the slight tension at the corner of Damodar's lips. "That includes your people who were here today. I'm certain you have more than enough of the brutes to take their place."

"As you wish, sire." Damodar said, swallowing his rage, knowing he had given himself away. He looked from Profion then, relieved to see one of the mage's liegemen coming swiftly across the stone floor. With a startled glance at the dead dragon, the man bowed before his master.

"My lord, forgive the disturbance. I thought you should know—"

"Know what?" Profion said, making no effort to hide his irritation.

"The Emperor, sire. I must inform you he is dead."

"How terrible," Profion said, darting a look at Damodar. "How could such a thing happen?"

"The physicians feel it was poison of a sort, my lord, though none can name the potion or how it found its way to the Emperor's favorite wine."

"And our lovely princess?" Damodar asked.

"Mourning her loss, sire. She has, of course, been quickly sworn in as Empress of all Izmer."

"We share her sorrow," Profion said. "Now leave us. And say nothing of what you may have seen here."

"Yes, my lord."

Profion waited until the courier was out of sight.

"Well and swiftly done, my friend. When we're rid of her, I'll see you are suitably rewarded."

"To serve your needs is all I ask, lord. However, if I may dare to observe, ridding ourselves of the girl may not be a simple thing. After the Emperor's . . . *accident*, the palace guards will be around her like bees about a hive."

"I expect you'll think of something," Profion said, jabbing a finger in Damodar's chest. "Surely one of your costumed apes can squirm his way past the palace guard."

Damodar's flesh crawled at the mage's touch. No one in the Empire, not even Profion himself, had ever dared lay a hand on him before. He could not abide another's touch, as he was certain Profion was aware.

"And while my *ape* is slicing the lady's throat," he blurted out before he could stop to think, "perhaps I should have him pick up the imperial scepter as well?"

Profion showed him a wicked smile, delighted at Damodar's obvious discomfort.

"I forgive your outburst," the mage said. "I know you meant no disrespect, Damodar. You are much too wise and cautious for that. Leave the matter of the scepter to me. I'll take care of that. Summon the Council of Mages, immediately. Do so at once, and do it quietly, if you will."

"It will be done."

Damodar backed away and stalked quickly out of the hall. His guards followed, relieved to be away from dead dragons and mad magicians. It was not the kind of duty they craved, not the special, more enjoyable tasks Damodar had trained them for.

"You will not catch me sleeping again," Damodar muttered to himself as he made his way out of the chamber and down the spiral stairs. If only I didn't need him for a while. What a pleasure it would be to watch a dragon snatch him up.

A sudden, most interesting thought appeared in Damodar's head. Profion had said he wanted no one left alive who had seen his disastrous experiment. The young courier who'd brought the news of the Emperor's death . . . He hadn't actually *seen* very much. Still, best to follow Profion's orders, was it not?

He thought, then, of a way to keep the members of his own Crimson Guard alive. They would be sent at once to a far outpost of the Empire for a while. As Profion said, they were ugly louts, every one, no one would argue that. Who, then, could tell one horrid fellow from the next. . . ?

* * * * *

The great chamber was empty except for the stiffening carcass of the dragon crushed beneath the heavy metal door. Corruption of the flesh had already begun. Color had fled from the bright crimson scales, leaving a dismal, powdery shade of gray.

The odor of putrefaction was intense, an almost visible pall that would soon spread far beyond the chamber itself. The workers had been ordered to hack the body up and remove it, but they were slow to return, and no one in charge of the lot was anxious to lead them there.

It wasn't long before immense black rats scuttled out of the rocky walls and began to tear hungrily at the ruined flesh. On their heels came a horde of carrion creatures—beetles, roaches, fat blue flies.

A small trail of dragon's blood began to spread across the stone floor. It reached the mage's abandoned rod, stained it rusty red, trickled past the cobblestone hollows, out of the chamber, and down the spiral stairs. It was joined by another turgid stream, and then another, and another after that.

The stream moved faster, as its growing strength swept it down one level and the next, until it poured with a rush into the dimly lit room that held Profion's waterwheel.

As the bloody tide met the surface of the underground river, it hissed in protest, writhed like a living thing, boiled and sizzled, then burst into flame. With a great explosive rush that woke the new Empress from a troubled sleep, the fiery river raced through every tunnel, every sewer, every passage, every hollow it could find on its swift, relentless path down, down, and ever down, through the very roots of the ancient city itself.

CHAPTER 4

Ridley awoke with a start, waking just in time to duck. The crock full of wine shattered inches from his head. Rolling quickly over the hard stone floor, he went to his knees and scrambled for the door. Ridley could always find the door. Awake, asleep, in daylight or dark, a person who takes things from others and never gives them back has to know his way in, and more important still, he has to know his way out.

This time though, he was puzzled somewhat, for he hadn't stolen anything at all. The girl with green eyes and spiders in her hair had given him a kiss, and he'd given one back. Nothing more than that. They'd danced half the night at the Ferret and Fox, later at the Dog and the Duck, and somewhere else after that.

The lady liked to dance and didn't want to quit, but Ridley was dead on his feet and had to stop. All he remembered was coming back to her place, dropping to the floor, and taking a little nap.

It might be, he thought as another crock missed him by a hair, that she was somewhat upset about the nap.

"I'm sorry," he said, backing into a corner as she reached for a rather large pot. "I dozed off a minute, Elweeda, and I apologize for that."

"You *napped* on my floor an hour and a half," she shouted back, "and my name's not Elweeda! It's Alycia, you miserable oaf!"

"I really loved the dancing," he said. "You're light as a feather on your feet. If we could try again some time—"

The pot was already in flight, but Ridley was half a second faster and made it out the door. The missile shattered, and Alycia called him something he'd never heard before.

"I hate a misunderstanding," he muttered as he stumbled down the broken wooden stairs. "Takes all the cheer out of life, and spoils the day besides."

Outside, a sickly yellow moon was lost behind gray and somber clouds, clouds the color of a dead man's hide. Ridley guessed it was still a good hour till dawn. A thief preferred to work and play at night, have a nice breakfast, and then sleep the light away. This particular night, however, hadn't ended in a very pleasant way. Maybe, he thought, if he talked to Alycia, maybe stole her something nice, they could get back together again.

Stopping at a fountain in a narrow alleyway, he cupped his hands, splashed cool water in his face, and ran his fingers through a tangle of dark, thick hair. He was neither tall nor overly short, a man with rough-hewn features, nut-brown eyes, and a disarming smile that seemed to put everyone at ease. Well, most of the time, he thought, except for this one unfortunate night.

His clothing wasn't new, just this side of worn. A cape of mottled gray topped a vest, trousers, and shirt a dull brown. Leather gauntlets and boots that were comfortable—again, unless he'd danced the night away—were better than they looked. Across his waist he wore a thick crossbelt with a sword on one side and a dagger on the other—arms that were common to many a man who wanted to survive in such dangerous and unforgiving times.

This was the Ridley he wanted everyone to see, the Ridley no one could recall. No one remembered his features or his dress moments after they passed him in the street. A thief nobody forgets, Ridley knew, was a thief whose carcass would rot on a gibbet one day.

He yawned, flexed his hands, and stretched his aching limbs.

Breakfast seemed a good idea. Two plover eggs, fresh sugar-bread, and a slab of red beef that didn't smell bad. Badger Bob owed him for a fine bolt of cloth he'd filched from a silk caravan. The cloth was another chapter in Bob's eternal quest for the hand of the widow Gill.

"You need to see to that nail in your boot," announced Ridley without turning around, "the left one, I think, though I might be wrong about that."

"I know about the nail," Snails said as he approached. "I don't need you to be checking my boots. I can handle that myself."

Ridley knew Snails like he knew the back of his hand. He knew, at once, from the timbre of his voice, that his friend had a bone to pick and even knew what it might be.

"All right, let's get it out," he said. "I should have told you I might be a little late. I sort of forgot the time."

"You don't have to tell me. I'm well aware of that."

Ridley perched on the edge of the fountain, picking at a string that was hanging from his shirt. If I pull it, he decided, the whole thing will likely unravel. A shirt with a string is better than no shirt at all.

"You knew I was going back to the Ferret to meet a lady there.

You saw me doing that. Besides, Snails, when did I have to start checking my life with you? I'm fully grown; you might make a note of that."

A black cloud descended, settling on Snails, and with it a look in Snails's eyes that told Ridley there was more hurt than anger there.

"Look," he said quickly, "now I didn't mean that, I—"

"I sat up in that damned tree half the night," Snails said, "perched like a bloody bird on a limb. It was *cold* up there, Rid. I 'bout froze solid. Finally, after the guardsman near spotted me twice, I had the good sense to come down. If I hadn't, I guess I'd be up there still."

Ridley looked bewildered. "What were you doing sitting in a tree? Of all the dumb—" It suddenly struck him, and it all came back. "By the gods, Snails, I straight out forgot!" He groaned and slapped his head. "I did, friend, and I can only confess I'm a miserable soul and not worthy of you at all. Would you like to hit me, knock me to the ground? I'll give you a shot. No, now, I'll give you two. It's two I deserve, and maybe more than that."

"I wouldn't need two, and the offer's tempting, Ridley, I won't deny that. The fact is, I'd rather we'd gotten our hands on Meister Jax Winkit's brass candlesticks, which there's no chance at all of doing now, seeing as how he'll be back from Gonnetz Town this very day."

"I said I was sorry."

"You did. I heard you say it clear."

"We could have used those candlesticks, Rid."

"Surely we could."

"I believe that's what I said. I don't see as you need to be saying it again."

Ridley didn't answer. Snails stuck his hands in his pockets, kicked at the ground, then looked at Ridley again.

"So. How was your evening with the lovely what's-her-name?"

"Alycia. Not Elweeda, and why I called her that I'll never know."

"Women don't care for that. They like it when you truly know their name. Is that all you did? I've a feeling there's some more than that."

"I laid on the floor and took a nap."

"Took a *nap*. . . ?"

"I couldn't help it. We danced a great deal. I simply meant to rest for a while. That woman is possessed, Snails. There's a demon in her toes that won't let her stop."

Snails shook his head. "Doesn't sound to me like a love that's destined to last."

"You can safely say that."

"Sorry it didn't work out."

Ridley looked at Snails. He was almost certain that his friend's words were less than sincere, that instead, they betrayed a sense of pure delight.

"She's too tall for you. I think I told you that."

"I recall that you did. It appears, though, from what you've said, the lady's not looking for *height* as much as she is for a man who can stay awake a while."

Ridley looked at Snails's somber face, then burst out laughing and slapped his friend solidly in the chest.

"You've the best of me, as ever, Snails. Breakfast today is on me. Anything you like."

Snails frowned. "We're not going to eat at the Badger's, are we? I'd as soon do without as step in there again."

"The Badger?" Ridley looked stunned. "You think I'd take my dearest friend to a sewer like that? I'm hurt, Snails. I can't believe that even crossed your mind."

* * * * *

Night seemed reluctant to creep away. Only the shyest edge of dawn, a weak luminescence scarcely akin to light at all, found the river below the ancient walls.

Ridley and Snails were mere shades in this moment, neither daylight nor dark. Ridley was clad, as ever, in brown and a cape of mousy gray. Snails, hardly visible at all, was a crosshatch of every dull shade it was possible to wear. Patches on his jacket, patches on his shawl, patches on his worn mustard tights. Patches on the leather bags and sacks that hung loosely from his belt. Patches appeared on patches themselves.

Still, if anyone should doubt he could give as well as he got, they would do well to look at the well-dented sword that was always at his side.

"I feel," Ridley said, "it was just as well we missed Meister Winkit's candlesticks. I've given the matter some thought, and I'm no longer sure those items were really brass at all."

Snails smirked. "If they're not, what is it you think they are?"

"They might be pewter or some base metal made to look like brass. People do that all the time."

"Some people do, but why Meister Winkit, Rid? He's got more money than the king of the elves."

"I wouldn't go as far as that."

"No, but you would go far enough to make me think it was wise of you to while away your time with what's-her-name and not steal anything at all."

"Alycia. And I meant nothing of the sort."

"I am not as dull-witted as you think, Ridley. I might seem the fool, but that's simply a guise. I believe you have said many times—"

"I know what I've said: That it's wise to put honest folk at ease. And I don't think you're a fool, Snails. I cannot imagine you'd even think such a thing of me. All I— Double damnation, *what's that?*"

Ridley stopped. A fierce tongue of fire abruptly blossomed halfway up the city wall. As the two watched in awe, the flames hissed and roared, then spilled down the wall in a bloody waterfall, rushed past the battlements, and spilled into the river, where they steamed and sizzled for an instant before setting the water afire.

"Well," Snails said, "that's something new. I wonder what the fools dumped in the sewage up there."

Ridley and Snails took their cups and walked out the tavern door. "Whatever it is, I wish they wouldn't dump it down here."

"Now where else you think they're going to dump it, except on the poor? That's the way of life, the way it's always been."

In only a moment, the river quay was crowded with people, some still in their bedclothes, shaking their heads in anger and disbelief at the burning river coursing by.

"I'm telling you," Ridley said, "this has to be some twisted magic experiment gone seriously wrong. One of those crazy magicians up there. Some fool in a robe drops a snake in his pot when he should've dropped a frog. Likely happens all the time."

Snails made a noise in his throat. "Anything goes wrong up there, you blame it on mages. Every time it rains, it's somebody's spell."

"Well, when was the last time you saw a river catch fire?" Ridley watched the bright reflection of the river on the faces of the crowd. "Answer me that. You think the royal louts up there care if we all burn up down here? Take my word, friend, they surely do not. The people of Oldtown are good for taxes and working till their backs give out, and that's all."

Snails raised a brow. "When did you pay taxes? As far as that, when did you ever use your back?"

"Never to both, but a lot of good people do, and I respect them for that."

"Someone's got to do it, or else there'd be nothing to steal. Say, look at that! Strike me blind if that's not a pretty form and face."

Ridley watched, as a lady who clearly didn't belong in Oldtown at all stepped gracefully out of her carriage, sighed in desperation, and stomped her tiny foot. Her liveried driver scratched his head, gazing at the broken wheel. He plainly had no idea what to do, and no one in this part of town seemed anxious to help.

"She's a beauty, that's a fact," Snails said, "but the purse she's likely left in that carriage is prettier still. Go talk to her, Rid. Pretend to help the dolt with the wheels. While you're doing that—" Snails stopped, waving a hand in Ridley's face. "Are you there, friend? Are you hearin' what I said?"

"I am," Ridley answered, "but I'll tell you now, robbing that lady's a precious waste of time."

"It is? You mean, like me sitting up in a tree all night? Wasting time like that?"

"I said I was sorry, but I don't intend to say it again. You got a decent breakfast, and that's all of that." Ridley looked down at his boots, then up at the city walls. "We talked about this last night, remember? I said we're not going to be small timers anymore. We're going to be major thieves, Snails, and all the major thievery's up there."

Snails let out a breath. "I remember, and you know what *I* said: That I was perfectly happy stealing little things down here."

It was clear that Ridley's thoughts were far away, and Snails didn't like that at all. He felt the same queasy, empty feeling he'd felt the night before. Ridley was thinking again as he stared at the burning river, and that was always bad news.

"Ridley, old friend."

"The magic school. That's the thing to do."

"What is?" Snails looked pale. "Rid, you're scaring me. Please don't do this again."

"You gave me the idea yourself. About magic up there. You're a genius, Snails. You've hit it right square, and I'm proud of you, lad. I'd never have thought of it myself." Ridley paused and grinned. "We'll only do the one big caper, instead of all the smaller jobs. That makes a lot more sense than stealing Meister Winkit's candlesticks."

"Huh-uh. Not me, no sir." Snails raised his palms to shove the idea away. "I'm not going *near* Sumdall City, and I'm certainly not breaking into the magic school. That's absolutely insane, Rid! Just put the idea right out of your head."

"This is absolutely perfect," Ridley said, as if no one had spoken at all. He pointed out to the burning river. "Look at that, will you, Snails? Everyone will be busy putting out the fire, and do you think our precious mages will care if anyone gets hurt? I'd love to find a way to give those mages some payback."

"Oh, yeah," Snails said soberly. " 'Ridley the Savior.' That'll be the day. Look, Rid, things are the way they are, and there's nothing we can do to change it. All right? You got your haves and your have-nots. We are your gotta-gets."

"Hey, come on." Ridley gave Snails a friendly tap on the shoulder, which Snails just as quickly brushed away. "Think of the treasures they must have up there. Gold, for sure. Mages love gold, and likely precious gems as well. Buckets full of gems—diamonds, rubies, every kind there is. We'll never have to work again."

"No, we won't," Snails said soberly. "You don't work if you're dead, not even in Izmer. No one can make you do that."

"Come on, friend. I'm standing you another cup of ale, maybe three or four. Trust me. Everything's going to be fine."

Snails had an answer to that, but he knew it was useless to bother Ridley with reason, logic, or truth of any sort.

CHAPTER 5

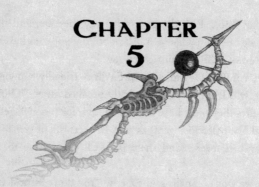

The Council room was immense. Great oaken beams rose up in breathtaking arcs to a high, domed ceiling. At the center of the dome was a circular window of multi-colored glass inlaid with the runes, signs, and mysterious symbols of the great mages of the present and far distant past.

In the center of the room, directly under the dome itself, was a raised dais and several magnificently carved chairs of raven-wood, harder than iron itself—a wood that was no longer found anywhere. Surrounding this dais like the arcs of a wheel, like the perfect structure of the room, was a gallery for the Council of Mages, those wise and eminent seers, prophets, philosophers, and masters of spells for the Empire of Izmer. In truth, some would say, here was the true power of the empire, and thus of most of the known world.

At the moment, Azmath, a dark-robed mage with a precisely cut goatee, was addressing the council from one of the raven-wood chairs. Seated beside him was Profion, and standing next to him, properly servile and beautifully dressed, was the wily Damodar—standing, because no one but council members were allowed to sit in this hallowed hall.

"There is much to talk about," Azmath said, whose voice, fortunately, was perfectly audible in this perfectly acoustical room. "Much to talk about, and much to do. We have a new Empress on the throne. As our powers have warned us, we have a troublesome cycle of years ahead. We have, of course, suffered greatly from the fire. I am pleased to tell you, however, that the Royal Palace and the Library of Alchemy suffered only minor damage, and repairs are under way now."

Cries arose from the gallery, cries of anger and fear, one mage shouting over the other, so that none could clearly be heard.

"What about my lands, my estates?"

"My property! My homes!"

"Who's going to recompense me for my losses? My entire collection of ancient silver urns is gone!"

"What about my—?"

"Please, Brothers!" Azmath held up his hands. "I understand your concerns. We have all lost precious possessions, but we have not lost our lives."

"No, we have not," Profion said, "and we should be most grateful for that."

The council went silent as Profion grasped the arms of his chair and let his dark, penetrating eyes sweep across the faces of the seers. There he saw concern, rage, fear, and—perhaps crowding all other emotions out—the almost visible stink of greed. Poor, benighted fools, thought Profion. You have no knowledge of what grand schemes, what daring, glorious deeds are under way before your unseeing eyes.

"Your losses are not the reason I called you here. There are far graver problems facing this body today, problems that must be dealt with at once, if we are to survive."

Profion paused to let his words sink in, to prepare them for the cunning tale, the enormous lies that he intended to plant in their addled heads.

"I must tell you," he went on, "a terrible, shocking truth, one I can scarcely credit myself. I regret, Brothers, that I must tell you the first official act of our new, esteemed *Empress* Savina is to disband this worthy council and rule Izmer without our good wisdom and advice!"

Every mage in the gallery rose as one—all but the oldest and infirm—to stamp his feet and shake his fists.

Once again, Azmath managed to turn an unruly rabble into a council of dignified, respected old men.

"You make a shocking accusation!" one shouted as a semblance of order returned to the room. The mage's eyes bored into Profion's. "I trust you have some solid proof of what you say. It would be well if you do, sir, for this council demands it!"

This time, no one spoke. No one wanted to miss what Profion had to say.

Excellent, Profion thought, fighting to keep a triumphant smile from his lips. They are furious now, and ready to be angrier still. . . .

He stretched out the silence, letting the tension come to a boil. Bringing one hand to his chin, he frowned as if in deep thought, then rose and stared up at the brilliant glass dome, as if invoking higher help.

"I am wondering, with the rest of the members of this council, what will become of our property. Who will repay the losses we have suffered? In your concerns, Brothers, do you not wonder how such a terrible conflagration could have started? Has that question crossed you minds?"

The councilors stirred like so many waking bees, but all ebbed quickly into silence.

"How, indeed?" Profion spread his hands in wonder. "Not even the power, the magic of fifty of us combined could have caused such devastation." He swept his gaze across the gallery again. "No, this was not magic, my friends, not the magic of *our* kind. This terrible fire was caused by the blood of a dragon. I know this is so, because we discovered its blazing, rotted carcass washed up on the shore downriver."

The very room itself seemed to hold its breath.

"Dragons die," Azamath said, breaking the intense silence. "That alone is not proof our Empress is responsible. It is unthinkable, Profion, to imagine that she is."

"They die, yes," Profion said, "but who has the power to control such a creature? More, how to bring about its demise? I ask you: Unless this near immortal beast were summoned by the Empress's scepter, what would it be *doing* here?

"And, if the question cannot be answered, it is harder still to imagine how this monster died on the very shores of Sumdall City. Yet, if logic and reason is not enough for this distinguished gathering of mages, the wisest of the wise, hear the truth for yourselves."

With that, Profion paused, swept one hand slowly to his right, and let it point directly at the patient Damodar.

Damodar nodded with respect, then walked to the center of the dais, head bowed, hands interlocked across his chest. He had even left his startling, crimson uniform behind. Here, he was telling them in silence, is not the head of the feared Crimson Brigade, but a simple, loyal servant of the Empire.

No one, Profion thought, can give a better imitation of an angel than the devil himself.

"I am honored to be in your presence," Damodar said, "and grateful to the Lord Profion for asking me here, yet I come to you saddened and reluctant to speak, for I take no pleasure in what I must say."

"Don't push it," Profion said under his breath. "Some of these men are fools, but many of them are even more cunning than you."

"During the dark of night," Damodar went on, "upon hearing of the Emperor's tragic death, I went at once to watch over our blessed Savina, heiress to the throne. Much to my bewilderment, I chanced upon her slipping quietly out of the palace with only the smallest complement of guards.

"Soon, it became clear to me that she was meeting with others, that this was a clandestine appointment. She was not meeting with a gathering of sages like yourselves, but with—I hesitate even now to speak the word—with *commoners,* the worst kind of rabble from the sinkholes of Oldtown. Rebels, if you will, known for their seditious acts. Members of my Crimson Brigade have watched their activities for some time, but never, never amongst this filth, did they see a princess of the Empire.

"You know who these people are. They have always been with us, the unwashed herd dedicated to bringing about our destruction, the destruction of Izmer itself." Damodar paused, as if it was most difficult to continue this shameful story. "I saw, I witnessed myself, the Empress summoning up this dragon, showing the rabble the power she could bring to their cause. And, summon the monster she did, but in so doing, she also caused its agonizing death. It was clear to me the lady was careless in the use of her instrument of power. She did not understand the strength that lies within the scepter. To her—if you'll forgive me—it seemed a mere plaything for a young girl's idle hours."

Damodar let the silence stretch for several heartbeats before continuing. "Forgive me, Lords, but it was a sight I had sooner never seen."

The gallery stared at Damodar, too stunned to speak.

Finally, it was Azmath himself who broke the silence.

"And what became of this dragon's carcass? It is clearly not there now."

"The rebels, the commoners she gathered there, disposed of the thing at her command. And none too happy at the task, if I might add."

"Come, Azmath," Profion said, slapping at the arm of his chair. "Let's be honest here. We have all watched the young lady grow up. We have all heard her misguided chatter on . . . *justice for all,* I believe. Commoners, beggars, the lot. You can blame her fool teacher for that. The honorable Vildan Vildir, who, I note, has shunned us again today.

"The Empress Savina is too young to know her heart from her mind. I will not condemn her for that. She should be raised under the thoughtful guidance of this council, as royals have ever been in the past." Profion shook his head in wonder. "And if she does not have our guidance, what will she do when she *does* learn how to use the monarch's scepter to enforce her will? On the people? On us? Your fate is in the hands of this child. Ask yourselves: are you willing to put your future in her hands?"

The council broke into loud discussion. Profion let them stew a while. Finally, the mage Ferilanius stood.

"What are we to do, then?" he asked. "You cannot remove an Empress from her throne. That goes against our sacred laws."

"By all the gods, no." Profion pretended horror at the thought. "I only intend that we remove the threat that hangs over our head, that we vote to *insist* she give up the scepter so the future will be safe for us all."

"And if she does not agree?" asked Azmath.

"Then we will know her true intentions—" Profion's countenance melted into a mask of sorrow— "and we must do whatever is necessary for the sake of keeping Izmer strong. So, what say you?"

As he expected, as he knew, the entire council was on its feet, shaking their fists and crying for action at once.

Profion lowered his head, as if in obeisance to the inevitable will of the mages of Izmer. He did not risk a look at Damodar, and he prayed that serpent could restrain himself until the vote was done.

CHAPTER 6

The day seemed long, and the sun was masked by a pall of smoke from the fire that had swept down the river. Fishing boats, barges, and trading ships that had sailed upriver from the sea were now no more than charred, skeletal masts rising above the water's foul and ash-covered surface. The hapless crewmen of these vessels had been consumed in flame in the blink of an eye.

Warehouses, businesses dependent on the river, were victims of the fire as well. Most of these structures were owned by the rich of Sumdall City high above. The greater number of people who perished in the river of flame were the poor, those who lived in the overcrowded—and highly flammable—tenements along the riverbanks of Oldtown.

Ridley and Snails, along with many other citizens of the lower city, spent much of the day helping dig through the ravaged remains, recovering few of the living and many of the dead. There were many opportunities for "salvaging" items that no longer belonged to anyone, but Ridley and Snails would have none of that.

"We are thieves," Ridley explained to Snails, "not looters. Those fortunate souls who have *not* been affected by the fire, well, that's a different thing."

Snails felt there was little difference in taking things that didn't belong to anyone, and things that did. He didn't mention this to Ridley, who clearly had his mind set.

"Besides," Ridley reminded him, as they finished a very late supper at the Hoof and Hair, which served a marrow soup Ridley liked, "we are not simple cutpurses and snatchers anymore. We have graduated to greater things."

Snails looked pained. "I'd hoped the grim events today had sobered you, Rid, and flushed you of this ridiculous scheme of yours. But I see that isn't gonna happen, and if that's so, I must sadly tell you I can't rob the magic school. I *won't*. I'm sorry, but this is the most witless, suicidal plan you have ever come up with! I have gone along with your fool ideas in the past, but I won't let you talk me into this."

Ridley waited, but apparently that was all.

"That was a fine, remarkable speech. I believe it's the best—and the longest—I've ever heard you give."

Snails lowered one brow. "If that's all you think it was, then you missed the point, Rid. It was not intended as a speech. It's more in the order of a declaration, and I didn't intend it as a joke."

"And I didn't take it as one. I know you meant every word you said. And I can't tell you, Snails, how it grieves me to hear that I won't have your support, wise counsel, companionship, and, ah—all your other fine qualities I can't quite recall. I don't know how I'll manage to continue alone. All I see is a dismal and lonely road ahead."

Snails looked pained, the look he usually got when he ate bad fish. "Lonely and dismal? Because I'm not there?"

"Worse, if that's possible, though I can't see how it could be."

Ridley gave a deep sigh, full of sorrow and regret. He stood, then, dug in his pocket for a copper coin, dug and found another, and laid the pair on the table by his empty bowl of marrow soup.

"I would pay for yours if I could," he told Snails, "but that's truly all I have." He held out his hands. His eyes glistened with tears. Either that, or he was bothered by the sun. "Good-bye, old friend. I've never had a finer companion and don't hope to find one half as good again. I trust, when I come home safely from my task up there tonight, we'll have a chance to chat once more."

"Tonight?" Snails drew back his hand. "You're going up there tonight?"

Ridley shrugged. "Of course. Why not?"

"Uh, what's the rush, you know? Why not wait for another night, give it a little thought before you go?"

Ridley ran a hand through his hair. "We talked about this. Everyone up there will be occupied with the aftermath of the fire. We'll slip through their hands like grease. They won't be expecting any trouble at all."

"You mean *you*, not *we*."

"What?"

"You said 'we.' I'm not going."

"Yes. I quite forgot." Ridley turned away and sighed, staring past the grimy window of the inn, apparently at nothing at all.

Snails felt a tug below his heart. Was it possible, or was the light simply bad? Was there a sadness in his old friend's eyes that he'd never seen before? That, and moments ago, the faint possibility of a tear?

"I . . . wish there was some other way," Snails said. "I truly do, Rid."

"No, now don't be wishing that." Ridley shook his head. "In truth, I think you've made a wise choice."

"You do? Honestly, Rid?"

"Yes, I do. I've talked you into some pretty shaky schemes in the past, and I'm not proud of that. You don't need to be hanging around with a scoundrel like me. You need to get a new life, find your own way . . ."

Snails shook his head. "I don't want a new life. I want to steal things, like I always have. I just don't want to do it up *there.*"

"And I don't think you should. It's a foolhardy mission, like you said. I doubt very much I'll come back. I don't want your death on my hands, friend. I'm much too fond of you for that."

Snails drew in a breath. "But you didn't say that. You said we'd be fine."

"I lied. I lied because I wanted you to be there with me. I was selfish, Snails, and beyond that, if we *did* come back with riches beyond compare, I wanted you to be a part of that."

"Rid—"

"No, say no more, dear companion. It will only hurt me the more." Ridley drew Snails out of his chair and held him to his chest. "I doubt we'll see each other again."

Before Snails could speak, Ridley was gone. Out the door of the Hoof and Hair, out into the evening's smoky light.

For a long moment, Snails simply stood there, watching the spot where Ridley had disappeared. He felt that familiar tug again. He knew in his heart that he was right, that this scheme was clearly a disaster in the making, far worse than any Ridley had dreamed up before. Though Snails earnestly wished he could put the thought aside, there was another, greater reason he didn't want to go up to Sumdall City or anywhere near it.

He was scared, plain frightened out of his wits at the mere thought of that place. It was *bad* up there. The people were powerful and rich, and they practiced strange and evil ways. There was magic everywhere, and now there was this story of a dragon, which everyone said had started the fire.

Snails felt a chill at the back of his neck. Dragon's blood—blood that could set a whole city on fire. What else might there be up there?

Whatever it was, Snails didn't want to find out—not even if he was feeling so lonely already that he hurt all over, just wondering what he'd do with himself. Since Ridley had come into his life, he'd never had to think about that.

CHAPTER 7

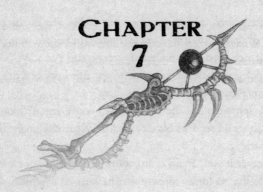

The chapel always smelled of candles, not the foul and odorous candles made of animal fat—the Empress Savina had never even seen such a candle as that. The candles she knew were made of the finest beeswax, sweetened with the faint perfume of flowers and spice, the heavenly scents of fir and pine. For as long as she could recall, Savina had thought of the gods of Izmer as beings made of cinnamon, roses, and mountain lilies pale as ice.

Now, kneeling before the great altar, beneath the marble pillars and golden light, she did not feel the presence of the gods, only a dark and lonely emptiness, a cold, eternal night.

Why did you leave me, Father? I am not ready. I cannot take your place. Send me a sign, Father. Tell me, what I must do . . . please.

No answer came. In truth, none had ever come before. She had not expected the gods to speak to a young and foolish girl. They had better things to do. But her father, surely he could help. The dead were said to have all the time that was and could ever be. What was there to do in the afterworld, more important than answering a frightened daughter's prayer?

As hard as she tried to stop, the tears began to flow again. She was flooded with shame and quickly wiped her sorrow away with the edge of her long sleeve.

"I am an Emperor's daughter no longer," she reminded herself. "I am the Empress, and the Empress cannot afford the luxury of tears."

She turned at the slight sound of the chapel door opening behind her. Vildan Vildir stood there in a simple green robe, his hands folded in his sleeves. He started to bow, but Savina rose and ran to him quickly, holding him to her instead.

"My child," Vildan said gently. He wiped fresh tears with the touch of his finger to her cheek. Savina thought he had the bluest eyes she'd ever seen—bluer surely than the eyes of the gods themselves, though that might not be the proper thing to say.

"I shouldn't cry," she said. "It is unseemly for me now."

"You cried when you skinned your knee as a child," he said, stroking her silken hair. "Do you think you are less a human now? Or possibly something more?"

Savina gave him a curious look. "I am the Empress. I'm not supposed to be like anyone else."

"I know, child." Vildan leaned in close to whisper in her ear. "Don't ever tell anyone, but you are."

He guided her to a bench and sat beside her. "You are not alone, Savina. I am here with you, as I was with your father before. And there are others who are with you as well."

"And many against me, too."

Vildan shook his head. "The council has committed a great

sin in voting against you—a sin they will deeply regret. Anyone with half a wit knows you do not consort with dragons or set cities afire. That's nonsense, and everyone knows it."

"Vildan—"

"Hush, now." He laid a finger to her lips. The sight of her nearly broke his heart. She was eighteen, and as beautiful as her long-departed mother, but now she looked like a helpless child. How could he make her strong against the forces that faced her now? That was a job for the gods themselves, not a weary mage who'd nearly lost his powers.

"Listen to me. The palace counselors will come to you, Savina, but you must shut your mind to their advice. They, too, have betrayed your father, and they will not hesitate to betray you. They are weak-kneed, frightened fools in the hands of the Council of Mages now. You must *not* give up your scepter just to keep peace with that gallery of selfish old men. That is the last thing you must do. That, indeed, would be the end of Izmer and the beginning of chaos, the end of all that is good in men . . ."

Savina held him close and gazed up at the soaring marble columns and the bright golden dome. She spoke to Vildan, but did not look at him.

"It's Profion, isn't it? He wanted my father's throne, and now he wants mine."

"He plays on the fear of others, and he does it quite well. He has the serpent Damodar by his side." He ran a hand across his silvered beard. "I don't have to tell you that your concept of an Empire where even commoners have a voice is not popular in high places."

"But it's a good concept, Vildan, and a *right* one. I will not walk away from it. I'll die before I do that."

And so you might, child, and take all of us with you as well. . . .

Vildan stood. He searched the dark corners of the chapel, clutched his robes about him, and gripped Savina's shoulders in his hands.

"There is only one way to beat Lord Profion. You cannot meet him head on. You have to outsmart him. You must force him to show his true intentions and give himself away before the council."

Savina frowned. "He will never do that."

"He will, if he thinks he's won." Vildan caught the Empress's gaze and held it. "If you give up the scepter as he asks—as I said you must never do, I know—if you do this, he'll *think* that he's won."

"No!" Savina stared at the mage and drew away. "He'll be right. He *will* have won. How can you counsel me to do such a thing?"

"Lady, I do not counsel surrender. Those words will never pass my lips." He leaned in closer still. "You will not be defenseless, Savina, if you have a weapon greater than the one you give away."

Savina started to speak, but Vildan cut her off. "Listen, Empress. For centuries, those close to the Emperors of Izmer have kept a great secret. It has long been known that there exists an ancient artifact called the Rod of Savrille. This wondrous instrument is said to hold the same power as your scepter, but for a single difference. . . ." Vildan paused, and the hint of a smile touched his wrinkled features. "This rod, Savina, gives its owner control over red dragons."

Savina gasped, startled at his words. She was sure she had misunderstood. Such a weapon was surely an unholy force, no less evil than the frightening spells Profion used to maintain his power.

"I've followed the trail of this instrument for half a century,

Lady. Now, I have a scroll in my hands that reveals where the rod is hidden. Do you see my reasoning here? If you obtain this rod, it would mean nothing to give up your scepter. You would have in your hands an even greater protection against Profion and his followers."

"Yes, I see, but . . ."

"If he doesn't know you have this instrument of power, he will proceed with his plans. He will trap himself, Lady, expose his evil in front of the Council of Mages."

Vildan looked down at the young Empress. Light from the multitude of candles danced in her sea-green eyes, flickered across her dark brown hair. He breathed a silent sigh of relief and sent a prayer to the gods of the afterworld. For the first time since her father's tragic death—his murder—he saw, instead of a frightened, callow girl, the beginnings of a woman, the iron strength of her father, the indomitable will of her mother.

He reached out, then, drew her close for a moment, and then held her away by her shoulders.

"Red dragons are among the most evil of all creatures. This is a truth from which I cannot shield you, but you are the Empress now. I see that mantle of greatness on your shoulders as surely as if it were a jeweled cape of ermine and the fur of the northern bear. I have done all I can in this, my Lady. I fear that whatever wisdom is left in this weary head is of little value to you now. I have the scroll, and I will do all I can, but we must have the help of another to discover where this miraculous rod is hidden."

Savina nodded but said nothing.

"I have sent word to one who will come to you soon. She is one in whom you can fully trust, one who has shown her loyalty to your family for generations past."

Savina's eyes brightened. "Norda! Yes! Am I right, Vildan?"

"You are indeed, Empress. The elven tracker is the one I have chosen for this task. She will come in silence, and you may be certain that not even Profion with all his spells will know that she is here. He could as easily hear a whisper from the moon or the breath of a star."

"Norda." Savina spoke the word, the name a thing of magic itself.

Vildan sensed her new confidence, her exhilaration at the prospect of meeting Norda again. He did nothing to dispel this joy, the strength that had now replaced her tears. He knew, though, for he had seen as clearly as others see the coming of the day, that all would not come to pass as easily as the young Empress now believed.

* * * * *

The chapel doors closed behind the Empress and the old man. As the sound of their footsteps faded, something moved behind a pew in the back of the chapel. From the shadows it stirred, daring into the flickering light of the hundreds of candles. Shaped like an emaciated, diminutive dragon, the imp hissed in pleasure, having heard every word of the exchange between the slip of a girl and the old man.

Taking to the air on its frail wings, the imp began to spin, faster and faster until it was only a shadowy blur. The wind from its flight caused the nearby candle flames to flicker and sent shadows dancing on the marble columns. The breeze ceased, the flames steadied, and the imp was gone.

CHAPTER 8

If night is dark and day is light, if black is black and white is white, then no two places of worship could be farther poles apart than the golden chapel of the Empress Savina and the grim walls and tainted altars where dwelled the likes of Profion the Mage.

Here, the pale, ragged columns that stretched up into foul darkness contained a pattern of skeletal arms, one dry and wasted hand clutching at the next, circling ever higher, higher, and higher still, until the fearsome column swept into a bent and twisted arch of broken spines, spines that appeared like dead and tortured vines reaching for another bony tower across the room.

There were six gray columns and six high arches, the brittle remains of countless souls who had failed, offended, or angered Profion—or often had simply served to amuse the great mage for an idle moment or two.

The far wall of the chapel was called the Hall of Heads, one white skull placed flush against the next from the ceiling to the floor. It was spoken in whispers that Profion knew the names behind every grinning mouth, behind every empty eye. Some said he talked to them at times, and even brought them back to life, fleshed and frightened as before, so he might have the pleasure of hearing their screams again.

No one knew if this was so, and no one ever dreamed of asking the man who knew if it was true.

Now, the mage himself stood in this dark chamber of the lost. Red light flickered across his face, light from the open skulls of bullocks, goats and multi-horned creatures no man alive had ever seen before. The sweet, cloying scent in here was neither blossom nor spice. The only odor here was death.

Profion stood alone, his thoughts, for the moment, far beyond the grim chamber itself. He was angry, in a rage, in a fury past all imagining in the minds of ordinary men. When such a mood struck him, no man with his wits about him cared to face the mage.

Finally, he turned, so quickly his great cloak wrapped around him like a shroud. Damodar, a vile little imp perched upon his shoulder, stood well apart and wisely kept his silence, his gaze upon the floor beneath his boots. Behind him, cowering in the dark, were four hooded figures, their faces pressed to the ground.

"I detest bad news," Profion said, his voice so harsh, so strangled with hate, that the hooded figures trembled at the sound. The imp gave a frightened squeak and scuttled off into the darkness. "Somewhere, hidden in some . . . some hollow, some cavern, some dungeon in the blasted Empire, there is *another* rod that supposedly brings the red dragon to its scaly knees." Profion threw back his head and laughed, laughter that chilled the bones of everyone in sight. "Imagine that, Damodar.

Another rod somewhere, a rod that would bring us power unconfined . . . or send us all to hell!"

Damodar remained silent. In shadow, he was nearly lost from sight, his crimson cape faded to black. His face was barely visible in the hollow of the jeweled green cowl that swept up in a high, magnificent arc, framing his gaunt, pitiless features and hairless skull. His shoulders, arms, and even his gauntlets were festooned with curved and sharpened spikes.

"If what Vildan said was so, Lord," he said finally. "Imps are not the most reliable messengers, but I do not doubt the story of the rod is true. Vildan is one of those rare people who imagines himself above a lie." Damodar shook his head, as though this was a near unheard of quality in a man, an act against nature itself. "If the Empress should actually come to possess this instrument, I fear there is nothing you could do that will overcome her powers. We will, Lord, have a bloodbath on our hands."

Profion shot Damodar a killing look. He didn't like to hear words that might harbor a fight he could lose.

"Find this cursed rod, then, wherever it is. I'll take this girl-child down, and that council of fools as well. I sicken of *asking* my beloved *brothers* what I am to do. I know what I will do, and I will not tolerate the so-called wisdom of old men!"

"Your wish, then, my lord?"

"What do you *think* I wish, you idiot? Pay a visit to the magic school, and see our friend Vildan. Find this scroll he babbles about."

"Indeed, Lord. And may I say I sense that better days are soon to come?" Damodar couldn't resist the suggestion of a smile. "Your wall is heavy with relics, but we will surely find room for several more."

He bowed, then, took a step back, and began to fade into the chapel's shadow.

"And Damodar?"

Damodar paused, bowing, and said, "My lord?"

"Make sure that Vildan is no longer around to give our young Empress any more advice."

Damodar bowed lower, turned, and proceeded up the stairs. Profion watched him go, following his motion long after the man was out of sight.

"Perhaps a trophy you hadn't counted on, my treacherous friend," the mage whispered.

A viper is useful for ridding the house of mice, Profion thought, but once the rodents are gone, I do not wish to have an idle serpent around.

CHAPTER 9

Snails decided the best thing to do was fall. If he simply let go from such a height, he would only have seconds before his body struck the ground, and in those few seconds, he could think how lucky he was to have perished before he found another handhold scarcely deep enough to hold the corpse of a gnat. Stretching for the next tiny crevice, Snails's heart nearly stopped as he slipped and started sliding down the side of the high stone building.

It was a joke! Can't any of you gods take a joke?

Ridley's strong hand snaked down and grabbed Snails by his wrist. Snails shut his eyes and hung there in the dark.

"Put your foot somewhere," Ridley whispered. "I can't do this all night."

"I don't *have* a somewhere. Don't think about me. Let go and save yourself. Oh, wait—there's a good spot. Thanks for not listening to me, Rid."

Ridley let out a breath. "Now why would I ever do that? Be

careful, will you, please? The climbing part's a walk in the park. We get up there, the place will be crawling with traps."

"This is the easy part?"

"Well, yeah, I guess it is."

"This whole thing is crazy, is what it is. No one in their right mind would break into the magic school. What does that say about us?"

"Don't talk. Climb."

"I hate you, Ridley," Snails said as they resumed their ascent. "Before we get skewered, hung, quartered, or whatever it is they do, I want you to know that. I want you to know I don't like you at all. I don't think I ever did."

"All right, Snails."

"You know what else? If I ever get out of this, which I won't, I'm going to look up that girl at the Ferret and Fox. If she doesn't like you, it stands to reason she'll be crazy about me."

"How do you figure that?"

"Because we both don't like you, Rid. That's the way it works. Two people who despise you, they've got a lot in common; they're bound to be friends. Or maybe more than that. Maybe love and romance. I can see us— Rid? Damnation, where are you? Where did you go?"

"I'm up here at the top. Shut up and give me your hand. We're almost in."

"Can't we just rob the first floor next time?" Snails asked as he reached for a more secure handhold.

"Sssh!" Ridley hissed. "Quiet!"

"Great gods above, if you can hear poor Snails, turn me into a bird so I can fly out of here. An eagle's fine. A crow's all right with me."

"You keep babbling, I'm not giving you half of the treasure, Snails. I'm keeping the Cloak of Invisibility for myself, and the Gem Finder, too. And the Sniffer. I'm hanging onto that."

Snails blinked. "What cloak? What are you talking about? What's a Sniffer? I never heard of that."

"A Sniffer's for when you forget to wear your cloak," Ridley explained. "A Sniffer tells you if a guard or somebody's around so you can get away fast."

"Where'd you hear all this? You don't have any idea what's in this place."

"My point exactly." Ridley grabbed Snails's shoulder and grinned. "We *don't* know what's in there. Think how wonderful it'll be when we really find out."

Snails risked a look down and felt his stomach begin to do a flip.

"We don't have to, Rid. We could go home and go to bed."

"Too early to go to bed," said Ridley as he began to explore the wall. "Sunrise is hours away, and we— Here!"

"What?"

"Quiet. Down here."

Squinting in the near dark, Snails saw his friend slide through a narrow window and disappear. He took a final look at Sumdall City. Even at this hour, it was lit by a thousand yellow lights. Was everybody still up? Didn't anyone sleep in this devil's town?

He muttered a prayer, the only one he could recall, and crawled into the blackness where Ridley had disappeared.

CHAPTER 10

The room smelled of dust, old paper, rotting leather, and mice. It was a fine, comfortable smell, the best smell there was to those who spent their lives here, puttering through the past, searching along the high wooden shelves that lined the walls, shelves packed to overflowing with thin, fat, ancient books, and even some that were new. There were books with covers and books without, scrolls and books laid flat, books about this, books about that, books of every conceivable sort.

The room was well-lit or badly lit, depending upon where a reader chose to sit. In addition to an ample supply of thick, slow-burning candles, there were immense oil lamps with mirrored tops, the mirrors a clever device designed to ease the strain on weary eyes. These massive lamps hung from chains linked to the ceiling high above. On this ceiling, beneath a coating of grime, was a painting that depicted a grand and bloody scene of battle from a war now long forgot.

Crowded into the center of the room were long wooden tables

and scattered highback chairs. The tables and chairs were covered with large, open books and scrolls, tomes with lofty titles such as:

Dragons: A True and Precise Anatomy of Scaled and Flying Beasts
Various Engines of Siege and Other Machines of War
Alchemy for the Beginning Student, Volume 329

Not for the first time, Vildan wished he could simply have his body strapped to the library ladder and stay there all the time. He had strengthened the tendons and muscles in his legs for sixty years, climbing up and down in this very room an uncounted number of times. Now though, late in his eighty-seventh year, his legs had turned against him, as had everything else in his tall and withered frame. Nothing irritated him more than waiting below while others searched the crowded shelves above.

"It's up there," he grumbled. "Unless you *moved* it somewhere, Marina, this is where it has to be."

"Yes, it should be," Marina said patiently, "and I'm sure it'll turn up soon."

"Maybe *you* are sure," Vildan muttered. "I'm surely not."

Marina sighed. She had many duties in the Library at the school, but the most important task of all was following Vildan about and taking the blame for everything the mage lost.

"Ah, a moment. I see it now," Vildan said. "There. Right under your nose. How anyone with eyes to see could miss it, I couldn't say. Marina, my dear, why was it there with the books on Alchemy? It clearly belongs in Dracology. Anyone would know that."

"I really couldn't say, sire."

Because you put it there yesterday yourself, that's why, she thought. Because you climbed this very ladder and nearly fell when you thought I wasn't looking.

"Huh!" Without even glancing her way, Vildan took the yellowed scroll from her hand, crossed the room, and set the ancient document on a table already crowded with dusty tomes.

At once, he began fussing about with vials, pots, mortar and pestle, and the countless jars of evil-smelling potions that were always scattered about, sometimes tipping over with horrid results.

Marina wondered why magic was such a foul, odorous profession. Just once, why couldn't someone make a spell that *smelled* good?

While Vildan worked, she busied herself with cleaning up the area where he'd worked the night before. Learning from a master magician was an endless, near hopeless task, not nearly as exciting as she'd pictured. Still, who else could she stand to work for? Who else would want her, for that matter?

She shuddered at the thought of even getting near one of those foul-minded mages who would eagerly take her on.

"Gods protect me," she whispered to herself. Before she'd do that, she would simply give up magic and scrub floors somewhere.

No one who knew Marina or had any knowledge of her goals would mistake her for a scullery maid. She was a tall, slender woman with silken hair the color of dark autumn leaves swept gracefully atop her head. Her eyes were dark as river stones, and her skin was fine ivory tinted with gold, reflections of her birthland in the far mountain reaches of the north.

She dressed in a simple, plum-colored gown under a black cowl sewn with a golden pattern of runes. On one wrist, she wore a breathtaking bracelet adorned with a brilliant green stone the size of a pheasant's egg. Marina came by her love of magic naturally, and the bracelet was a gift from her father, a mage himself like his father before him. She carried herself with a regal bearing, and many who saw her were certain she was somehow of royal birth.

Many men who admired her beauty passed her by with much regret, thinking her somewhat haughty glance reflected a lady too distant and cool to even approach. In truth, quite the opposite was true. Marina simply had little desire to expose her emotions and masked them from the world. This, too, was a part of her heritage, for one learned early in a mage's family to betray no weakness that others might use to pull them down.

She watched Vildan with her usual calm and forbearance. He could be surly and overbearing at times, and completely forget that she was there, but she loved the old man like a father and would put up with anything as long as he allowed her to stay.

I hope he never guesses the truth of that. If he does, he will drive me completely mad.

There was another aspect of the mage that made Marina doubly proud to be a part of his busy life. Vildan, above all others, had been close to the Emperor, and now that he was gone, Vildan was the strong right arm of the Empress Savina herself.

"And the gods know she needs all the strength she can get," Marina said beneath her breath. "Especially in such dangerous times as this."

Bending closely over a particularly ancient scroll, Vildan squinted at the fading runes and sprinkled a pinch of nightblack over the surface. He then stood back and waited. After a moment, he scowled and muttered inaudibly. Adding a pinch of ground adder, he tried agai.1. This time, the scroll gave off a faint shimmer, which quickly faded and died.

Vildan brought his hand to his waist and straightened his weary back.

"I swear all the demons of the underworld are set against me this night, Marina. I have never seen a scroll so determined to hide its secrets. It is clearly protected by very ancient magic."

"It must be, sire, if it defies your powers."

"Yes, well . . ." Vildan frowned at the wrinkled, fading parchment that dared to resist his efforts.

"Let's try something else. Bring me some manticore wing, if you will."

"I fear we're out, Master," Marina said with regret. "I sent the old woman, Lethine, to the eastern border for that and other potions, as you'll recall. I don't expect her back until—"

"Great gods of the wind!" Vildan shouted, pounding his fist on the table and raising a cloud of dust from ages past. "Isn't there *anything* that works in this place anymore? What am I supposed to do, make up spells in my head? Get me some raven's eye, then. That will have to do for now. It's in the red pot next to the gall."

"Yes, I'll look for it right away," Marina said, knowing full well that Vildan had used up all the raven's eye months before, making a horrible smell.

"Help me," she said softly, with a quick glance above, addressing any spirits who might be lingering about. "I've *got* to tell him, and he isn't going to like that at all."

* * * * *

"Come on, Snails!" Ridley whispered as loud as he dared. Snails was still dangling from the window high above the hard floor.

"I thought you said this was going to be easy."

"No," Ridley replied. "I said this wasn't impossible."

"See?" Snails yelped as he almost lost his grip. He climbed back up to the window sill and steadied himself. "That's the same thing you said when we robbed that little halfling's house." Ridley rolled his eyes, and Snails continued. "And who did he catch? Who? *Me!* And who'd he beat from the waist down? Me."

"Are you gonna jump or dangle and complain up there all night?"

"Are you gonna catch me?"

"I'll catch you. Now, will you hurry?"

Snails didn't seem convinced. "Promise?"

"Yes!" Ridley said in a whisper that was growing steadily louder. He held his arms open. "I promise. Now jump."

"All right." Snails closed his eyes and steadied his nerves. "Here goes."

A noise that sounded disturbingly like a very large animal came from somewhere beyond the opposite window just as Snails let go. Ridley tensed and turned toward the sound. Snails hit the ground behind him and screamed.

"Sorry." Ridley winced. "I thought I heard something."

"You did!" Snails said angrily. "Me hitting the ground, you dolt!"

Ridley turned, already putting the incident behind him. A faint sliver of light from outside cast an eerie pattern over a glass tank of angry red scorpions, and another of giant beetles.

"Oh, wonderful," Snails said as he got up. "I've got bugs in my bed at home. I didn't need to come here."

Ridley didn't hear. He gazed about the dark hall, trying to see every wonder at once. "This place is a veritable treasure house,

Snails. There's a fortune here, more than I ever dreamed."

He made his way carefully across the room, stopped, and studied one glass tank, one cage, after another. One cage held hideous giant rats, each with a single ruby eye. A glass tank was writhing with a nest of silver vipers, serpents with heads on both ends. They hissed and struck at the sides with a terrible rage.

"No wonder they're mad," Ridley said. "I would be, too."

There was cage after cage of creatures Ridley had never even imagined before. How many were natural beings, he wondered, and how many the result of magic?

"This is it, truly, my friend. We've stumbled on the mother lode of every thief's dream. *Anything* we take out of here is worth its weight in gold."

Snails let out a breath between his teeth. "I can't argue that. Look what I found here."

Snails reached up on a dirty shelf and held out a gleaming, bejeweled paperweight. "If those aren't sapphires, I'll eat my hat. This thing's worth a—"

With a bright explosion of lightning, the giant, chalky skeleton of a dragon suddenly appeared, looming over Snails.

"Rid—Ridley!"

Snails dropped the paperweight, turned, and stumbled away from the horrid creature shimmering in the dark.

"Snails, watch it!"

"Huh—wuuuh!"

Ridley cringed as his friend ran headlong into a stack of wooden boxes, sending them tumbling to the floor.

"It's an illusion, Snails! Look! It's gone. Get up from there."

"It looked real enough to give a fellow a stroke," Snails said, pulling himself to his feet. "By the gods, Rid, steal something and let's get out of here."

"That's the problem, you see? And a finer problem we never faced, my friend. There's so much treasure here, it's hard to decide what to steal. Gold is best, of course—always is—but it's heavy, and we've got to climb down again. Gems are nice, and they weigh scarcely anything at all, but how can you tell in the dark if they're real? That's important. You've got to know if they're real."

"What treasure? Where?"

"What?"

"I don't *see* any gold. I don't see any gems. All I see are bugs—and ugly bugs at the that."

"Well, of course you can't see any treasure. It's hidden. Even mages don't leave their goods lying around. We've got to look is all. Look, and I promise you we'll leave here rich as—"

Ridley froze, turned, and stared as light suddenly spilled into the room. Standing against the brightness of the now open door was a woman so dazzling, so lovely, Ridley almost forgot the trouble he was in.

"Evening," he said, "we're the new—"

"—Cleaning crew!" Snails finished. "We'll be out in a minute, my lady—soon as we get this mess straightened up. You don't mind me saying, someone needs to go through this place, sweep up, sweep out—"

"Shut up," Ridley said without taking his eyes off the young woman. "This lady's not feeble-minded, Snails."

"No, I'm not," the woman said, shaking her head in disgust, "but you two apparently are. Just stand still, both of you! Don't even try it!"

Halfway to the window, Ridley and Snails froze in their tracks. A green pulse of eerie light leaped from the woman's bracelet and circled the pair in its grip.

"Look now, don't do this," Ridley protested. "We won't hurt you, I promise."

"Oh, how marvelous," she said, delighted and somewhat surprised by the power of the green stone. As she spoke, the shimmering band vanished, replaced by a common strand of ordinary rope.

"Miss, there's been a misunderstanding," Ridley said.

"There certainly has," Snails added. "We don't belong— Uh, what I meant to say was, we won't be *long* here, if you'll just forget about this and let us go."

The woman shot a fiery glance at the pair. "Where you're *going* is the city dungeon, a place you've likely seen before, unless I miss my guess."

"Oh, the city dungeon!" Ridley said. "What a relief! I'll thank you when they cut my head off."

"You should," the woman replied. "It would be an improvement."

Ridley laughed, mocking her. "There's that superior intelligence you mages are so famous for. What wit!"

"We aren't common thieves, miss!" Snails broke in. "Don't think we are!"

"No?" she raised a brow, a gesture Ridley found most appealing. "What are you, then?"

"*Un*common thieves," Snails said. "We're a lot better than your ordinary thieves. I could tell you some astonishing stories, criminal deeds that even I scarcely believe."

The woman shook her head. "Are you two feeble-minded, or

what? What kind of genius would break into a magic school? You'd have to be really stupid, or—"

"Or what?"

"Or really . . . *really* stupid, that's what."

"She's got us there, Rid. Can't argue with that."

"There, see?" Ridley said. "You've hit upon it, my lady. We're not too bright, all right? You can't hold that against us; that's the way we are. It's not our fault. We grew up in the streets, we never went to school, we . . . Uh, you get the picture, right?"

"Oh, I certainly do." Marina showed him a sour smile. "Now, if you'll stay right there—which you will—I'll find a city guard. There's usually one right—"

The woman's words were lost in a harrowing scream from the other room.

"Master!"

The woman's eyes went wide with fear. Turning quickly, she raced out of the room. Ridley and Snails came after her with a sudden jerk as the power of her spell nearly swept them off their feet.

CHAPTER 11

As Marina came upon the library, she stopped short, taking in the horror before her in a single glance.

"No, please," she cried out, "he's an old man! Let him go!"

She gasped and raised a hand to her breast, almost too frightened to move. Vildan, sprawled on the floor in a tangle of books and scrolls, looked up at her with a great and terrible sorrow in his eyes. Around him, in full armor, were eight troopers of the Crimson Brigade, their faces hidden behind hideous masks. Each held a stubby crossbow pointed at Vildan's head.

"Well . . . company," said the Brigade Commander as stepped out of shadow into the room. "And very pretty company, too." He paused to look behind her, and frowned. "Except for that pair. What on earth are they doing here?"

"I know you," Marina replied with all the calm she could muster. "I know what you are, Damodar. Let's talk about this, please. Whatever you want, I'll try to help. But don't hurt him! He can do you no harm."

Damodar threw back his head and laughed. "One more time, old man. Show me which of these damnable scrolls I'm looking for, or I'll finish you off right here. And your charming friend as well."

Vildan looked directly at his captor. A pale blue glow sparked in his eyes, and a quick spell left his lips. Damodar deftly stepped aside, as a lance of blue pain drilled a hole in the wall behind his head. In that instant, a scroll rose off the table in a blur and slapped itself into Marina's hand.

"A very nice bit of magic," Damodar said, "one you'll pay dearly for, old man." He turned his eyes on Marina. "Now, I think you'd best give that to me."

Before Damodar could act, a green beam of energy shot from her wrist, striking the Brigade Commander squarely in the chest. Damodar staggered and caught himself, his face filling with a rage he could scarcely contain.

"I don't believe it!" the taller of the two thieves shouted "You just zapped—"

"—the head of the Crimson Brigade!" the other finished for him. "I'm extremely sorry I got you into this, friend."

"You two, quiet!" Damodar squinted at the pair in disgust. "Get rid of them. I'm getting bored with this."

A pair of Damodar's troopers went quickly to the two thieves. Damodar clenched his gloved fists, eyes blazing, as he turned all his anger on the old man.

"That's it, Vildan. The girl has your scroll, and I have her. I don't need you now."

With scarcely a glance at his prey, he reached down and grasped Vildan's head in both hands.

"No!" Marina cried.

It was over, quickly done. Marina drew a ragged breath as she heard the bones snap. The mage's head jerked back on his shoulders and he sagged to the floor.

In that instant, Marina's hand moved, almost of its own accord. A handful of red and silver dust suddenly clouded the air. A shimmering portal, like a door into some other world, hummed into being before Marina and the two thieves.

"Come on, time to go," Marina said, biting back her tears as a magical portal opened before her. "It's not going to get any better in here. The streets of Sumdall!"

In a blink, the room was gone as something drew them through the bright circle and out of the room.

*   *   *   *   *

Ridley blinked, sniffing the night air of Sumdall City.

"Nice trick," Snails said. "I don't mind saying, you call 'em a little close for me, lady."

"Shut up," Marina growled. "Don't say another word to me."

Ridley could almost feel the anger in her eyes.

"A good man died back there, a better man than you'll ever be, thief."

"I'm sorry," Ridley said. "I really am, and I'm grateful for what you did."

"We are," Snails said. "That's as true as it can be."

She looked over her shoulder and swept back a strand of tousled hair.

"I can open that thing, but I don't know how to close it. We'd best get out of here."

She turned away, and Ridley followed her down a dark alleyway, still bound to Snails. Half a moment later, he heard the call of angry soldiers, the clang of their armor, the rattle of their arms . . .

Ridley raced through the twisted alleyway as fast as he could, hampered by the spell that held him to the girl. Once, she took one pathway in the dark, and Ridley and Snails took the other. The jolt cut into Ridley's gut and nearly threw the pair to the ground.

He cursed the girl, the ridiculous spell that chained him to her, and at the same time, reluctantly blessed her for setting them free.

"If we get out of this," he muttered, "I'm having a talk with that lass. This is more than humiliating." He turned to Snails. "Will you please keep in step? We're closer than unborn twins, whether we like it or—"

"Huuup!"

All the breath left Ridley's chest as a short, stocky figure struck him just below his waist.

Ridley and Snails bounced off a grimy wall but managed to keep their feet.

"Where in the demon's unholy breath do you think you're going?" the small man demanded. "I ought to slit your throat for that!"

Ridley rubbed his belly and stared at the absurdly short, unseemly figure with a flaring red beard who blocked his way. He wore a ridiculous, ornate horned helmet made of skulls, broken teeth, and bits of precious metal.

"Look, whoever you are—"

"Ridley!" Snails shrieked.

A masked, Crimson Brigade trooper appeared around the alley corner, came to a halt, stared at Ridley and Snails, then leaped at the smaller of the three.

Before Ridley could blink, the little man swung a battle axe as long as himself and nearly cut the guard in half.

"You," the woman shouted, "look to your back!"

Her warning nearly came too late. Damodar stepped over his dead warrior and loosed a crackling bolt of raw energy at the short man's head.

The small warrior ignored him, waving the spell aside.

"Are you blind, you oversized oaf? I'm a *dwarf*. Your childish magic doesn't work on me!"

"So be it," Damodar said. "Iron kills just as well."

The dwarf moved faster than Ridley would have dreamed such a being could. In a blur, he dropped to the ground and side-kicked Damodar just below the knees.

Damodar yelled in fury and went down hard. The dwarf gathered up his axe and smashed the blunt end into the side of his foe's head. Damodar looked surprised, bewildered that such a thing could happen to him. His helmet saved him, but he staggered back, stunned by the blow.

"Where'd he come from?" the woman asked.

"I don't know," Ridley shouted, "but get this spell off so I can help!"

For a moment, Marina seemed reluctant. Ridley wasn't sure she wouldn't simply leave him and Snails bound together forever, but as the woman rubbed her bracelet, he felt the tension let go. The rope simply vanished.

Ridley moved away from Snails, and Snails backed off from him. Friends were one thing, but inseparable twins were something else.

Just then, two more guards appeared, pausing for an instant to stare at their downed leader and dead comrade before they came at the dwarf.

It was only the small part of a moment, but time enough.

Ridley, rushing in, downed one of the soldiers with a thrust to the throat. Snails took the other on the end of his blade.

"There's no one coming," said the dwarf, peering around a corner of the alley, "but this feisty fellow will come to his senses soon."

"I should run the devil through," Ridley said. "Make a lot of people in Oldtown happy, and I'd guess a few up here as well."

"But you won't," the woman said. "He's unarmed and out of his senses. That's not a proper thing to do to any man. I'll admit it's a temptation. If I wasn't a moral person, I'd kill him myself."

Ridley gave her a curious look. "That isn't a man. That's a walking hunk of slime, and I wish I didn't have the fine set of morals that *I* have."

"I don't have any," the dwarf said. "I'm free of such silly human traits. You want me to take him off your hands? No problem, friend."

"Yeah, it is," Ridley said. "Look, just leave him. Let's get out of here. I'm sick of Sumdall and tired of smelly alleys as well."

He noted, then, that the alley wasn't truly an alley anymore. In only a few steps forward, the narrow way began to arch overhead, and the cobbled street very clearly slanted downhill. If anything, the way ahead more closely resembled a sewer than anything else.

"You folks want to stand around and talk," the dwarf said, wiping the blade of his great axe against his trousers, "that's your concern. Me, I figure more of them uglies'll turn up lookin' for the rest."

"Any suggestions would be greatly appreciated," the woman said as the four of them entered the dank and dripping entrance to the sewer. "You appear to know your way around here."

The dwarf scowled. "I'll overlook that, seein' as how you're likely under a strain."

The woman sighed and turned to the dwarf. "Please forgive me. I'm most grateful for your help. Don't think I'm not."

"Yeah, well never let it be said I haven't got manners myself. Glad to be of service, lady." The dwarf swept the grand helmet from his head, revealing a bald and shining dome. "Elwood Gutworthy, of the Oakenshield Clan. And you?"

"Marina of Pretensa, daughter of the Ninth Level mage, Farnoff, and Nalrid of the House of Staverid, founder of the—"

"Fine, whatever," Ridley growled. "It's been fun, miss, but Snails and I haven't had supper yet, and I'm dipped and bedamned if I care to search for suitable inn down here."

Marina didn't answer. For the moment, she was clearly lost in thought. It was nearly dark in the fetid passageway, but Ridley was almost sure he saw a tear course down her cheek. One hand absently touched the sleeve of her gown, and, in a dim splinter of light, Ridley saw the tightly rolled parchment in her grasp.

"That thing means a lot to you, doesn't it?" he said. "That old man back there, he was willing to die for it, and I think you are, too. You mind telling me what it is?"

Marina seemed to return from wherever her mind had taken her for the moment.

"Everything," she said softly, looking at him in the dark. "I think it means everything there is."

CHAPTER 12

The room was cold, for no fire had burned in the night. A lamp had been lit, but for the Empress Savina, this weak intrusion only added to the sorrow, to the gray morning light.

Nothing could erase the presence of death. Once that pale and chilling wraith, that harvester of souls, left his mark, it would linger there forever, and all who passed that way would say, "Someone left the roses in the room too long. They should have taken them away. . . ."

Poor, sweet Vildan. First they take my father, and now they have come for you. If this is the beginning, then I pray I'll not live to see the end. . . .

"He was loved by all, my lady. He will be sorely missed."

Savina, as she knelt before the cold corpse of her friend, turned and faced the hooded mage who stood above.

"How do you say he was loved by all, Azmath, when they did this to him? And how 'sorely missed,' when the one who killed him will not miss him at all?"

Azmath stroked his beard and pretended to stifle a cough.

"I'm sure you know, Empress, that I was speaking for all who did love him well. And of those there are many."

"Yes, of course."

The Empress came to her feet. Azmath bent to help her, but she swept his hand away.

Several more mages and soldiers of the Crimson Brigade stood by the door far from the Empress and the silent figure on the floor. Savina had covered Vildan with her own cloak, and now dark stains appeared on ermine and royal blue.

"See that he is interred in the royal vaults, Azmath. Next to where my father lies."

"We share your grief, Majesty, but he was not of royal blood. Such a decision may send the wrong mess—"

"Mage. . . !" Savina turned on him so swiftly that Azmath took a step back. "He was family. You *will* do as I command."

"Yes, Empress."

"And find that girl who was with him. Bring her here at once."

"The Crimson Brigade is searching the city as we speak, Lady."

"I'm certain they are." Savina glanced at the hideous figures in shadow and quickly looked away. "Leave at once. All of you."

Azmath bowed and took his leave. His brother mages followed him from the room. The soldiers of the Crimson Brigade turned and closed the heavy wooden door.

For a moment, Savina was alone once more, then someone stepped through a curtain at the far end of the room.

"This one, this Marina, she is not a girl who would kill her master, Lady."

The gentle voice brought the beginning of a smile to Savina's face. She walked across the room to take the visitor's hand.

"Indeed she is not, Norda, but she was with Vildan when this happened. I am certain. She seldom left his side."

"I see. That tells me she is likely in some danger herself."

"Or past it," Savina added, gripping the woman's strong hands.

Her hands, Savina thought, were as kind and gentle as the woman herself. She was slight of figure but held herself with the confidence and grace of a trained athlete, a person who ever strives for mental and physical perfection. She wore blue silver armor over soft brown leather and a rose-colored vest. A sword hung about her slim waist, and a silver helmet was drawn down about her face.

"Azmath is not pleased with me," Savina said. "He did not expect an Empress with a will."

Norda smiled. "Few men like a princess who does not play with toys. You will have to be strong, Savina. And cautious."

The Empress led Norda out of the room where Vildan lay and into a small study off the large expanse of the Dracology Library. It was a comfortable place and almost excessively neat.

Savina sat and motioned Norda to a chair as well.

"Vildan spoke with you, I know."

"Yes, he did. I know what it is you seek."

From a fold in her robe, she drew a small scroll. Sketched on its surface was a well-conceived sketch of Marina. Norda read the look of concern in Savina's eyes and took her hand again.

"I *know* how to do this, Savina. I have been your family's tracker since your father was a child. Our kind do not age the same as yours. I'm sure you know that. I will find the woman, and I will find what I hope and pray she carries, as well."

Savina felt a chill at the mere mention of the scroll that had caused the old man's death.

"The survival of the Empire, perhaps the world, lies in that single parchment, Norda. By all the gods, it cannot fall into Profion's hands. If it should, if we should fail . . ."

"But we will not. Do not imagine that we will."

A moment later, Savina looked up to answer, but Norda was gone, and the Empress was alone in Marina's empty room.

CHAPTER 13

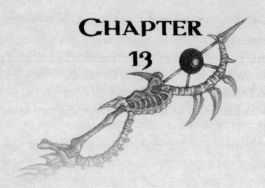

In the darkness of the Chapel of Bones, the foul stench of fear was stronger than the smell of rotting flesh, sharper than the copper taste of blood, more fetid and intense than the scent of death itself. Here were Azmath and the cunning Damodar, in company with a low and merciless band of villains from the Crimson Brigade, cruel and heartless fellows who would, for their master's favor, do any deed he might wish, be it mayhem, murder, vile desecration, or crimes so terrible none dared speak of them.

Now, though, no man in this place was either confident or bold of demeanor, for even the most wicked among them quailed before the wrath of Profion.

"I vow I will bring you the scroll, Lord," Damodar said, his eyes to the ground. "It is only a question of time before you will hold it in your hands."

"Time, Damodar? What sort of *time* are we speaking of here?"

"Scarcely any time, sire. Truly. You need have no worry, no concern at all."

"No? You dare to tell me to have no *concern?*"

The strength of Profion's rage clutched at Damodar's chest and nearly stopped his heart. Even Azmath, who had great powers of his own, staggered and caught his breath. Among the crew of killers Damodar had brought along, all cried out and went to their knees. Many of them retched, and several of the weaker spat blood.

"You let that *girl* take the scroll from you, and now the Empress has put an elven tracker on its trail? And I am not to be *concerned?*"

"Lord—"

"You sent this band of idiots to search for the most precious scrap of parchment in the universe? Tell me again, Damodar, is this not what you did? Did you come within reach of the prize only to let yourself be bested by a *dwarf?*"

"It will not happen again, Lord."

"No, it will not! And you shall now understand *why.*"

Profion's eyes turned silver. His face drained of blood. He spread his hands wide and spoke words so ancient they had scarce been heard in ten times ten thousand years.

Even Azmath clamped his hands against his ears.

Damodar staggered under the full brunt of Profion's will. He fought against the horror, conjured every shield, every spell his desperation brought to mind, then at once, he felt the cold presence of the thing that had found him. He felt its evil, felt its joy, felt it gnawing through his skull, felt its hunger and its need . . .

Damodar went to his knees, screaming. His body jerked in spasms, ripped, tore, wrenched in mortal pain.

Azmath turned away, sickened by the sight. Damodar's head began to swell, ripple, and heave in awful convolutions, as if some savage creature were trapped in there, fighting to break free. His eyes bulged, and his features stretched in grotesque imitation of the highborn, arrogant being that had ruled there moments before.

Then, as if the worst were surely done, something dark and wet poked its snout from Damodar's nose. Something pale as death slid from his ears. Damodar shrieked in terror as the mindless, ropy things snaked out of his head, hissed, coiled in anger, then struck at one another, struck at his mouth, struck at his eyes . . .

"I am sending a *companion* along to remind you not to fail me again," Profion said. "A gentle reminder not to make anymore mistakes, my friend. I suggest you take a lesson from your foes and follow the Empress's tracker. She appears to be somewhat more proficient in her work than you. She will lead you to our missing friends and the scroll. And this time, Damodar, *do not fail me.*"

Profion paused, watching as Damodar writhed in hellish pain. He found great pleasure in the sight, for he saw a fine irony in what this man had become. Damodar, who masked his evil with the handsome features of a fine aristocrat, now faced the world as the monster he truly was.

"The beast is in us all," Profion whispered, "and it takes little magic to bring the creature out."

CHAPTER
14

The Rusty Sword was the second oldest tavern in the Empire of Izmer. The first, the Gutted Bear, had been burned to the ground by its patrons some four hundred years before.

Graphiot, a former soldier and a man more cunning and cruel than the worst of the brutes who dared to guzzle ale in his place, had not made the same mistake as the hapless owner of the long forgotten Gutted Bear. Graphiot's tavern was built in a circle of many tiers, much like a stadium. Crowded in this loud and odorous inn was a drunken horde of elves, halflings, dwarves, humans and orcs, each in the tier set aside for their particular race.

In theory, though murder and assault were commonplace, a creature could only slip a blade into the belly of his very own kind. Not a perfect plan, but no tavern-keeper wanted a repeat of the Gutted Bear again.

Coming here had seemed like a good idea at the time.

"Stave off hunger," Ridley had said, "get some ale to drink . . ."

Wearing the dark, hooded roles of the mage class, they could hide in plain sight in the dark, huddle at the edge of the crowd. Who would look for them in a place like the Rusty Sword?

Marina had pointed out that Elwood was a little too short to mix with humankind, but no one, sober, sodden or in between, really wanted to share a table with mages. You never could tell what they'd do. First class mages or rank amateurs, they could all cast spells.

"This place gives me the creeps," Marina said. "Honestly, I never even *imagined* there were dumps like this."

"Hey, take it easy," Snails said. "We come here all the time."

"My, what a surprise."

"Don't knock it," Ridley said. "It's a lot safer than walking around on the street."

"The eatin's better too," Elwood said around a mouthful of food. He paused to tear another roast bird in half and stuff it his mouth, bones and all.

Marina made a face. "That's the most disgusting sight I've ever seen. My mother always warned me: Don't smile at an orc; don't watch a dwarf eat."

"Smart mother," Elwood said, waving a drumstick larger than his head. "That's true as it can be about orcs. You don't want to have nothin' to do with their kind." He paused, swallowed, and wiped a sleeve across his mouth. "So, as I understand it, if we find this, uh, rod thing, the Empress pins a medal on us an' gives a lot of gold."

"This is not about gold," Marina said coolly. "This is about saving the Empire."

"Big deal," Ridley said. "We do all the sweating, and what does the Empire do for us while all of the royals and the mages get rich?"

"And the thieves. Don't forget the dedicated, hard-working thieves."

"At least we've got respect," Ridley told her. "Honor among thieves, I guess you heard of that. Not like a bunch of backstabbing mages that don't give a blink for anyone but themselves."

Marina turned on him and glared. "That's just the sort of half-baked, illiterate drivel that proves commoners really *are* . . . common."

"Uh-huh." Ridley drew a thick roll of parchment from his belt and slapped it on the table. "So who you think's nailing this up all over the place?"

Marina's face turned crimson red. She grabbed the paper and jerked it out of sight. It seemed like a nightmare, a terrible dream that had happened to someone else. She didn't have to read it, she knew it by heart:

TO ALL PERSONS OF THE EMPIRE OF IZMER

Marina of Pretensa, Student Mage, is sought for the brutal murder of Vildan Vildir, Master of Dracology. Her magic powers are low to moderate. Her accomplices are bloodthirsty, depraved criminals of the vilest order, and they should be slain on sight. A generous reward will be paid for their remains.

"It is not the Council of Mages that's behind this," Marina said. "I will not believe that. They've been deluded by Profion. Most of them are really very nice."

Roast fowl exploded from Elwood's mouth at that. Marina gave him a frosty look and turned her fury on Ridley.

"If none of you believe in this cause, why don't you simply go and leave me alone? I'll find the rod myself."

"Hey, right." Ridley slapped his mug on the table. "Smartest thing you've said all day. Snails, friend Elwood? You want to look for magic rods or take a nap somewhere?"

Neither Elwood nor Snails looked his way. Both looked around for something else to do.

At once, Ridley was sorry he'd shot off his mouth. He thought she was out of her mind, sticking her nose where it didn't belong and likely getting everyone around her hung up by their heels. Still, he couldn't help the fact that he was fascinated by her, couldn't take his eyes off her for a moment, even if she couldn't stand the sight of him.

"Ah, listen, what I said . . . We're all under a strain, all right? Stuff comes out that you wish you hadn't said."

"*I* don't."

"You don't what?"

"Say *stuff,* as you put it, that I wish I hadn't said."

It was Ridley's turn to feel the color rise to his face. "Can't anyone be nice to you? Anyone says a kind word you've got to slap 'em in the face. Uh, what's that, what're you doing now?"

Marina turned half away and unrolled the scroll she'd retrieved from Vildan's dying hand. Holding down the edges with empty mugs, she hummed to herself as if no one else was there.

"What I'm *doing*," she said finally, "is getting to work. I have a lot to do, and it seems I have to do it by myself." She looked up then, as if she were surprised to find him there. "Oh, you still with us? I thought you'd gone to take a nap."

"I am. Quite soon. Do you mind if I get something in my belly first?"

Marina shrugged and turned back to the scroll. Ridley leaned over her shoulder and watched. This close, he could smell the flowery essence in her hair.

"Those little red marks there? They look a bit like the locks my father used to put on the plans he drew for carriages when he wanted to keep 'em secret. You know, so no one else could steal his ideas."

"Please," Marina sighed, "this is an ancient, very precious scroll. It is not a blueprint for buggies."

"Oh, well excuse me." Ridley backed away in mock horror. "See, I thought you didn't know what you were doing, so it wouldn't matter if I put my two coppers in."

"What? What are you talking about?"

"Like this, see?" Ridley put down his drumstick and grabbed the scroll. "My pa used to put his finger like this—"

"Get your greasy hands off this right— Oh, oh dear."

Marina went suddenly quiet, as the runes on the parchment began to move, slowly circling about one another and arranging themselves in a totally different design.

Ridley let out a breath. "Then he'd say something like, uh, *Alinor salla . . . bebara . . .* No, no . . . *bedara,* that's it. *Alinor salla bedara.*"

Marina stared at the scroll then peered up at Ridley. "So? Now what?"

Ridley shrugged. "Hey, you can't blame me for trying. You weren't getting anywhere, you know. At least I— *Holy dogs and cats!*"

For an instant, Ridley's finger glowed. His eyes went wide, his whole body trembled, and then he was gone. All that was left was the sound of distant thunder and a whisper of steam where he'd been.

"Oh, no, no. . . !" Marina bit her lip, then quickly planted her finger on the fading red marks. *"Alinor salla bedara!"*

At just that moment, Snails turned and saw the girl vanish before his eyes.

"Absolutely amazing!" he said. "Can you imagine that?" He peered under the table to see if Ridley was there. "I suppose he's gone as well. He's taken with the lady, even if he doesn't yet know it himself."

"I can imagine another mug of this lovely ale." Elwood yawned. "How about you, friend?"

Snails didn't answer. He stared at the runic lines on the scroll, watched in wonder as they seemed to dissolve into a small, flat drawing of the very room where Vildan had died. Now, within this room, two tiny figures moved about.

"Flat amazing," Snails said. "A marvel's what it is!"

"You said that," Elwood frowned. "Why are you sayin' it again?"

"Well, they're *in* there, that's why," Snails said, pointing a finger at the scroll. "Both of 'em, the girl *and* Ridley!"

"Humans," Elwood grumbled. "They'll get themselves stuck somewhere and never get out. I seen it happen a thousand times."

"Don't say that. I don't want to hear that."

"Don't matter if you don't or you do. It's true, is what it is. You'd never see a dwarf fall in a damned scroll, I'll tell you that for sure."

* * * * *

Down below, somewhere between the here and over there, Ridley became aware of a somber darkness above him, like a storm cloud blocking all the light from the sun. Peering up, he saw two enormous faces staring down from a blurry sky, watching him and Marina intently, like bugs in a box.

Marina rubbed her eyes. "I can't believe you did that. What I'd like to know is how. You're not a mage. You're a common, ordinary thief!"

"Neither common nor ordinary, and sure enough, it's a mage talking now. No one can do something right if you haven't been to school, if you haven't got your official mage *robe.*"

"Anyone can . . . stumble into something, I suppose. I strongly doubt you could do it again."

Ridley looked past her and studied the room. It looked just like the great library, only nothing seemed real. Nothing seemed right.

"See, that's what they told my father after he invented a carriage that could fly. He figured it out for himself, but the mages, of course, they couldn't have that—a plain old commoner, who'd never been to magic school. He did something they couldn't, so they— So they took it out of him. They erased it right out of his mind."

Marina looked away. "I'm sorry, Ridley. I really am."

"Forget it. It's ancient history now."

"No. No, it's not. It's very real, and it's something that shouldn't have ever happened."

"It shouldn't, but it did. In case you hadn't noticed, there're a lot of things in this world like that. I guess that's the way it'll always be. I don't see it getting any better."

"Maybe it will, though," Marina said. "Things do get better sometimes."

"For your kind, maybe. Not mine."

Ridley looked at her a moment, then quickly glanced away. It was difficult to look at her for very long. Too long, and he began to think of things that might happen, days in the future where the two of them might be together, might have a life that was nothing like the life they had now, a life where they were two different people than Ridley the thief, and Marina the mage. . . .

Shaking the thought aside, he toyed with a small wooden box on the table, absently turning it this way and that.

"People in Oldtown don't change a lot," he said. "If you're born into something, that's where you'll likely stay. Like me. What am I going to be but what I am? My father tried, and look where it got him."

Ridley ran his fingers over the ivy and thorns carved into the top of the box. A very pretty design. He wondered if he could do something like that. Work with his hands, make something nice . . . He lifted the lid and looked insi—

"Whoooooa!"

The tiny box exploded, swelling into a dense, vaporous mist, a dazzling white cloud that quickly consumed the room.

Ridley grabbed Marina and stumbled back. The mist whirled about them, twisting and curling into a trembling wraith.

"Who calls upon the Rod of Savrille?"

"Uh, I'm Marina. Marina of Pretensa, daughter of Farnoff and Nalrid, student mage of the—"

"You are not the seeker of the rod. Only the person who first enters the scroll is the seeker of the rod."

Ridley stared at the thing. It made him dizzy to watch. It was there, and then it wasn't. It winked in and out like it truly didn't know just where it ought to be.

"See, I don't want it. *She* does. Let her be the seeker, not me—"

"NO!" The wraith's breath was like the chill of polar ice. "The one who enters the scroll must seek the rod. Why do you seek the rod?"

"We seek it because our land is threatened," Marina said, gripping Ridley's hand, something she'd certainly never done before. "We need it to stop some men who are . . . who are determined to destroy everything."

The wraith seemed to inhale itself, drawing its misty form into a hole somewhere then blowing it out again. An impossible act, Ridley knew, but the phantom did it anyway.

"The rod is a force of evil. Famines, plagues, death . . . It was the cause of the great war of ancient times, a war no longer remembered, a war in which much was lost . . ."

"That doesn't sound like anything we want, does it, Marina?"

"It's not what we want, it's what we have to *have,*" Marina said, looking straight at the wraith. "We don't have any choice, it's what we have to do!"

The wraith seemed to sigh.

"If you choose to seek it, know that you must complete the quest, or you will be eternally cursed."

"What kind of eternal curse?" Ridley asked, "Is this a really *long* eternal curse or a—"

"SILENCE! What is your choice, boy?"

"No," said Ridely as he began to back away. "No, I don't think so. Can we go now?"

"We'll do it," Marina said, giving Ridley a scathing look.

"What?" Ridley turned back to the wraith. "No we won't! Don't listen to her!"

The wraith swirled, turning itself inside out again.

"The box you so foolishly opened contains a map that will lead you to the Rod of Savrille."

"Fine," Ridley said as he reached in to find the map. "We'll give it a look, that's as far as I'll go right now."

"WAIT!"

Ridley dropped the box and stepped back.

"It is not that easy, boy. First, you must go to Antius City and obtain the Eye of the Dragon. Only through the Dragon's Eye can one see where the rod does lie."

"That figures," Ridley said. "A riddle. I hate riddles. What does this eye look like?"

"It is a ruby as big as your hand."

"Really? I find this thing, I can keep it, right?"

"Ridley—" Marina began.

"No!" the wraith thundered. "Do not be lured by the dragon's treasure, for in it lies great sorrow, not pleasure."

With that, the wraith vanished as quickly as it had appeared.

"I hate a curse that rhymes," Ridley said. "Things that rhyme get you into trouble all the time."

"But you'll do it?" Marina's eyes were so deep, so soft and shadow-dark, Ridley wanted to fall in and drown.

"No. You think I'm an idiot that I'll listen to a cloud?"

Marina's warm and pleasant eyes turned to ice.

"Oh, all right," Ridley said, wishing, for an instant that he'd never been a thief, never opened boxes that didn't belong to him, wished he hadn't done a lot of things and done a lot of things he never had. "It won't hurt to think it over. I can live with that."

CHAPTER 15

A nyway," said Elwood, "there I was, minding my business, when this orc comes stompin' up—he's drunker than I am, see?"

"Hard to believe," said Snails.

"Don't interrupt me. Someone stops me in the middle of a story I tend to lose my place. Uh, where was I?" The dwarf raised his tankard of ale, emptied it in two noisy slurps, half of it running down his tangled red beard. "Ah, that's better," he said, wiping the foam from his mouth. "I'm recalling the whole thing now. This giant fella, who is uglier than sin by the way, which is what every giant thrives to be, he's pullin' out this sticker which is maybe twenty, thirty feet long, and terrible sharp it was, too . . ."

Snails, though, didn't hear a word the dwarf said. He was awed, shaken by the vision that had just walked through the tavern door. She was tall, slender as a reed, dressed in rose-colored leather, and armor the color of a winter sky. He was totally enchanted, stricken by her charms. The woman didn't *walk*, not like an ordinary woman, she just sort of *flowed* in an unearthly manner, as if her leather boots never even touched the ground.

"Idol of idols," Snails said, when he was able to breathe again. "I never believed that a dream could come true, yet there you stand, just as real as you can be."

"Like I was saying," Elwood went on, "this giant, who had to be eighty, no, I take that back—ninety feet tall if he was in inch, he— Now where you going, Snails? Get back and sit down! I'm not half done with this."

Elwood snorted in disgust. Snails was out of his chair and halfway down the gallery before the dwarf could draw a breath. The dwarf watched him go, and when he saw where the thief was headed, he scowled.

"Smitten by an *elf!* You've got to be daft, friend. There isn't any meat on their bones—nowhere to get a grip. Now, you take a fine, two-hundred pound dwarf lassie with a little sprig of hair on her chin you can hold on to . . ."

*   *   *   *   *

Snails reached up and straightened the collar of his coat, wishing, for the moment, he'd worn his other jacket, the dun-colored one where the patches seemed to match, the one that nearly fit.

The woman seemed to sense he was near, for as he approached she turned and granted him a smile that nearly brought him to his knees.

"Why, hello," Snails said, as if he'd suddenly come upon her there. "I hope you won't think I'm out of line, but what's a beautiful lady like you doing in a terrible place like this? Looking for someone in particular, or are you just looking for . . . somebody?"

"Actually," the woman said, in a voice that sent a shiver up Snails's bony spine, "I was looking for someone just like you."

"You—you were?" Snails felt his mouth go dry. "What kind of coincidence is that? I've always been looking for someone like you. I'm Snails. That's what everyone calls me, anyway."

"Norda," she said, reaching out to take his hand.

"This calls for a bottle of the very best wine," Snails said. "You're not going to find any here, so why don't you and I go looking somewhere else?"

"Snails . . ." Norda paused, and he saw her eyes sweep warily about the room, a practiced gesture that told him she missed very little, even in a crowded, noisome tavern like the Rusty Sword. "I would really like to spend some time with you, Snails, but I think we'd best meet your friends as well."

Snails hesitated, wondering if he shouldn't have been more cautious approaching someone he didn't know. Even if she was the answer to his dreams, what *else* might she be?

"My, uh, friends? How did you—? May I ask just how you know I'm with friends? I mean, in case I am."

"You may, and you have every right to, Snails." She paused, darting a look past his shoulder again. "But I have to ask you to trust me for now. Please. I don't feel right about being here, and I don't think your friends should be here either."

Norda paused and moved closer to him, so close he could see his reflection in her eyes. What he saw there was honesty, courage, and something he couldn't name, something so alien, so different from anything he'd ever seen before. She was an elf, of course, and that accounted for much of her ways, but there was more, a great deal more than that.

"You don't have to ask for my trust," he told her. "You have it for sure. Come with me and meet my friends, if we can *find* them, that is. I think they'll be glad to talk with you."

*　*　*　*　*

Elwood Gutworthy had consumed an enormous quantity of ale, but not that much for a dwarf. His senses, as ever, were intact. His mind was perfectly keen and ever alert. Thus, when he turned to squint down at the entry to the tavern, he already knew what was there. He saw, with the clarity of an eagle who sights a fat salmon far below, that something was greatly amiss, something was terribly wrong.

He saw, in that instant, the brigand in the shadows by the door, saw the gold pieces vanish in his hand and disappear. Half a second later, the shadow man was gone. The other, though, the man who'd given away the gold, was still there, and when he turned to face the room and Elwood saw his face, the dwarf squeezed the heavy clay mug so hard in shattered in his hand.

"Damodar! By the gods, it's him! But what foul monster ate his face?"

Elwood didn't pause to look for an answer. Grabbing his helmet, his axe, and the precious scroll, he was up and darting quickly through the twisting tiers, even as Damodar dispatched his corps of uglies through the door.

The dwarf offended everyone he passed, elbowing humans, halflings, and anyone else not swift enough to move out of his way. He left them all with a dwarvish curse, the same one he always used, which began with "Shrivel up and die, whoever you are. . . ."

A table of orcs, four big brutes with scarred purple hides, stood directly in his way.

"Move," Elwood said. "I mean to get by."

The orcs looked up and stared. Orcs can be dense, but it was clear to these four that it would take a good dozen dwarves to make a single worthy foe. One began to laugh, and the others joined in. Orcs at other tables howled, pointing at the bearded little man.

Elwood didn't blink. "Right," he muttered to himself, "don't say I didn't ask."

No one saw it coming. No one saw the great axe until it cleaved the table neatly in half, sending foul ale and fouler foods showering through the air.

Orcs spilled onto the floor. One tried to catch himself, flailed his arms about, and tumbled off the tier into a horde of halflings down below. The dwarf was momentarily forgotten, as angry halflings scrambled up the gallery, swinging clubs, chairs, and mugs at the startled orcs.

Elwood cut through the crowd, spotted Snails and the elf, walked up, and tapped his friend on the back.

"What?" Snails blinked in surprise. "What are you doing down here?"

Elwood didn't answer. He grabbed Snails by the belt and hauled him toward the rear of the inn. Norda followed quickly on their heels.

An orc flew through the air and landed senseless at her feet. Norda stepped nimbly out of the way and ran into a large, angry human with a tattooed face. The man snarled at her and shoved her roughly aside.

"Hey! Stop that!" Snails shouted, pulling away from the dwarf. "I'm deeply in love with this person, and I won't stand for that!"

Elwood made a face. "With an elf? They think humans are a joke."

"This one doesn't. This one doesn't care if we're different. She cares about me."

"Sure she does." Elwood took a sharp turn to the right. He'd spotted Damodar's brutes bulling their way through the crowd.

The whole inn was in a uproar now, everyone fighting or running for the doors.

Cleaving his axe through the air, the dwarf carved a wicked pathway to the back door. An orc came at Snails, swinging a notched sword. Snails ducked under the blow and kicked the orc squarely in the gut. The brute gagged, clutched at his belly, and retched on the floor.

One of Damodar's henchmen slashed at Snails, who was busy fighting another orc at the moment, but Elwood stepped in and struck both with the flat of his axe, sending them smashing through a wall.

Jerking the door open, he held it while Snails squeezed through, then slammed it shut with the heel of his boot.

Half a second later, three barbed arrows thunked into the panel, followed by several more.

Snails followed Elwood, stumbling through the foul-smelling alley in the dark. It irritated Snails that the dwarf could run so fast. He thought of himself as a fairly good sprinter. As a full-time thief, he had run a great deal in his life.

Elwood wound through one twisting passage then the next, finally barreling through the city gates and coming to a halt in a thick growth of reeds near the murky waterway. Trees hid the stars and cast deep shadows across the water.

Snails pulled up beside him out of breath. "I hope you're happy now," he said. "I wait all my life for the perfect love, then you and your orcs come along and foul it up!"

"Next time I won't, you damned fool. Did you happen to see who was after you back there? Damodar it was, and you moonin' over an elf."

"Damodar? Truly?"

"Truly indeed. Only somethin' horrible has happened to his head. It's all twisty-like, and there's awful things a-hanging out."

"What kind of things?"

"Things I never saw the like of, friend, and I've seen a lot."

Snails felt the side of his belt. His sword and dagger were still intact. "I'm grateful for your help, Elwood, but I've got to go back. I expect things have settled down some at the Rusty Sword, and I have to see that Norda's all right."

"Don't be a bigger fool than you are, Snails." Elwood shook his head, and offered Snails the kindliest look he had. "I know you won't believe it, but I'm sure she's just fine. I don't care for their ways, but an elf can take care of herself."

"That's easy to say, us standing safe out here ourselves. Talk all you want, friend, I'm going back."

"I could stop you, I guess, but I won't. It's your hide, and if y— Hey, now! Stop it! Quit doin' that!"

Snails backed off, reaching for the weapon at his side. The scroll stuffed in Elwood's belt began to jerk and twist about. Elwood cursed, then pulled the paper loose and tossed it on the ground.

Twin wisps of steam hissed up from the scroll. The steam disappeared, and Ridley and Marina stumbled out, dizzy as drunken cats.

"I thought we'd lost you two for sure," Snails said, brushing dust off his friend's coat. "Wait'll we tell you what happened back there. I met this very nice elf, a woman the Fates simply dropped into my lap. I've got to go and get her now."

"What we've got to do is move, and move fast!" Elwood broke in. "It's Damodar, and he's after us."

Ridley rolled his eyes. "We've got a lot more trouble than that." He blinked, getting his bearings, aware of exactly where they were now. He quickly explained their encounter with the wraith and showed the others the crude map that led to the Dragon's Eye.

When Snails saw where they were going, he groaned and slapped a hand against his brow.

"Antius City? Are you out of your mind? That's Xilus's stomping ground. *Nobody* goes there."

Ridley looked hurt. "Hey! I'm a thief, too. He'll be glad to see us. He'll likely *give* us that Dragon's Eye, if he knows where it is."

"It's a solid ruby," Marina said, "the size of your hand, or so the wraith said."

"Oh, fine," Snails said, "he's got a map from a wraith. Our troubles are over now."

Ridley turned to the dwarf. "What about you, friend? Do you care to come along? You'd be right welcome, you know."

"I don't see as I've got any choice," the dwarf muttered. "The Empress wants me for murder, and Damodar wants my head. Say, did I tell you about *his* head? Like nothin' you ever saw or hope to see again."

"Tell me later. As you say, we've got to get out of here."

Snails hesitated a moment, after the others were gone. He looked back into the darkness, thinking of Norda, a picture of her elven beauty so clear in his head that he could almost feel her presence there.

I can't go back, Snails thought. I know that. You've got to stick to your first friend and look for your true love after that. Lousy rules, but you've got to stand for something in your life, you truly do.

After a moment, he sighed and followed the others, unaware of just how close that presence had really been.

CHAPTER 16

Antius was a city even older that Sumdall itself, a city built atop a city and a myriad of cities under that, going back to even before the great war. Antius contained all the faults, all the smells, all the dangers of Sumdall, and few of its benefits. It was a cramped city with a crumbling fortress wall perched atop a steep hill. The place had nowhere to go but up. A stranger approaching this kingdom of thieves was awed by the towers and keeps that seemed to push one another aside, stretching high into the low clouds, struggling like thirsty plants, fighting for a single drop of water, a single breath of air.

No one in Antius, it seemed, had ever had a bath. Everyone, man, woman, and child alike, was so filthy and covered with ragged clothes that there was often no way to tell what sex they might be.

Ridley thought the citizens of Antius were, if possible, an even louder, coarser, more vulgar breed than the worst ruffian of Old-town Sumdall.

In the humid marketplace, everything imaginable was for sale—
vipers, vegetables, swords, dirks, flagons, food, and pots. Melons,
birds, monkeys, and frightened slave girls were all crammed into
rickety stalls topped by gaudy awnings.

Marina was horrified. She had scarcely dreamed there were
people who lived like this. If there weren't bugs of every sort
crawling beneath her clothes, there might as well have been, for
she truly imagined they were there.

Elwood looked longingly at a booth selling wines and ales
where a big-bellied man was squirting wine down his throat from
a bloated leather bladder. Much of the liquid entirely missed his
mouth.

"Forget it," Marina said. "We don't have time for that."

"I'm a dwarf," Elwood said. "Dwarves have a great thirst at
least several times a day."

"Some dwarves do. You don't."

"Hmph. Humans. I don't see why the gods had to make 'em
at all."

A few steps ahead, Ridley poked Snails in the ribs, and Snails
stopped to look. A brute with three bloodshot eyes, his great
body thick with purple skin, very deftly snatched a heavy purse
from a merchant passing by.

"Huh-unh, I don't think so," Snails said. "Not him."

"Yeah, him," Ridley said. "We don't have time to look for
handsome thieves."

Before Snails could stop him, Ridley stepped up and grinned
at the ragged horror, choking on his ghastly smell.

"Fraternal greetings, Brother," Ridley said, using the thieves'
hand signals as well. "I'm Ridley Freeborn, fellow practitioner of
the larcenous arts."

Three-Eyes blinked and spat on Ridley's boot.

"Yes, well, at any rate, I'm looking for your esteemed Guild-master Xilus. We thought perhaps you might know him?"

"No."

"What?"

The enormous purple man—or whatever it might be—bent down and breathed on Ridley.

"I said no. The only thing I know is you oughta take your business out of town before you end up with the words 'Outsiders Not Appreciated' branded where your nose used to be. Got it?"

"No, but thank you for your time. I appreciate that."

The giant stomped away, leaving behind an odor of sewage, muck, pollution, slime, and stomach disorders of every kind. Ridley held his breath as long as he could, but it didn't seem to help.

"Nice going," Marina said. "That worked out rather well."

"You can't get along with everyone. That fellow doesn't have a lot of social grace. I expect he comes from a bad home."

Marina made a face. "I imagine he comes from a hole in the ground."

"I hope he didn't hear that. He's got feelings like everyone else."

Marina blew out a breath. "You are hopeless, Ridley."

Ridley turned to look at a shop full of cages. There was every sort of creature there—everything that made a hoot or a hiss, a jabber or a squeal. The place reminded him of the room full of crawlies and slitheries in the mage's back room.

"There, look at that," Snails said, nodding toward a shabby looking structure made of rotting timber and mud. "That three-eyed what's-it just went up those outside stairs."

"Good work," said Ridley. "That's him. Let's go."

"Go where?" Marina said.

"Wherever he's going. You can bet he's on his way to report us to Xilus right now."

"He's going to get a big club, is what he is," Elwood said.

Marina moaned. "He doesn't *need* a big club."

Ridley looked her in the eye. "You want to get that big ruby or not? We can turn around right now."

"All right, let's go. I never could say no to a charmer like you."

"Keep it up," Ridley said. "You're doing fine so far."

* * * * *

Ridley sniffed the dusty air. The odors inside the ancient structure were worse than the miasma outside. The stairway led to an empty room, and the empty room led to a hall. The hall led nowhere at all.

"There's got to be a way in somewhere," Ridley told Snails softly. "A monster like that can't vanish in the air."

"Even if you want him to," Snails replied.

They had studied all the walls twice and then twice again. If there was any way in or out of the place, no one could say where.

"All right," Ridley concluded, "if it's not in here, it's back in that room somewhere."

"I don't think so," Marina said.

"You don't?"

"No, I don't. Stand back a minute, will you?"

Ridley gave her a bow and a wicked smile. "Please, be my guest."

Marina closed her eyes, turned around twice, shivered, gasped, and put her hands across her mouth, then took them down again. Without even opening her eyes, she walked straight toward the dwarf. Elwood got out of her way, and Marina touched the stone wall, ran her hands up, then down, then far to the left.

A tiny green light flickered in the gem on her wrist. The wall gave a rumble, a ragged line appeared among the stones, then swung back to reveal a wooden door.

"Hey, now how'd you do that?" Ridley gasped.

"I'm a mage, Ridley, as you'll likely recall. Only a student, but we learn to do things like that the first year."

"Did you ever think about the burglary trade?"

"No, of course not." Marina sniffed the air. "Mages use their powers only for good." Everyone's eyebrows raised. "All right, most of them do."

"Elwood," Ridley said, "I'd be grateful if you'd stay here and keep an eye on our back. You never can tell in a place like this."

"Good enough, friend." Elwood licked this thumb and ran it across the blade of his axe. "I can handle anything that comes from the front or the rear, sideways or upside down."

Ridley suddenly felt extremely tired, weary of dragons, rubies, wraiths, and mysterious rods.

"It was your idea to break into the magic school," Snails said, guessing his friend's thoughts.

"Don't remind me," Ridley said. "You do, I'm likely to brain you with Elwood's axe."

CHAPTER 17

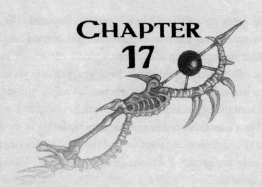

The vast, underground chambers of the Thieves' Guild were a maze of many rooms. They were designed to delay, confuse, and trap unwelcome intruders. A stranger might wander about for days and go virtually nowhere at all.

Ridley grudgingly had to admit that without Marina's magic skills at discovering secret doors and the right paths to take, they could have wandered about forever. Both Ridley and Snails marveled as they passed through one torch-lit room after another, crowded to the ceiling with stolen goods of every sort. Here was a sample of everything a stealer could possibly steal. And some, Ridley saw, that no one but a master of the art could have managed to spirit away.

"I feel awful," Snails confided. "It doesn't make apples and barber shears look like much, does it?"

"And chairs," Ridley added. "Don't forget ordinary chairs."

"You can shame me no further, Rid. I can see my failures all around me. I might as well have gotten a—a *job* somewhere, like a clerk or a worker on the docks." Snails stopped and looked at Ridley as if his heart had skipped a beat. "What am I saying? I could never do something as hideous as that!"

"Never fear, friend. You never will. You've given yourself a fright, is all. You'll be yourself again soon."

Marina, walking just behind them, shook her head and sighed. "I have never heard quite so disgusting a conversation in my life."

"Really?" Snails looked bewildered. "Oh, I have. Any number of times. You really should get out more, you know."

They could hear the babble long before they reached the vast chamber, a noise so deafening, so raucous, so rife with chaos and strife, the very stones of the corridor trembled with alarm.

The sight that met their eyes left them stunned. None of them had ever seen so many thieves before. All Ridley could think of was an ant hill someone had stirred with a stick. Brigands, hooligans, outlaws, and felons by the score. Villains, smugglers, robbers and muggers, crooks of every sort and every kind. Crooks buying, crooks selling, crooks stealing from other crooks as well. Crooks so caught up in the game, they were even stealing from themselves.

"Look at that!" Snails said. "This is thief heaven, Rid. There's nothing like it anywhere."

"Over there." Ridley pointed. "That's the great Toland him-self. He stole a glass eye right out of a prince's head, and the fellow was wide awake as well."

"*The* Toland?" exclaimed Snails. "The Toland who kidnapped the Duke of—?"

Marina frowned. "Who'd want to steal a glass eye?"

"There's a market for those things," Snails told her. "Praise the gods, why, *everyone's* here."

"Good. Then one of these characters can help us find Xilus.

I'd just as soon get that ruby and haul out of here."

"That's what I told you to do: Get out of here. But you wouldn't listen, would you, two-eyes?"

Ridley started as the purple three-eyed creature suddenly appeared at his side.

"Say now, great to see you again," Ridley said. "I thought we'd lost you back there. Just the fellow I was looking for. I'd like to ask you again, do you know where— *Ulllp!*"

The three-eyed creature lifted Ridley by the collar, jerked him off the ground, and breathed the essence of sewage in in his face.

"You goin' to see Xilus right now, little fool. An' I can tell you for sure, you'll wish he hadn't seen *you*."

With that, the odorous giant dropped Ridley to the floor, turned to several large brutes, and said, "Take 'em away!"

"See," Ridley said, "I told you we'd make a connection. You've just got to know the right people to see."

* * * * *

Xilus, Guildmaster of Thieves, was a wiry, bleary-eyed fellow with a cock-eyed jaw. He was festooned with rings—rings on his fingers, in his ears and in his nose, rings on his dirty bare toes, rings everywhere a ring might me, and possibly places no one had thought about before.

He lay in trashy splendor on the pelt of some very large creature—a beast, Ridley was sure, that had died of some terrible skin disease. Behind him was a blinding array of gaudy loot from every corner of the Empire and beyond.

"Well," Ridley said, poking out his hand, "you must be Guildmaster Xilus. It's an honor and a privilege, sir. I'm Ridley Freeborn, practitioner of the larcenous crafts, member in good standing of the Sumdall Guild. It's a pleasure to meet you."

Xilus raised a finely arched brow, looked Marina over from head to toe, and then looked her over once again.

"Tough town, Sumdall," Xilus said with a yawn. "All that magic and spells. Bad for business, I say."

"And I'd be the first to agree," Ridley said.

"Fine. So what do you want with me?"

"I can see that, sir. I'll cut this short and get out of your way. I understand you've got the Eye of the Dragon here. I'd like to talk you out of that little trinket if I may."

The thieves gathered close about Xilus broke into laughter, but Xilus stopped them with a many-jeweled hand.

"Never mind these fools, my friend. A perfectly reasonable request. Always happy to help a fellow thief. Especially one from out of town." Xilus found something under a fingernail, gave it a curious look, and bit it with his teeth. "While you're here, there's some interesting sights you ought to see. There's the Ever-Flowing Fountain, though I don't believe it's running right now, the Museum of Blood, and—say, have you ever heard of the Antius Guild Maze?"

"No, I can't say I have. Sounds like fun, though."

"Oh, it is." Xilus shot a lewd wink at Marina. "What's even more fun, if you make it through that is, is that the Eye of the Dragon is the prize."

Ridley felt a sudden chill. "Uh, has anyone ever finished it before?"

"Not exactly, no, but they all *died* trying."

The assembled smelly louts thought this was a riot. They laughed until they cried. It occurred to Ridley, though, they might simply laugh at whatever their leader said.

* * * * *

"You don't have to do this," Marina told Ridley, who was standing before the iron gate the barred the way to the famed Guildmaster's Maze. "We'll get the ruby some other way."

"Oh? Just what did you have in mind?"

Ridley, standing at the entry to the maze, knew how a bullock felt as the butchers led him to the slaughterhouse. The very same gawkers lined the high wall above, waving and cheering the dull-eyed victim on.

"You think of something," Ridley said, "you let me know, but you'd better make it fast."

Marina bit her lip. "I feel just awful. I got you into this."

"Yes, that's true. You certainly did."

"Ridley—"

"Hey! No problem. I do this all the time."

"You do?"

"What? You think I'm out of my mind?"

With that, he stalked down the narrow corridor, waved to the crowd, and kicked open the gate to the maze.

CHAPTER 18

Blue beams of light sliced across one stone wall to the other. Aside from hundreds of tiny dust motes dancing softly through the light, nothing moved in the chamber. Everything seemed perfectly safe. Too safe. Ridley paused, studied the scene, and thrust one hand through the first beam. A frighteningly sharp spike sprang up from the floor and stopped inches from Ridley's crotch. Ridley froze, startled, but ever so grateful that the spike had not proceeded another two inches. Eyeing the floor for more traps, Ridley cautiously stepped around the spike and continued down the hall.

Another beam of light pierced the shadows just ahead. Standing well away, Ridley waved his hand through the sparkling dust motes, then took a quick step back. A great, crescent-shaped axe with a shiny iron blade swung out of one wall. Ridley jumped back, and the blade neatly parted his hair before swinging back again. Ridley leaped up and slammed his boots against the floor, halting only inches from the next beam of light. The axe swung back, but Ridley wasn't there.

The crowd above roared, a din that deafened Ridley down below. He could see nothing ahead of him now, only the beams of light, and that worried Ridley a lot. Something was there, and he could only guess what. He could sense the danger, feel it in the hairs on his arms, in the tingle of his legs—

He threw himself quickly aside, hard against the right wall, and clambered into something—bones! Ridley stared at them in horror. He'd fallen into the long-dried remains of the last person who'd braved the maze.

Peering down the shadowed corridor, he grasped a long dusty bone from the pile and sent it twirling through the lancing beams of light. One massive blade, then another, and another after that—six in all—whirred out of the wall.

"These guys are crooks," Ridley muttered to himself. "This game is fixed, and I'm sliced meat."

Drawing a breath, cursing life and cursing death, he grabbed the haft of the nearest axe as it swept past his face, pulled himself atop, balanced there an instant, then made his way dizzily from one swinging weapon to the next.

The crowd went mad. They loved the action, the danger, the suspense . . . as long it was happening to somebody else. Some moaned in anger; some cheered in delight. Some tore up useless bets and tossed them like snowflakes in the air.

* * * * *

"A thousand gold pieces he makes it!" Snails said, shouting at Xilus and taking a good long look at the maiden stroking the Guildmaster's head.

"Why, I'd be delighted," Xilus said, showing Snails his teeth. "You'll lose, of course. The fellow doesn't have a chance."

Marina leaned in to whisper in Snails's ear. "Do you have a thousand gold pieces?"

Snails looked appalled. "Of course not! I don't imagine there are half that many gold pieces in the world!"

* * * * *

For a moment, Ridley could sense no obstacles at all. The room was absolutely bare, but lavishly decorated for all that. Walls and floor were completely covered in hundreds of large ornate tiles, and on each tile were strange markings and symbols. Ridley could see no two alike. Other than that . . . nothing. A doorway beckoned on the opposite side of the chamber.

Ridley took a hesitant step into the room, and in an instant, both ends of the corridor blossomed into flame, stranding him square in the middle of it all.

"Filthy cheats!" Ridley shouted, shaking his fist at the audience above. "You won't give a man a chance. It's not bloody fair at all!"

As the flames continued to roar only a foot over his head, Ridley drew his sword and began an awkward crouching walk forward, studying the colored tiles before him. He spotted a blue one and pressed it with the tip of his sword. The flames intensified.

The air was stifling, painful. Another minute, and the air would be too hot to breathe. Steeling his nerves, Ridley pressed down on the next tile, a red one this time. Nothing happened. Desperate to be out of the room, Ridley leaped onto the red tile.

As suddenly as they'd begun, the flames stopped. Ridley grinned just as a sharp click echoed in the chamber, and the smile dropped from his face. With a sickening grinding sound, the wall behind him began to move forward at an alarming speed, and the door on the other end of the room began to slide closed. Left with no other choice, Ridley leaped, landed, and lurched into a desperate run.

He half-felt tiles sinking ever-so-slightly beneath him, and again flames erupted from the walls. He ducked and dodged his way through the flames and refused to look back. Over the roar of the flames, he could still hear the incessant grinding of the wall only a few paces behind him.

Ridley stumbled and fell, his sword clattering beside him. His foot landed hard on a red tile, and there was a faint hum, then an audible click. The red tile flipped over, and this side was a yellow that glowed like bronze beneath the flames. He was about to pick himself up when all of the red tiles in the room began flip in rapid succession, each revealing a bright yellow.

Not caring what that might mean, Ridley retrieved his sword and made one last desperate lunge for the door. Flames roared around him, and he dived through the doorway, rolling as he hit the ground. The door slid shut behind him, cutting off the roar of the flames. Ridley inspected himself, sure that he'd been scorched in a dozen places. The sleeve of his jacket was smoking slightly, but other than that, he seemed to have escaped unscathed.

The room in which he found himself was small and dimly lit by a cold blue light for which he could see no source. In the center of the opposite wall was an intricate lock upon a vast door. Ridley had never seen such a locking mechanism. In the midst of wicked-looking iron jaws was a large stone hand holding a fat hourglass, bigger than his head.

He felt the short hairs climb the back of his neck. Wiping the sweat from his eyes, he peered into the darkness above. He couldn't see them, but he knew they were there, ringed about the high wall, all of them silent now—Marina and Snails waiting for him to try, Xilus and his odorous crew waiting for him to die.

"All right!" he shouted. "Let's do it! It isn't going to get any more fun than this!"

He stepped forward, but before he was within an arm's length of the lock, the stone hand turned, and sand began to flow. He couldn't believe it was flowing so fast. Damnation! Couldn't they get any coarser sand than that?

As Ridley approached the lock, a low rumble reached him from above, and he looked up. From the ceiling, a grate of iron spikes began to descend into the room, and in front of him, the sharp iron jaws surrounding the lock began to chomp open and shut, again and again.

"That's it?" Ridley yelled, waving his fist at the unseen audience above. "Nothing else? You can't think of anything more than that? How about some vipers? Got any cobras, something like that? Maybe some spiders? I *love* spiders—the big hairy kind! Hey! Send that purple lout with three eyes down here! He looks like a spider! That's close enough for me!"

Ridley knew he was wasting precious time and really didn't care. He was beat, worn to a frazzle. His head was exploding, and his knees wouldn't work properly. His hands were shaking and wouldn't stop.

He bent to the lock, knowing he couldn't do it, but knowing he had to try. He knew this was clearly the final stage of the maze. The builders had saved the most cunning, devious tricks for this final act. Ridley felt strangely calm. The time for fear was past. He knew this last challenge for what it was: impossible to solve. There was no reason, no logic, no pattern here at all. And that, he knew, was what the maze builders had in mind. If any man got this far, the final trick would break him, let him know he'd been a fool to try. Before him, he saw the last of the sand begin its way down the slick surface of the hourglass. He had a few seconds at best.

Ridley stopped and took a deep breath. Whatever he did would kill him. Whatever he did would be wrong.

He slowly backed away from the device. The sand in the hourglass was nearly gone. The spikes were so close that he knew he'd feel them begin to bite at any moment. He wondered if Marina and Snails were watching, if Snails had the sense to try to get her out of there before the end.

The spikes touched his skin. Ridley turned his head aside, took a breath, and saw the hourglass. The barest whisper of sand remained, and just like that, Ridley saw the solution. He'd know in half a second if he was right, know if he'd live or die . . .

With one swift stroke, Ridley brought his sword around in a hissing arc and shattered the glass. With a shriek of metal gears, the iron jaws froze wide-open, and the grate stopped and began to rise again. Ridley turned to see the studded face of the heavy iron vault spring open wide.

He knew that he'd won, that he'd guessed the last dirty secret of the maze.

He could see his prize there in the next chamber. Nesting on a black velvet cushion, bathed in a warm red light, was a blood-red ruby, the Eye of the Dragon, glowing with a fiery, inner light of its own.

CHAPTER 19

They gathered around him in Xilus's dungeon, a cheering collection of thieves resplendent in silks, rags, or scarcely anything at all. Each told Ridley he was a great, fine, most respected man, that he would surely never be forgotten as long as Antius stood, as it had for a thousand years.

Then, as a body, as a single breath, they ran to Xilus's big gaudy bar for another mug of ale. The losers, those who'd bet against Ridley living, were already there drowning their sorrows and empty purses in ale and sour beer.

Marina gave him an almost tender hug. Snails, with tears in his eyes, told Ridley how relieved he was to see his old friend and what a joy it was to win more than ten thousand pieces of gold from a number of thieves, including Xilus himself.

"Well, I'm glad I could make your fortune," Ridley said. "Mind if I take a look?"

"I don't have my winnings yet, but everyone's promised to pay this afternoon."

"In other words, you'll never see a copper," Ridley said.

"I know," Snails said, "but I *did* win, and that's almost the same."

Xilus, totally exhausted from watching Ridley's ordeal, was back on his tasteless couch, eating peeled grapes from a girl in a gown that was formerly a drape.

"My most sincere congratulations," Xilus said. "Very clever. Well done, you. That last little bit, you know, I've always liked that. You were absolutely marvelous." Xilus gave Ridley a sly and crooked grin. "Not easy, you know. One has to be an idiot to try it, yet smart enough to win."

"And I came along."

"Bless you, lad, you did! And I couldn't be happier that you made it out alive."

"Thank you," Ridley replied.

"Oh, no, no, no," Xilus said. "Thank *you*. You know, I've waited fifteen years for someone to come along and pick that lock." Xilus threw back his head and laughed. As ever, the laugh was echoed by the fetching young women and the unwashed thieves, who mirrored Xilus's every emotion, every possible need. "Now, my friend," the Guildmaster said, leaning forward and brushing a maiden aside, "now I would be most grateful if you'd give me what's rightfully mine."

Ridley gave the man a weary sigh. "Now why am I not surprised to hear this? Still, it hurts me to see you break the code of honor among thieves."

"Honor's for fools, my friend," Xilus replied with an almost genuine smile. "Quite a romantic notion, but do you really think I could have amassed all this wealth if I worried about honor?" Still smiling, Xilus extended an open hand to Ridley. Several of the thieves behind him drew their weapons. "Now, if you don't mind, hand it over. *Please."*

"Marina," Ridley said without taking his eyes off of Xilus, "I told you there's no place for magic in the stealing profession. It's possible that I lied. If you would, please turn all of these odorous louts into lice. It shouldn't be too hard. They're all halfway there already."

"I can try," Marina said. "I'm not real sure that I—"

Xilus's jaw dropped, the smile gone. "Halluk! Hugo! Get her out of here, now!"

Two burly thieves detached themselves from the crowd and came at Marina on the run, but before they had crossed half the distance, two crimson arrows buried themselves in their throats.

An angry roar erupted from the crowd. As one, the band of thieves turned to look behind them, swords and sharp axes already in their hands.

Ridley stood at Marina's side, weapon at the ready, Snails protecting his back.

"Whoever it is," Ridley shouted about the din, "I think we're going to be best friends!"

"No!" Marina gasped. "Oh, no!"

Marina's fingers bit into his arm. Ridley looked past her. The horde of cutthroats had suddenly gone quiet. They hastily stepped aside, and Damodar marched through them, a squad of crimson-armored killers at his back.

"Well, isn't this fine?" Damodar said. "All of you together! Thieves among thieves. I trust you're in good health?"

"Who the hell is he?" Xilus demanded, struggling to his feet. "Who the hell are you? I don't know you, sir, and I don't *like* people I don't know."

"Patience, or you'll know me too well." Damodar turned to Ridley. "This is very tiresome to me. I'll take the map if you will, and that lovely stone as well—then we can talk about how quickly you die."

"Sure," Ridley said, "it's too big for a ring, anyway."

He tossed the stone high into the air. Damodar and every soldier, thief, and parasite in the place looked up to follow its flight. Before they could glance down again, Ridley drew the scroll from his belt, grabbed a torch from Xilus's wall, and set a corner of the parchment afire.

"Got you!" Snails grinned as he caught the red stone coming down.

Damodar's ruined face turned hideous shades of purple and red.

"Put it down," he said softly. "Put it down now, or you'll wish you'd never been born."

"Sure, try to sweet talk me. Won't do you any good."

Ridley held up the smoldering map for everyone to see. "Here's the map you'll need to find the rod, friend. Clear a nice, wide path for us, and I'll *think* about putting it out."

Damodar didn't hesitate. "Do it," he ordered, and his warriors moved aside.

"Marina! Snails!" Ridley blew out the small flame but kept the torch close by. "Everyone, we have to leave, but I hope you'll all stay and enjoy yourselves. The party's on Xilus and his Ugliness here."

Damodar glared and clenched his fists. The taught skin of his head writhed and rippled, a living thing.

Snails shuddered. "You look awful, friend. You ought to see somebody about that."

"Snails," Ridley said, "watch Xilus and his bunch. Marina, keep your eye on these crimson-clad uglies. We're going out the way we— Hey! No!"

From the corner of his eye, Ridley saw Xilus make his move. Damodar turned, too late, and Xilus bowled him over, slamming him to the ground.

The courtyard exploded in a riot of armored soldiers and ragged thieves. Snails struck whoever was standing close by. Ridley kicked a Crimson Brigadier in the belly, grabbed Marina, and pulled her away. She was shouting something he couldn't hear. He took two steps, and someone hit him hard, spilling him to the ground.

The scroll and the torch flew out of his hands. Ridley shook his head, gasping to get his breath back. Marina was gone. The scroll was out of sight, lost somewhere in a forest of kicking, slashing boots and dirty bare feet. He saw the torch, grabbed for it, and missed. It rolled away and stopped at a pink and green satin wall-hanging.

"Uh-oh," Ridley said. "Time to leave."

Before he could fight his way to Marina and Snails, flames raced up the dry, rotting fabric on Xilus's wall. In seconds, thick, blinding smoke filled the courtyard, catching the melee of rioters unaware.

* * * * *

Scarcely two thief-lengths away, Marina crawled through the bedlam, the map clutched tightly in her hand. Snails had been beside her a moment before, but now he was gone.

"Ridley!" she shouted frantically. "Ridley! Snails!"

"Here! Quickly, take my hand!"

Marina reached out blindly. A strong arm grabbed her and held. A sword slashed its way through the crowd, leaving bleeding victims behind. Almost at once, there was hardly any smoke at all, and no one else to fight.

"Ridley! Thank the gods! I thought I'd—"

"What? Lost me forever? Not a chance of that, my dear."

Marina tried to scream, but the sound froze in her throat. Damodar, enraged face writhing, smiled down at her and snatched the map from her hand. Marina tried desperately to pull away. She imagined a thousand worms rippling beneath his pallid skin.

Damodar caught her expression and fondly brushed a lock of hair from her cheek.

"I'm not pretty anymore, I'll grant you that, but the mages say beauty comes from the soul. I believe that, don't you?"

"*Ridley!*"

Marina spotted him then, fighting two of Xilus's henchmen, but Damodar tightened his grip and drew her roughly away. Pressing a dagger to her throat, he dragged her toward a heavy wooden door.

*   *   *   *   *

"Marina!" Ridley shouted as ducked under a lethal swipe of his opponent's blade, but in that instant she was gone.

His heart beating painfully against his chest, he slashed his way through the angry crowd, choosing escape over victory. He struggled to reach the door where Damodar and Marina had disappeared. He heard Snails call out behind him, and as Ridley turned, a thunderous roar filled the courtyard, shaking the very walls.

Ridley saw a welcome, wondrous sight. Elwood, no higher

than the shortest thief's belt, lurched through smoke and fire, a sawed-off demon with a dirty red beard. With a frightening battle cry, he swung his murderous axe through soldier and thief alike. Some dropped their weapons, scattered, and ran. Some stood and died on the spot.

"You blasted oversized cowards!" Elwood roared. "You dare start a killin' spree and don't invite *me?* You'll wish you were dead before Elwood Gutworthy's finished with you!"

Ridley, awed by the dwarf's fierce assault, looked away an instant, caught the side of a blade, and went down. Knowing death was half a heartbeat away, he looked up in time to see a gauntleted fist come from nowhere to smash his assailant to the ground.

Snails looked down at Ridley and grinned. "You all right, Rid? Thank the gods! I thought you were dead."

"So did I. Thanks for the help." He stood and grabbed Snails's shoulders. "Damodar's got Marina! I've got to find her!"

Snails looked over his shoulder. "Someone's got to help the dwarf."

"Absolutely. You get Elwood. I'll go after Marina."

"Why me? Why do I always get the dwarf?"

"Shut up! We're wasting time. Go and get the dwarf."

* * * * *

Outside the high wall, the night was black as ink. Ridley could see scarcely anything at all. A chill touched the short hairs on his neck. Marina was gone, nowhere in sight. A great storm was racing across the horizon to the north. From the compound past the wall came the cries of dying men, and a black column of oily smoke rose to the somber sky. Ridley wanted to retch, but there was nothing but a dull, hollow ache where a pleasant meal should be. He tried to recall when he'd last tasted food.

Once more, he scanned the dark horizon. Would Damodar take Marina back to Sumdall City? Most likely, he decided. Damodar would keep her alive until he got the map, which was likely back there in the compound, burned to a crisp. And where was that damned great ruby now? He'd tossed it to Snails, but what had happened to it after that?

Ridley held onto the thought. Slim as it was, it was better than nothing at all. Damodar needed the map *and* Dragon's Eye. Until he had both . . .

He turned, then, weapon at the ready, as Elwood Gutworthy and Snails emerged from behind the high wall. Both of them were ragged, bloody, and covered with soot.

"Glad you made it," Ridley said. He shook his head and looked at Snails. "I can't find her. She's gone."

"We'll find her, Rid. You can count on that."

"I'm sorry," Elwood added, "but if we don't get out of here fast, we'll be finished as well."

"She's not *finished*," Ridley said harshly. "Don't say that. I'll bring her back, and she'll be all right."

"No offense, lad." Elwood glanced over his shoulder at the high wall. "Even so, we'd best save ourselves. We've no friends in this hellish place."

"He's right, Rid. We're in a hornet's nest here."

As if in answer, a horde of howling thieves burst out of the courtyard door and swarmed over the wall and into the darkness below. They came in all shapes and every form—fat thieves, skinny thieves, thieves with two noses, thieves with three eyes. Some swung down on shoddy ropes. Some jumped and fell.

There were even a few who tried to fly.

Ridley spotted Xilus bringing up the rear, waving an enormous jeweled sword, a dozen maidens on his heels, spilling plates of fruit, sweetmeats and flagons of wine.

Ridley, with no idea of just where he might be, on possibly the blackest night he'd ever seen, raced for the nearest alleyway, Elwood and Snails trailing along behind. The alley came to a narrow avenue of shabby homes and shops. Ridley turned left, changed his mind at once, and veered right.

"Where are you going, lad?" Elwood shouted. "Hold up there!"

Ridley didn't answer. Another street over and he saw a familiar sight: the marketplace where they'd entered Antius City earlier in the day. Dark and empty now, he knew if they kept a straight path they'd reach the city gates.

And who'd be there to greet them? He wondered. More bloody thieves? Damodar's guards? No time to wonder with Xilus's bunch biting at their heels half an alleyway behind.

"*Ridley!*"

Ridley didn't stop. Snails ran up beside him, breathing hard now. "Not that way, friend! Left! Left!"

"You sure about that?"

"Absolutely. I don't know much, but I know my alleyways."

"Fine. Why not?"

Ridley jogged into the narrow avenue, his companions close behind. Timber and wattle houses leaned drunkenly over the street below, shutting out the feeble moonlight.

"All right, great navigator," Ridley called out, "what next?"

"What's next, friend, is you don't move a muscle or you're dead."

Ridley came to a sudden halt. Looming out of the dark were at least a dozen hooded figures, each armed with stubby crossbows, and every one of them aimed at his head.

"Look, we mean you no harm—" Ridley began.

One of the figures laughed. "I guess we can see that. Get down on your bellies. Now!"

"Damned if I will," Elwood protested. "You can kill me just as easy standing up."

Three of the cloaked figures stepped forward, holding their weapons on Ridley, Elwood, and Snails. The others held fast.

"Now," their leader said quietly, "fire!"

A dozen deadly iron bolts whined through the air.

Ridley cringed, waiting for signs of the afterlife. Nothing seemed to change. Finally, he risked a look, turned around, and saw bodies sprawled in the cobbled street behind them, some still, some thrashing about. One, he saw, was a shaggy giant with three eyes. One eye wore a feathered bolt; two were still intact.

Coming quickly after the first, a second volley dropped another band of thieves. There was little need for a third, but the bowmen sent their deadly shafts winging through the dark.

Ridley sat up and blinked. Snails was staring into the night, all the color drained from his face. Elwood was cursing in the sharp, throaty language of the dwarves.

"All of you," said an archer, "on your feet! We must be quickly out of here."

"Why?" Elwood grumbled. "So you can murder us somewhere else?"

"Bind them," the leader said. "Gag the short one as well. I can stand most anything but a foul-mouthed dwarf."

CHAPTER 20

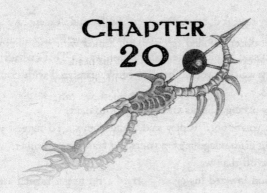

Even from the deep cover of the forest, Ridley could see a bright glow low in the eastern sky, a light that told him that the fire had spread far from Xilus's keep. He knew that the city was a tinderbox, and it wouldn't take long to burn Antius to the ground.

Ridley stood under the heavy branches of a thick-boled oak that was likely as old as the world itself. The hooded crossbow-men had taken no action against them, and Ridley felt that was surely a positive sign. There was no need to drag them out in the woods to kill them when they could have done the job in Antius.

"Don't get your hopes up, boy," Elwood said. "This bunch is wearin' hoods. They likely got some secret rites to perform, before they do us in."

"Like what?" Snails wanted to know. "What kind of rites are you talking about?"

"Oh, the usual." Elwood ran a hand through his tangled beard. "Torture, to start. Strange and terrible things like pluckin' out eyes and snippin' off toes. Horrors even worse than that."

"They haven't done anything yet," Ridley said, "except save us."

"Well, of course they haven't." Elwood gave Ridley a painful look that said he pitied the man's foolish ways. "That's what they do. They wait till you're 'bout to break, paralyzed with doubts and fears."

"It's working," Snails said. "I'm getting there."

"No, you're not," Ridley said. "And you, sir, I'd suggest you keep your grim imaginings to yourself. I fear there are others who are worse off than we."

Elwood lowered his eyes. "Sorry. I tend to get carried away. It's both the failing and the glory of a dwarf. I'm terrible sorry about the lady. As you say, she might not be lost after all. We can't know that."

"I won't believe she's back there with that filthy lot."

Ridley let the words fade away. Snails, standing in silence beside him, reached out and gripped his friend's arm.

"I hate to pile any more stones on your back, Rid, but they may be coming to start that eye-poking, finger-chopping part the dwarf was warning us about."

Indeed, five of the hooded crossbowmen were approaching from across the clearing.

"I think it might be best if we gave them the chance to speak first," Ridley said, aiming his words in Elwood's direction. "They seem to prefer a more courteous approach over cursing in uncouth tongues."

"I reckon you'd be referring to me," Elwood growled.

"I am."

"For your information, lad, *uncouth* is a point of view. Human speech sounds like cattle peeing on gravel to me."

Ridley had an answer to that, but the crossbowmen were well

upon them, so he kept his opinion to himself and prayed the dwarf would do the same.

"I regret you were ill-treated," the tallest of the figures said in an obviously feminine voice. "There was little choice at the time. Moreover, the short fellow here appears to have no manners at all."

"Listen, now—"

"Shut up," Ridley said. "Right now."

"If I offended somehow," Elwood muttered, gazing at his boots, "it's 'cause I'm not used to being bound up and killed in some awful secret rite."

Suddenly, the hooded figure broke into laughter, a sound to Ridley's ears like the chiming of silver bells. The hood came off, and Ridley stared at a most angelic face framed by pointed elven ears and short-cropped ebony hair.

Snails gasped. "It—it's you! Norda!" He shook his head in wonder. "I can't believe it!"

Ridley raised a brow. "You know her, then?"

"Yes, I do, Rid!" The sly smile that creased his face said he'd just found a bag of gold he'd forgotten he'd hidden away. "We're quite well acquainted, Norda and I. Our relationship goes way back."

"Not *that* far back, and not that well acquainted," Norda said.

"Hmph." Elwood sniffed. "Is this that elf you were moonin' about 'fore I had to come and save your hide?"

"I wouldn't put it quite like that, but yes, this is certainly the one."

"They all look alike to me."

"Pardon me," Ridley said, "my friends here know you but I don't, and while I'm grateful you got us out of a terrible mess back there, I'd like to know what *for* and what we're doing here. We've lost one of our own, and that maniac got her. Meanwhile, you're risking her life by keeping us here."

Norda took a step closer to Ridley. "Who? Who is lost, and who has her? Tell me the rest of this, and quickly."

"Marina," Ridley said, "Marina of Pretensa. Though who she is no concern of yours."

Norda's eyes flashed. "In that you are quite wrong, human. My concern, as you put it, is to place you, your companions, and the woman known as Marina Pretensa under royal arrest and return you and the precious map you stole from Vildar Vildan, advisor to the Empress of Izmer."

Ridley gave her a hollow laugh. "You're a little late, I fear. Another keeper of the royal *law*, the renowned leader of the Crimson Brigade, already has her in his care."

"Damodar?" Norda stared. "Damodar has her?"

"You've got it, and the bad news is, he's not working for the law, if indeed he ever was. He belongs to Profion of Tarak. He's the thief here, not us."

"These are things I did not know." Norda looked off into the dark. "This path has been deliberately muddied, I fear, hidden from me . . ."

"Well it ought to be *un*muddied now. So why don't you do your job instead of standing here?"

"My friend is not abusive by nature," Snails said. "He is, ah, under some strain right now, and rightly so, you'll agree. I hope when all this is straightened out that you and I . . . what I mean to say is—"

"Not now, Snails," Norda said gently. "Another time, perhaps, we'll cross the same path again."

Snails's smile faded. "Yeah, that'd be fine with me."

Norda looked at Ridley. "I fear we face more troubled times than you can imagine, if indeed, we have any future at all."

She walked away, and Ridley saw her disappear in shadow past the dying fire. He wondered how many other beings had misjudged this slight and seemingly harmless female? None, he imagined, who had seen what lay in those deep elven eyes. She was not the demon Elwood saw in his wild imaginings, but neither was she even close to being human.

* * * * *

In a black and tangled dell, in the midnight shadow of great dreaming trees, Norda sat alone by a small trickling spring. From her robes she drew a crystal, clear and pure as morning air. As her hands passed lightly over its infinite facets and planes, the crystal began to glow, as if a tiny luminous heart had come to life inside. In a moment, a faint and shimmering image of the Empress Savina appeared. At first, Savina was startled, but then she turned to a mirror on the table by her side, a mirror cleaved from the very same crystal in Norda's hands.

"Majesty."

"Norda, do you have it? Have you found the scroll?"

"No, Highness. I have grave news, I fear. Profion also seeks the rod."

"How? How could he know?"

"I cannot say, but there is worse news still. Damodar has taken Marina of Pretensa along with the map. I have her companions here. What is your will?"

"I don't— I don't know, Norda. Seek out Damodar. We must have the Rod of Savrille, at any cost."

"Yes, Majesty."

"Time is running out for us, Norda. Time is nearly gone."

Norda watched Savina's image fade, then flutter and disappear. In the instant the Empress was gone, Norda felt a cold, unnatural chill, as if a wind from some alien world had reached out and found her.

Norda's whole life, her long years as a tracker for the royal house, as a student of strange and secret lore, had taught her that signs and portents were all about her, were with her all the time. A chill, a whisper, a sound in the night, small and insignificant, but it was said that one could read but a midge's breath of what they said could hold in their hands the destiny of the world.

CHAPTER 21

They were nearly lost in the mist that curled through early morning, clung to the heavy branches, and softly sighed over the forest floor.

Half of Norda's small force rode ahead and half behind, each astride a mount elven-trained and elven-bred. Snails rode with Norda herself and felt he was blessed to be so near this vision that had come into his life. The fact that he doubted she returned these feelings worried him not at all. Why would the Fates bring him this close to heaven, then close the door in his face? It stood to reason they would work this out somehow.

Ridley, some distance behind, tried to hold a strong image of Marina in his mind, the Marina who could charm him with her laughter, her eyes, the Marina who could irritate him with her stubborn, willful ways. Damnation, but he longed for a sharp and cutting word, a cheek flushed red, a pouty mouth and a nasty attitude. What a wondrous creature she was. How could he stand to be around her? And again, how could he not?

"Can't I just walk?" Elwood muttered. "I'm a dwarf, in case no one noticed. Dwarves are terrified of horses. A human wouldn't know it, but a horse'll stomp a dwarf to death while he's sleeping and eat him if he can."

"Nonsense," Ridley said. "Horses don't eat dwarves or any other living thing."

"Oh, and you'd know, I'll wager—a thief from the foul hovels of the city. Why, I'd guess there's little you *wouldn't* know about the ways of horses and dwarves."

"All right."

"Well, it's so, or I wouldn't have said it, boy." Elwood was silent for a long moment. He squinted into the misty dawn, then turned to Ridley again. "Look, friend, we'll find her. I swear."

"I thank you for your thoughts."

"Dwarves have feelings too, you know. We've got our loved ones, same as humans do—and elves as well, I suppose, though I don't think I'd take a large wager on that. The only creatures that don't have feelings are orcs. An orc's a hellish beast without a soul. It's out of all reason to imagine one of those lovin' something they couldn't eat."

"I've never spoken to an orc," Ridley said, ducking his head beneath a low branch. "I can't say I know what they think or what they do."

Elwood looked aghast. "Well, by the gods of the river, lad, why on earth would you ever want to?"

Norda reined in her mount, waiting for Ridley and Elwood to catch up.

"Damodar's people have followed the valley trail. If we cut through the hills up ahead, we can likely cut them off."

"Fine," Ridley said. "I'm game for whatever works."

Ridley Freeborn the thief doesn't know he's a
hero—yet.

Profion—a mage of frightening ambition and
overwhelming pride.

Damodar, Profion's henchman.
Straining beneath the control of his
master, he longs for his own power.

Elwood Gutworthy. The dwarf is a good fight-
er and a faithful friend.

The elven tracker Norda is a beautiful ally and
a deadly foe.

Pretending concern for the empress, Profion
addresses Sumdall City's Great Council of
Mages.

Be careful when you rob a mage. You might
get more than you want.

Alone in his workshop, Profion prepares the
Rod of Dragon Control.

Marina of Pretensa, apprentice mage, has little
time or respect for a pair of thieves.

To gain the Dragon's Eye, Ridley must pass
through the deadly Thieves' Guild maze.

Ridley seizes the Rod of Dragon Control,
which could determine the fate of Sumdall
City.

Xilius of the Thieves' Guild has no intention
of letting Ridley out of his maze.

No sooner does Ridley escape one trap than he
find himself in another.

Norda shows she can handle several opponents
in a fight.

The mages of Sumdall City summon dragons
for their final battle with
the empress.

Gold dragons—the most terrifying
creatures in the empire of Izmer.

Elwood nodded assent, and Norda rode on ahead. She looked at Snails again and smiled.

"You've never ridden a mount before, have you? Have you even seen a horse?"

"I've seen plenty. I even stole one once, but the beast ran away. I know horses all right." Snails took a breath. "Don't be angry with me, now, all I want to do is ask. As humans go, you know, you couldn't find a kinder, more understanding fellow than me. And listen, I love the way you track. I— Look, you wouldn't happen to be single, would you?"

Norda pretended to stare at a tree. "How old are you, Snails?"

"Twenty-three. Yeah, I know I'm a little young for you, but what if I got my hands on an aging potion, huh? I'd be glad to sacrifice a couple of years for you. A lot of people say I look older than that."

"I'm two-hundred and thirty four, Snails."

"Damn. I didn't mean that much of a change. Well, I know there's a difference in people and elves, but if we really care for each other . . ."

"Snails, you're very nice, but this really isn't going to work."

"Give it a chance. You're an elf, but you can't know everything. I know the mages say a person's life can take about a zillion paths, and we never know which it'll be."

Norda turned suddenly, as if his words had startled her out of a dream. The color drained from her face, and she quickly looked away.

"Now, what was that for?" Snails wanted to know. "I say something wrong or what?"

"Nothing, Snails. Truly. Sometimes I simply see more paths than I want to see."

* * * * *

His friends were phantom riders, still pale and indistinct in the gloom of pre-dawn light. Elwood, the shortest of the shadows, grumbled about some terrible beast, some horror that would snatch them up and turn them into lint. This, he noted, was not to be mistaken for the ratbat, which sank its fangs into the skulls of its victims and sucked their senses dry.

Snails, who was ever certain a "no" was quite possibly a "yes," spent his every charm on Norda the elf. Ridley, who could not help but hear, had never imagined such bold, heroic adventures, such breathtaking tales. Certainly, he could not recall taking part in these daring events himself.

As the night wore on and exhaustion began to take its toll, even Snails's eager advances began to come fewer and fewer, until the party rode in almost complete silence. The companions rode through the seemingly endless forest, accompanied by only the monotonous sound of their horses' hooves.

"So much for your expert tracking skills!" Ridley shouted to Norda, breaking the unnerving silence. His impatience had finally won out over his exhaustion. "This is worthless!"

"The path is right," Norda replied.

"What could possibly make you think *that?* We've been riding all night, and we've seen no trace of Damodar or Marina!"

"I sense Damodar's presence." Norda looked away and would say no more.

"This is a waste of time!" Ridley reined his horse to an awkward halt. "We should split up. That's the only way we're ever going to find him in this cursed forest."

Ridley, ignoring Snails and Norda's protests, spurred his horse away from the main group between a gap in the trees. Not even turning around to face them, he shouted, "I'm going this way!

Snails, you go that way! Elwood, you stick with Norda! Don't let her out of your sight!"

He could feel the eyes of the elves watching him as he rode away, and he thought Snails and Elwood might have shouted something, but he ignored them all. Damodar had Marina, and he could waste no more time dallying through the woods.

Weaving through the seemingly endless trees, which he thought might be beginning to thin, Ridley kept his horse at a brisk pace until dawn's light began to shimmer through the whispering leaves.

An eerie silence seemed to grip the valley into which he rode. His mount moved quietly through the depths of the forest, through sudden open meadows of grass so high, so lush and freshly green, that Ridley's leggings and his boots were as wet as if he'd forded a stream.

The day, indeed, seemed hushed and pallid gray, seemed to slow time itself to the pace of a dream. Leaving the meadow for the cover of the forest once again, Ridley felt as if the world might pause right there, hesitate forever in the magic moment between night and day. And if that should happen, he wondered, would those still abed simply live on in their dreams and never have to wake again?

Caught in this waking vision, he scarcely noticed that the woods had given way to a barren, rocky land, a place of dark and ragged spires of naked stone. There was not a breath of wind here, no hint of any life, not a single blade of grass. Only the grim and lonely crags against a cold oppressive sky.

Ridley drew his mount to a halt, sat in the saddle and looked about. Wherever this was, it was surely not the way. He had let his thoughts drift, let exhaustion and frustration rule his judgment, let himself get hopelessly lost . . .

Ridley felt like a fool. There was no use going ahead. The only thing to do was turn around, go back, and hope the stony landscape ended somewhere and took him where he'd been. He kicked the horse lightly and brought its head about. The mount refused to move. Instead, it jerked its head up and twitched its ears.

Ridley kicked again, not so gently this time.

"Come on, whatever your name is, don't start any foolishness with me. Just get us out of here."

The horse looked blankly at Ridley and turned away. Ridley cursed him and wondered what to do next. He had no knowledge of horses, had seldom ever thought about the beasts.

With a sigh, he eased himself out of the saddle, stretched his legs, and remembered how fine it was to stand on solid ground. If, indeed, the gods had meant for men to ride these creatures, they surely would have made them softer to sit upon.

As this and other thoughts drifted idly through his mind, he began to hear the sound. . . .

It was a rustling kind of sound, like the wind through autumn leaves, like birds taking flight through winter trees. It came from the jagged cluster of boulders to his right, or so it seemed. Ridley closed his eyes and listened, trying to link the sound to something he'd heard before. Nothing, nothing familiar came to mind at all.

Quietly drawing his sword, he left his mount and walked cautiously toward the barrier of stone. Very likely there was nothing there at all, but they were too close to enemy country simply to let the matter go.

Behind the field of boulders was the narrow entry to a high canyon wall. Ridley paused to study the way, but there was nothing but shadow to see. Dropping his cloak, he hefted the blade in his hand and moved slowly ahead.

The sound came again, the same soft rustle, only closer this time. Ridley took a breath, slid around a solid outcropping, and into the canyon itself.

* * * * *

She knew it was nearly time. She could feel the pulsing glow of the golden sphere that held her, bound her, keeping her safely warm.

Now, though, it was time to leave the safety, time to leave the warmth, time to claim her place among her kind. Once again she slashed at her bright sanctuary that was fast becoming a prison now—slashed, ripped, and tore in sudden rage and desperation at the strong and viscous globe that held her there.

She strained to break her great wings free, thrashed her scaly head about, screeched in fury as the poison in the shell, the acid in her veins, tried to kill her before she could rip herself free.

Now she could feel a deep, throbbing vibration in her belly, a strange oscillation that spread in a wave of awesome pain through her spine, through her breast to explode within her head. With no conscious thought at all, her shriek of desperation eased into a hum, the hum into a chant, the chant into a song, a song that spoke of mighty thunderheads, lightning on her wings, a song that spoke of hunger, spoke of needs, spoke of fearsome dragon deeds . . .

The deep, tremulous notes of the song began to throb in the creature's corded throat, through muscle, heart and lungs. The golden shell itself began to shiver, tremble with the sound. Tiny cracks appeared, spidery fractures that raced across the bright surface like lightning come to ground.

First, a taloned claw broke free, then the tip of a leathery wing. Great sections of the shell began to shatter and fall away, releasing beams of luminescent gold.

The dragon stretched her scaly neck, rammed her snout against the shell, and broke her head free. As she had in a thousand lives before, she opened her jaws and roared at the world, lifted her mighty wings, and tore them free.

Now, the light burst forth like the molten sun itself, like a great exploding star. As she shook her armored hide and flexed her lucid wings, the dragon became aware of the man. A vision of other times, of other human things, filled its head with killing rage. Men thought themselves masters, lords of the world.

She held the pale creature with her amber eyes. The thing didn't run, didn't turn and take flight. Instead, it looked back at the dragon, looked and held its ground . . .

The dragon, newly birthed again, had hazy memories of its past and knew this was not the ordinary thing a man would do. How did it dare not show its fear? How did it dare stand and look her in the eye?

She knew, at once, what she must do. The answer was stamped in every cell of her being, as it was in every dragon that had trod this ancient world.

Kill the thing. Rip it in two with one sweep of its claw. Shake it in her teeth and fling the ragged gouts aside, a feast for lesser beings, crawlers and flyers of the carrion kind.

Still, she hesitated, watching the man watch her. What, she wondered, held her back? Did it matter that the creature had been there at her birthing, seen her rage and seen her pain, seen more than any being had ever seen before? There was something, something she couldn't name, something so puzzling and alien that she thrust the thought aside, lest she pursue it anymore.

The mist of morning burned away, and the dragon felt the sun upon her hide, felt the flood of power in her veins. The man was no longer in her thoughts, a small thing of no great matter now. Clutching the earth in her claws, she beat her leather wings against the air, raising an ocher cloud and sweeping the ground clear of dust and tiny stones.

The sound of her wings was a drumming, a thrumming, a sound with such force that it rolled like thunder, like a hammer of air across this barren place. And then the great creature was gone, a creature of the earth no more. Now she was a great and soaring denizen of the air.

The man, felled by the power of the new dragon's wings, picked himself up, brushed off his clothes, and raised his eyes to the brilliant morning glare. The dragon was gone, a golden goddess lost in the glare of the greater golden sun.

CHAPTER 22

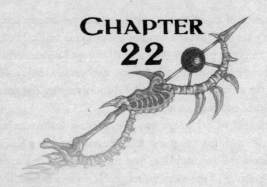

Ridley knew that the thing he'd seen was real, real and yet a
dream as well, for the birthing of a gold dragon could not
be wholly a thing of this world.

It was, he was certain, a miracle no man had likely seen
before, a thing no man was meant to see. Still, it had happened.
It had happened to him. Though he knew it couldn't be—that
his own imagination had played awesome tricks inside his
head—he felt as if he had reached out, tried to understand, tried
to comprehend this fearsome, alien thing, and that the dragon,
somehow, had reached out and found him.

Ridley walked back past the ragged columns of stone, past the
barren plain. His mount, grazing at the edge of the woods, gave
him a curious look and pulled up another patch of grass.

"I'm glad you found breakfast," Ridley said. "My belly's
empty as Elwood's cask of ale."

He wondered how far ahead his companions might be, and
how he'd lost the trail. He wondered what he'd tell them of the

marvel he had seen, and he knew at once it was something that belonged just to him, that he couldn't tell anyone at all.

* * * * *

"Where in the blazing underworld have you been? We thought you'd fallen in a hole somewhere."

Snails stood, munching a loaf of bread.

"I'm a city lad at heart," Ridley said. "I confess I'm better in a maze of alleyways than in a thicket of trees. They all look alike to me."

"They all look alike to me, too." Snails tossed him half a loaf of bread. "But I'm catching onto this outdoor life, and I find it suits me well."

"Maybe Norda can teach you elven ways, or you could live among the dwarves?"

Elwood choked on a slab of yellow cheese. "No offense, friend, but there isn't any way we could possibly let you in. Dwarves have got rules, and one of 'em is we don't like humans movin' in."

"Don't worry," Snails said. "I have no great desire to live among dwarves. Your people are safe from me."

"Like I said, nothing personal. We just got rules, and that one's at the top of the list."

"Fine. Put my name past the bottom somewhere, in case you change your mi—"

Snails didn't finish. He looked up as Norda appeared through the trees. It was clear from her features the time for resting was gone.

"We're moving out. Try not to make a sound from here on. My scouts have found Damodar's camp."

* * * * *

The castle was so ancient, the great black stones of its once high walls had wearied and begun to fall away a hundred generations before. The once proud keep with its arrow loops and fine crenellations had tumbled in upon itself, leaving only a hollow shell full of rocky debris.

Now, the castle heard the voices of men again. In the ruined courtyard, Damodar's troops, thirty-some uglies from his Crimson Brigade, had lit small fires and erected tents against the gathering cold.

These lawless, red-clad brutes, normally drunk with ale at such a time, were now unusually quiet, and none wandered far from the fire. They feared no enemy from outside their camp. They had no reason to imagine one was there.

The thing that had them edgy, fearful and out of sorts, was the great, ruined castle itself. Every soldier knew these dark and wasted towers harbored no life now, but those who had fought here, those who had died in dread and fearful ways, still lurked in every cleft and shadow and despised every creature still alive.

* * * * *

Ridley promised himself he'd never ride a horse again, or never sit, for that matter, even on the softest pillow he could steal. Not one pillow nor a hundred could salve the misery that plagued him now.

He had learned, to his regret, that an elf only speaks in the broadest of terms, not in precise detail, as a proper human does. Norda had said she'd found Damodar. No one mentioned they had found him several mountains away, across three rivers and a dozen rocky plains. Even when she announced they were close, just beyond a stand of trees, he found her words hard to believe.

"Fine," he said, easing his tortured body to the ground, "then let's get with it. If Damodar's got Marina there—"

"Oh, he does, Ridley. No question of that. But we cannot simply go in and get her, not until the time is right."

Norda walked away before he could answer, back to her elves across a narrow creek. As ever, she was as calm and fresh as if she'd just risen from a nap, an attitude that irritated Ridley to no end.

"I can't take this, Snails. We've come all this way, and *she* says the time isn't right. Tell me, just when is right? Marina's in there, in Damodar's hands."

"Trust her, Rid. She knows what she's doing."

"And how do you know? Because she's just as cute as she can be?"

Snails looked hurt. "No, though you're quite correct; she is. I know because I keep my eyes open. I saw her when she went off by herself. She peered into a crystal several times."

"A crystal?"

"Yes. If she says it's not time, believe her. Elves know these things, things we can never even guess."

"Uh-huh, fine. Maybe she'll let us in on some of these *things*, if we act real nice."

"I expect the lad's right," Elwood said, suddenly by Ridley's side. "I don't care for elven ways, but dwarves have such powers themselves, though I can't say more than that."

"Don't, then. I didn't ask."

Elwood closed a beady eye, and poked a stubby finger in Ridley's chest. "I'll give you room because you're a human and don't have respect for your betters, but don't be pushing a dwarf too far. Even one you think you know."

"I don't believe he meant anything," Snails said. "He's worried about the girl."

Ridley frowned. "I don't need anyone to speak for me. I can talk for myself."

"I know you can, but I don't see you're doing it right, if you know what I mean."

Ridley turned to Elwood. "What I said I meant. Take it any way you like."

"Here now, lad—"

"Poke another finger at me, and I'll fair cut it off."

"Why don't you give it a try? I'd welcome the fun, my boy."

"All of you," Norda said, coming up so quickly none of the three knew she was there. "I said I'd tell you when it's time. It is time now. The hour is right. The forest and those things within it are in the seventh hour of the day. The wind comes quietly now, and you must match its silence as well."

She looked in turn at Ridley and Snails. "You will go, and we will follow. When you have—"

"Wait a moment," Elwood said, "what about me?"

"What about you?" Norda said. "I send the wolves in, the stealthy ones, who hunt in shadow. The strong one, the ox, I keep at my side."

Elwood's scowl turned to a grin. "Really? An ox, you say? Well then, I'd guess you're thinking straight as you can."

He reached out a hand and gave Ridley a fearsome grip. "Don't have a fear, lad, Elwood Gutworthy, known far and wide as the Ox of the Earth, is ever at your call."

CHAPTER 23

They crouched low, sprinting across the open plain. Ridley kept the elf's image of the wolf in mind, moving with the wind, trying to make no sound, feet scarcely touching the ground.

At the ruined wall of the castle, Ridley waited, listening. He could hear the guardsmen's voices, but they were clearly on the far side of the courtyard near their fires. Ridley looked at Snails, nodded, and they tossed their hooks high above the wall, praying they'd make no sound at all. Elwood had carved the hooks himself, from stout crooks of oak, and he swore upon the honor of his clan that they would hold.

If they don't, Ridley told himself, we'll not be present to complain.

Ridley signaled Snails to wait then drew himself slowly to the top on strong elven rope. Most of the Crimson Guardsmen were huddled about their fires. Some cleaned their weapons, some spoke in huddled groups, and some simply lazed about.

Ridley nodded again, and Snails pulled himself up to the top.

NEAL BARRETT, JR.

"Now what?" Snails whispered. "There's a great crowd of uglies down there, and I doubt we'll be welcome for supper, though supper's a fine idea."

"It is, but I fear it's to come a bit late this day."

With an eye on the soldiers down below, Ridley carefully loosed a piece of stone from the crumbling wall. He glanced at Snails, who didn't have to ask what his friend had in mind.

The rock landed just past a pair of guards polishing their weapons by a fire. They looked up quickly, picked up their swords, and moved off to investigate the sound.

Ridley and Snails were over the wall at once, across the courtyard, and into the shadow of the ruined palace.

Pressed against the cold stone, they made their way toward the back of the great structure, Ridley in front, Snails keeping watch behind.

Ridley came to a halt. Just ahead was a doorway, and behind it, a patch of light. Ridley slipped carefully inside, waited, listened. He could smell the musty stench of the place, the dust of ages past. Past the doorway, a narrow stairway curved down into darkness. Ridley drew a torch from the wall, nodded to Snails, and started down into the depths.

The stairs seemed to twist down forever, deep into the bowels of the castle itself. Ridley could hear the drip of water, a rat or two scurrying about—then, the scrape of a boot, the murmur of a voice nearby.

Ridley held his torch low, retreated up the stairs. He could feel Snails's breath at his back. Below, two guards walked past, talking to one another. Their shadows made the shapes of twisted giants against the narrow wall.

In a moment, the pair were out of sight and sound. Ridley

and Snails took the last few steps down to the hall.

"All right," Ridley said softly, "I'll find Marina. You try the corridor where the uglies came from. Try to find the map."

"All right."

"We'll meet back here."

"Rid?"

"What?"

"How do you always get the girl, and I get the map? We've got to talk about that."

Ridley let out a breath. "Fine. We'll do that. Would you go?"

Snails didn't answer.

"And be careful."

Snails grinned. "You too, and next time—"

"We'll *talk*. Now get out of here."

Ridley turned away, a smile still crossing his features. Not for the first time, he reasoned that the Fates must choose a man's friends, for few men would pick the ones they got nor have the wisdom to understand how blessed they were to get them.

* * * * *

Elwood Gutworthy muttered to himself, poked his head above the dry brush, and scowled at the castle again. Nothing had changed. Not since the minute before, or the one before that. Something was wrong; he was certain of that. It didn't look right. It surely didn't *smell* right. There was trouble in there, trouble of the very worst kind, trouble that called for the strength, the cunning, and the courage of a warrior dwarf. Someone like Elwood Gutworthy, by the gods, no one less than that.

"No," Norda said, before he could ask. "No again, the same as no before."

Elwood looked past her to her crossbowmen waiting silently at the edge of the woods. He knew their prowess well, yet it angered him to see them resting there like children playing a game, a game where only shadows were the foe.

"We're waiting for what then?" he said, with a hint of mockery in his smile. "Something in the wind? That *crystal* of yours listenin' for spirits in the woods? Is that what we're waitin' for?"

Norda looked at him a long moment, then turned away. "You shame yourself with your talk. You and I are not the same, and yet we are. Your kind and mine are far closer to the earth than humankind. I don't have to tell you that. The dwarves know the signs in the forests, in the streams, in the wind that you so casually toss aside.

"You know these things, and yet you mock them out of anger, out of your taste for blood, which you cannot wait to shed. You know, do you not, that there will be blood soon enough? You do not have to chase so quickly after death. It will be here faster than you know, and all the world will be in sorrow when it howls out of the night. For it surely comes, warrior, comes on the very wind you so lightly jest away."

Elwood didn't answer, for he knew she spoke a truth he clearly could not deny. She was right in what she'd said. She had seen into his very heart. It was neither wisdom nor reason he sought, but a horde of warriors clad in red, shrieking out of that dark and stony ruin, coming at him with sword and lance and pike, thirsty for the great curved axe in his grasp.

CHAPTER 24

Snails passed several dark and empty rooms before he found one that literally took his breath away. It was a small, vaulted chamber lit by torches in the wall. One quarter of the roof had recently been repaired. The mortar between the stones was still white. However, the stonework was not what caught his attention, left him wide-eyed, left him astonished, left him rigid in his boots. Here, indeed, was a thief's paradise. The room was clearly Damodar's workroom, packed with a mage's secret goods: jars full of powders, full of dark liquids, full of ghastly animal parts, oils, unguents, and salves, alabaster, agate, and shiny crystal spheres. Thick tomes of magic filled shelves. Shelf upon shelf held old scrolls surely filled with ancient spells. A scarred wooden desk was stacked with mystic tools of every sort.

"Hard to tell where to start," he said, rubbing his hands together in delight. "Why, a person could spend a lifetime merely— *Yaaah!*"

Damodar! Looming right above him, not a foot away!

Snails took a breath, letting his heart slow back to its normal beat. Not Damodar, but his armor, great plates of shining iron, silver sheathes of mail, all hanging on a rack against the wall.

Snails walked around the thing, looking it over from top to armored boots. Such a pretty would bring a hefty price from a man who cherished armor such as this. Moving the thing though, getting it out of this damnable place, that would be a chore for sure.

At the rear of the iron suit, he paused and set his chin just inside the neck.

"I'm Damodar," he said, in deep and fearful tones. "I am the ugliest creature alive, and no man dares to say I'm not!"

Chuckling to himself, he moved across the room, taking a look at this and that. He slipped a pretty gem in his pocket, and another after that. Nestled among a clutter of bottles and vials was a small and dusty sack. He opened it and sniffed. It smelled like sage and heather, a very pleasant scent. He let some of the powdery stuff slip through his fingers, closed the bag, and dropped it in his pocket with the rest of his souvenirs.

"A little black magic," he muttered. "Nice to have around."

Looking about the room, he spotted a tangle of rope on the floor, bent to pick it up, and wound it into a coil. As he stood, he spotted a small table sitting by itself past a bubbling pot, past a gaily-patterned carpet against the far wall. On the table was a bottle of amber wine, a crystal glass, and a—

Snails drew in a breath. The scroll! There on the table, right in plain sight!

He grinned, clapping his hands together. "It's my lucky day!"

He crossed the room to claim his prize, one step forward, then the next, placed one foot on the colorful carpet and sank up to his knees—

Snails gasped for breath, stretched his arms and clawed

desperately for a hold on the cold stone floor. The patterns in the rug began to melt and slide away, sucking him ever deeper, past his waist and then his chest, deeper and deeper still.

His legs were next to useless, mired in a terrible, sluggish mass that drew him down into its depths.

I've got to understand this thing isn't real. It's an illusion's what it is. It isn't quicksand; it's quicksand of the mind. All you got to do, Snails, is figure that out in two or three seconds before that illusion covers up your head.

He felt it, then, seeping past his chin and into his mouth. He flailed his arms about, nearly went under, and spat out a choking glob of sand. He took a last breath and screamed as the muck came up past his nose.

"Well, little thief, having a bit of trouble?" said a voice Snails had mocked only moments before. "Need a hand?"

* * * * *

The long, narrow corridor seemed to go on forever, twisting left, twisting right, until Ridley lost all sense of direction. For all he knew, he could be walking in circles, getting farther and farther from Marina all the time.

He stopped and listened. He could hear the drip of water, rats scurrying about in the walls, rats and . . . something else. Something nearby. It took him a moment to identify the sound: Snoring. More than one man. Maybe three or four. Holding his blade by his side, Ridley reached a narrow archway and peered into a small room. Two soldiers slept on coarse wooden cots. Both lay on their backs, their mouths open wide.

Armor and helmets lay on the floor beside swords, boots, and a rusty vest of mail. One of the men wore a broad leather belt hammered with crude metal studs, and on the belt—

Ridley stared. *Keys!* One of the men had a large ring of keys looped into his belt. Ridley didn't hesitate, didn't let himself think. He laid his sword aside, went on his belly, and snaked his way into the room.

As bad luck would have it, the man with the keys was farther away than his friend. So be it, there was nothing else for it. Even if the man seemed a league away, Ridley knew he must have those keys at any cost.

Every scrape of his clothes across the cold stone seemed as loud as some rube dropping a keg of ale on the floor. Halfway there, the man by the door turned over, opened his eyes, and stared right at Ridley.

Ridley froze. The man didn't move, but his eyes didn't close. What was he waiting for? Why didn't he leap up, grab his weapon, and sound the alarm?

Ridley waited. The sight of the man gazing right at him made his blood turn cold. It seemed a full day, maybe three or four, before the lout turned over and began to snore again.

Ridley let out a breath. Every tendon, every muscle, every nerve was twisted tighter than a hangman's noose. He couldn't stay there, couldn't crawl another inch. Whatever happened, would happen. The Fates would handle that.

Bringing all the courage he had to bear, Ridley stood, crossed to the sleeping man, and drew his dagger. After slicing the leather belt away, he lifted the ring of keys, turned, and almost ran out of the room.

Still shaken by this very near miss, he made his way down the dimly lit hall. To his left and his right were darkened rooms, black maws that smelled musty and old. Ridley hurried quickly by. He didn't believe in apparitions, except for the ones a mage might conjure up, but why hang around and discover you were wrong?

Around the next corner, he stopped dead still. A real door this time, old, but with a fairly new lock. The first of his stolen keys didn't work. Neither did the second or the third. Ridley wiped sweat from his brow. The snoring guard could wake up any moment and find his keys were gone.

The fourth key stuck. Ridley held his breath, scarcely daring to try and force the thing out. If it broke in there—

Click!

The sound was like a blast of thunder in his ear. The key turned easily, as if the lock were a pot of axle grease. He opened the door cautiously and peered inside, weapon at the ready.

A torch flickered dimly on the far wall. The small chamber was nearly empty. A broken chair, broken stones, a bundle of rags against the far wall—

Ridley's heart nearly stopped. Marina! Knees drawn up to her chin, hands clamped tightly about her legs, she rocked back and forth, keening, mewling like a kitten lost in the dark.

He went to her at once, bent to her side, and took her in his arms.

"Marina. Marina . . ."

She lifted her head slowly, her swollen, frightened eyes lost behind a tangle of hair.

"Rid— Ridley. Is it . . . is it. . . ?"

"Hey, it's me. It's all right now."

She looked at him them, and her eyes told him she knew, finally, knew that he was there.

"Let's get out of here," he said, gently lifting her to her feet. "Come on, you're safe, now. You're safe, Marina."

"No," she said, her face buried in his chest, "not ever safe, Ridley. Never safe anymore . . . never again . . ."

CHAPTER 25

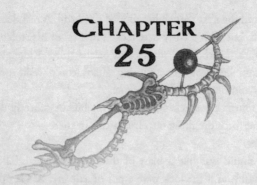

Snails shook his head and tried to get to his feet. There were three Damodars. One, or maybe two, had jerked him out of the mire and tossed him across the room. The third one—now somehow joining the other two—was stalking toward him across the stone floor.

Snails struggled. Something hard was stabbing him in the back. He drew it out and tossed it to the floor. A bottle, half empty, shattered against the stone. He knew where he was now, why everything hurt. Damodar had thrown him into the small table across the room, splitting it in half and hurling Snails to the floor.

The bottle on the table, the glass, the—

Snails bit his lip against the pain, turned on his belly, found it there, just where it had to be. A little worse for wear, a little damp from wine, but it was there—the scroll, the lovely scroll, and in his hands now!

Damodar spotted the prize at once, stopped, and showed Snails a lazy smile.

"Just like you, little thief. Always turning up where you shouldn't be. Always taking things that don't belong to you."

"I wouldn't push it, ugly," Snails said. "I'm not in the mood for this. In fact—in fact, I think I'm really getting mad. I think that's exactly what's happening. Right now. You can likely tell. My eyes get kinda . . . dangerous looking. Right, that's what they do."

Snails reached out blindly and found the sword he'd lost before the illusion sucked him down.

Damodar looked amused. "Oh, you want to play soldier? Truly? Are you certain, little thief, that's what you want to do?"

"Of course I am." Snails grabbed the far wall to help him to his feet. "I can't wait. How about *you?*"

Pushing himself off the wall, Snails charged Damodar, his blade slashing frantically at the air. Damodar didn't move, didn't try to get out of his way, but in the last heartbeat, his sword flashed in a blur.

Snails backed up, startled, staring at his hand. His weapon was gone. Damodar smiled and nodded at the ceiling. Snails looked up. His blade was there, the point still humming in wood.

"Right," Snails said. "Game's over then. You win. And a nice little move there, I want to tell you that. You've got to show me that when we've got more time."

Snails let out a bloody scream, turned, and stumbled out of the room and down a low flight of stairs. Damodar was on him in an instant. He jerked Snails up by the collar, held him high, and pounded him mercilessly across the face, one blow after the next with his armored fist.

Snails gasped, stumbled back, and went to his knees. Damodar reached down and pulled him upright again. Snails snaked a small dagger from his boot, grinned at Damodar through his ruined features, and lashed out in a blur, slicing his foe across the chest.

Damodar cried out, reeled back, and stared at his wound with disbelief. When he looked up, Snails was gone, lost somewhere along the dark and twisted paths of the dungeon that tunneled its way beneath the ruined castle.

Damodar roared in anger, his face turned black, and the fierce creatures that lived within his skull snaked out into the dark to coil about his features, to snap at his brow, to hiss and strike at his eyes. Damodar clutched his weapon so tightly that his hand bled through thick leather and mail.

* * * * *

Ridley knew he was lost, knew for certain the corner he'd turned only moments before was not the corner that would lead him up the twisted stairwell and back to the door where he and Snails had come in.

Snails . . . Where was he, and why had Ridley let him go off by himself? They *both* could have looked for Marina then searched for the scroll. It would have taken longer, certainly, but this way—

"Ridley . . ."

"We're all right," he told her, "we're almost there." It was a lie, and maybe she knew it, but he didn't have the heart to tell her anything else. He didn't know what she'd been through at Damodar's hands, and he knew he wouldn't ask, not unless she chose to tell him herself.

"I think I had a dream, Ridley, a really terrible dream."

"I think you did, Marina, but you're awake now. When you're awake, the dreams go away."

"No, no they don't, Ridley. They're . . . supposed to go away, but this one is real. This one really happened. It happened to *me.*"

He knew her words were true, knew there was nothing he could do, nothing but hold her, get her out of here, and get her as far from this place as he could. There was no time, no time to look into her eyes, no time to tell her things he hadn't told her before, for in that moment they were on him, howling out of the corridor ahead, coming at him in a blaze of crimson red, in an rush of ugly helms and slashing silver blades.

He met the first with a wicked slash of iron, driving the fellow back and watching the sudden horror in the man's eyes as he knew death was on him, that this was the moment he'd feared since first he'd dreamed of the killing, of the rage, of the wonder of a Crimson warrior's life.

Ridley took the second man as quickly as the first. The man knew how to hold a sword, but little more than that. He had loved the parades and the women and the wine—those were the parts of soldiering he'd liked.

"Ridley!"

Ridley, turned and ducked as Marina slammed the blazing end of a torch in the third warrior's face.

"Thanks."

"Any time," Marina said.

Ridley grabbed her arm, sprinting down the corridor toward a heavy wooden door. He backed off, quickly raising his blade as the portal suddenly opened in his face.

A guard half as big as a house stood in Ridley's way. He grinned, showed a set of broken teeth, and drew a short blade from his belt.

Ridley clutched his sword with both hands and took a step back.

"A little slow, friend," Marina said, and slapped him soundly with her torch. The guard blinked, slightly irritated. He caught the back of Marina's hand and sent her sprawling to the floor.

"Hey," Ridley shouted, "you can't do that!"

"Huuuka Pluuut!" the giant said, or words to that effect. He swung a massive arm at Ridley, but Ridley ducked and stepped on his foot. With a desperate shove, he sent the giant to the ground.

Ridley turned to flee and saw a sight that sent a chill up his spine.

"Snails!"

Snails didn't answer. He was stumbling down a set of stairs, running as fast as he could, his jacket flapping like ragged wings at his back. Damodar bounded down the steps only seconds behind him, shouting a fearsome cry, his great blade slashing at the air.

The giant picked himself up and came at Ridley again.

Ridley kicked him soundly in the belly, grabbed Marina, and didn't look back. He bounded up the stairs and stopped, startled to find that the steps ended, went nowhere at all.

"That's impossible," he said. "I saw them. They went this way!"

"Damodar," Marina said. "He's left some kind of a spell. There's a way here, you just can't find it."

"Damnation, I've *got* to find it. He's after Snails!" He turned, grabbed her shoulders, and looked into her eyes. "You're a mage, Marina. Do something. Get us out of here."

Marina pulled away and rubbed her arm. "I would if I could,

Ridley. He— He took something out of me. I don't have anything. That part of me's gone. It's there, but I can't find it anymore."

Ridley groaned. He took the hilt of his sword and started
pounding savagely on the stone walls, working his way from one
end of the corridor to the next, shouting, cursing to himself,
pommeling the rocky surface until the sweat poured down his
brow.

"You can't," Marina told him. "You can't fight him, Ridley.
You can't do it that way."

"Then show me another," Ridley said, his voice so choked
with rage that she backed away in sudden fear. "Show me a way,
or I'll tear this place down, stone by stone. *That's my friend he's
got out there!*"

CHAPTER 26

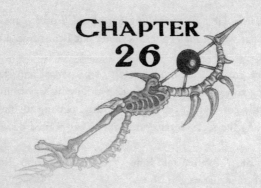

The castle was suddenly behind him, the broad courtyard below. Crimson-clad soldiers stared up at Snails, shouting in anger and waving their weapons about. Snails drew a ragged breath. Ahead was a crumbled tower, half its high turret hollowed by time or some ancient enemy's brutal siege. He didn't bother to look behind him. Damodar was there, stalking him, taking his time.

Snails made his way through the turret's debris. On the other side, if the Fates were with him at all, the narrow walkway would continue, maybe lead down the stone curtain wall to a notch in the battlement, a crenel still intact that would let him make his way down off the wall to the ground. With any luck he could find Rid again and get out of this mess.

Snails's heart nearly stopped. The wall past the crumbled turret was gone, crumbled away. There was nothing, only a deadly drop to the ground below.

All the strength, all he had left, seemed to drain away and

leave him hollow, empty. He fell to his knees, smashing his fists at the stone in hopeless, futile anger. So useless, so damned, totally *useless*—all of it a dull, useless, senseless life wasted, tossed away in a place he'd never even heard of, a miserable place he'd never meant to be.

"And what in all the hells for?" he muttered to himself. "What for?"

"For nothing, little thief. Don't tell me even you were unaware of that."

Snails looked up, the dust stinging his eyes, and saw the dark shadow as the figure shut away the sun.

"I could've told you." Damodar grinned. "You never asked, little thief. Now it scarcely matters anymore."

Snails drew himself up, blinked sweat from his eyes, spat blood from his mouth, and wiped it on his patched sleeve. He leaned down then, never taking his eyes off his foe, and drew the last of his small daggers from his boot.

"Come on," he said. "Let's do it. Let's do it right."

Damodar looked pained. "You can't be serious. Look at you."

"I've never been more serious in my life. And don't smile at me again, all right? You're ugly enough like you are, don't try to make it any worse. You're makin' everyone around you want to throw up, you know that? All that snaky stuff comin' out of your head—"

Snails came at him then, with no warning at all. Damodar shook his head, weary of this tiresome task. He thrashed out at Snails with a vicious blow to the face, then another, and another after that.

Snails gasped. Blood dripped from his mouth and the gaping wounds on his cheeks, on his jaw. He staggered back and dropped to the ground. In agony, he lifted his face, coated now with the dust of ancient stone.

"You're finished," Damodar said. "You know that as well as I. Give me the Dragon's Eye. I might decide to let you die quickly. It's a favor I seldom offer such as you."

Snails raised himself on one arm, the other now nearly useless. He could barely see the man now. His enemy's hideous face was a blur, his eyes tiny moons, lost behind a cloud.

"Go to hell," he said, spitting the words with blood. "You'll recognize the place. It's where your kind were spawned."

"You had your chance," Damodar said, "and I have to tell you I'm delighted you chose the more painful way. I much prefer to—"

Damodar was startled beyond belief. He backed off, nearly tangling one boot in the next as his blooded, dying foe, a man whose life flowed freely out of his veins, suddenly launched himself from an early grave and lashed out with a dagger in his weak and trembling hand.

"Fool! Damned little fool!" Damodar shouted. He grabbed Snails's arm with a one gloved hand, turned it with a nearly effortless twist, and plunged the weapon hard and deep into Snails's gut.

Snails staggered back, screaming in pain, both hands clutched at his belly. Damodar smiled, took one step, gave the blade a final, deadly twist, and shoved his victim roughly to the ground.

His rage, though, was far from gratified. Hatred still darkened his face, and the monsters within his head writhed and hissed about his features as he reached down and grabbed the limp form by the neck, dragging him roughly to his knees.

Raising his armored hand, he flexed the armored fist, closing and opening the iron, clawed fingers, the deadly wrist blades, again and again.

One blow, one slash of that hand and the little thief's face would disappear. One blow, and no one—*no* one, could be certain who he had ever been.

"Damodar!"

Damodar glanced up, a cruel smile creasing his features, not truly surprised to see the thief and the girl on the steps leading down to the turret wall.

"Not your usual punctual self, I see. Where's the Dragon's Eye? I'd be right in thinking you have it, would I not?"

"You would," Ridley said. "I have it. Right here."

Damodar gave the young thief a thoughtful look. Clearly, he had not suppressed the spells left behind to stop his way. From the boy's dusty, disheveled appearance, he had torn his way through the wall itself, nearly killing himself in the effort, solely to get to his friend.

"If you have the thing," he said, "I fear you must show me. Forgive the lack of trust, but you understand . . ."

"Let Snails go first. And then the stone is yours."

"Seems reasonable to me."

And in that moment, Ridley's eyes met Snails's. Snails showed his friend a painful smile, blood seeping now between his teeth, his face drained of color, white as new parchment off the artist's shelf.

Ridley knew there was something there, something in those quickly fading eyes, but their meaning wasn't clear, not clear at all until Snails's gaze shifted down to his hand, and there Ridley saw it, half-hidden beneath the blood-soaked shirt.

Ridley drew in a breath. The scroll! Snails had it clutched in his hand! In that instant, Ridley knew what his friend intended, what he meant to do—

"Snails, don't!" Ridley cried, but the scroll was already in the air, already on its way to Ridley's grasp.

"No!" Marina shouted, her fingers clasped against her face.

Damodar threw back his head in anger, raised his armored claw and plunged the iron wrist blades into Snails's back.

Snails's body crumpled. Damodar moved it with his boot to the edge of the turret wall and kicked it over the edge.

Ridley's voice cracked in a terrible, mournful cry. He came at Damodar, sword slicing the air. Damodar met him, blocking every blow with the edge of his blade. Ridley's arms were heavy as leaden weights. He called up every ounce of courage he could muster, meeting the mage's blows again and again.

As Ridley weakened, as his strength drained away, Damodar's power seemed to grow, as if the powers of darkness urged him on, adding their will to his. Ridley met one numbing blow and then another, and another after that. With a strike that nearly dropped him, his sword flew from his hand, dropping end over end into the courtyard below.

Damodar was on him at once, pressing his blade cruelly against Ridley's chest and forcing him to his knees.

"Make it easy on yourself," Damodar said. "One thrust, and it's done. There's scarcely any pain at all. Just give me what is mine."

"No," Ridley gasped. "I don't think I'll give you that pleasure. No, I won't do that."

Damodar grinned. "You're as stubborn as your friend. Whatever is the point in this false and foolish courage? It serves no end. Look at him. Look at your friend down there a moment, thief, and tell me what courage brought him."

With that, Damodar thrust, and the blade ripped into Ridley's chest, ripping flesh and cracking bone. Ridley screamed, crumpling to the stone, and Damodar raised his sword to finish the contest.

Marina couldn't take her eyes from the thing before her, couldn't look away. It was only a small, brown pouch, a thing that had clearly fallen from Snails's pocket before he fell to his death. Only a— She *knew* the thing, had seen such pouches a hundred times before, had seen them on Vildan's littered table, seen them on his shelves.

With a quick glance at Damodar, she snatched the small pouch, opened it, and spilled out a handful of powder in her hands. It smelled right, it looked right. Raising her palm slowly, she stared at the mage above her, opened her fingers and blew a small cloud of dust toward his face.

Damodar looked startled, stared, and, for an instant, his attention strayed from his captured foe.

"Vallice runsar kilose!" Marina mouthed the words Vildan had made her learn again and again, tossed the rest of the dust in the air, and threw herself at Ridley, cradling his body with hers.

A pale aura shimmered in the air, blurred, brightened, and then formed a wavery portal of blue.

"Take me," Marina whispered, "take me to Norda, wherever Norda may be!"

Damodar shouted in fury. His face turned black, and he took a step forward, slashing at the blue apparition with all the strength in his arms. His blade struck stone, ringing like a bell, but the portal was gone. There was nothing there, nothing at all.

CHAPTER 27

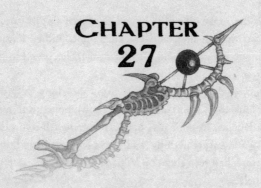

The storm had lashed the city all day, shrieking through the high towers, moaning in the streets and alleyways. People huddled in their homes, praying the gods would spare them, that the world would not end on this terrible day. Water quickly turned the narrow streets and cobbled avenues into swiftly rushing streams. Barrels, boxes, wagons, pans and pots, small animals and trash of every sort sped along the twisted maze of sewers down below.

For a minute and a half, the great waterways rushed the coursing flood along, as they'd been built to do. But that had been a thousand years before when Sumdall City was a bright and shining wonder high above a lovely blue river that flowed along below. The city wasn't a wonder anymore, and the river wasn't blue. The portals that spewed out water from the city filled with garbage at once, clogging every sewer and sending its foul cargo back up into the streets.

Late in the afternoon, the storm clouds vanished as quickly as they'd come, and the sun showed its splendor through a veil of amber-tinted clouds. The citizens of Sumdall opened their windows and ventured out, stunned by the beautiful sight in the sky, oblivious, for the moment, of the horrid stink that had risen up into their streets.

In the great council hall, an awesome array of brilliant light pierced the multi-colored dome and scattered beams of gold, red, green, and dazzling blue on the somber crowd gathered down below.

The dark-robed mages blinked their eyes and grumbled at this coarse intrusion of light. Mages did their work in shadow, in the dim glow of candles, in the flicker of a torch, set in a damp and stony wall. Besides, the mages lived by portents and signs, and they had no liking for the sight that appeared before them now.

For, as if the gods themselves had set the scene, the Empress Savina walked into the hall, veiled in an aura of luminescent light and walking through a bright slanting beam that was filled with dusty motes of gold.

Every mage held his breath, for the Empress was dressed in scales of pure gold, gold from her magnificent crown to the swirling gown that glittered in her wake. As the Empress climbed the nine runic steps to the dais, she spread her arms wide, revealing golden dragon wings of silk, wings that wavered from her fingers to the hem of her gown.

Not a word was spoken in the gallery of seers, and no man looked at another, for his brother might read some omen of the future in his eyes.

"This, I understand," the Empress said, "is the day you wish me to render my family's scepter of power to this council. You are gathered here, I presume, to hear my decision on this?"

"Aye, august Majesty, we are," Azmath said, bowing before his queen. "That is indeed our purpose here."

The Empress stood straight, royal and proud, her chin firm and strong, eyes steady and determined, no touch of hesitation about her this day. No one present, gazing on this monarch sheathed in gold, could mistake her for a child. She was, indeed, a woman grown, her father's daughter, no one's plaything, no one's regal pet, no one's weakling.

"Then," she said, her voice ringing out to every corner of the hall, "this day shall be remembered as the day your Empress defied this Council's decree. For I will *not* relinquish my scepter to you or to anyone else. Not today. Not ever."

Now the silence was broken as each man protested to his brother, showed by the anger in his voice, the frantic gestures of his hands, that he and he alone had truly seen the grim signs and portents of the day, that he had warned all the others that such a time would surely come, and now, as anyone could see, that awesome day was here.

Profion, standing in shadow, watched this drama play itself out through one dreary scene and the next. As the author of this bad piece of mummery, this sham with unworthy actors who mumbled through their parts, he simply waited his time. For he and he alone among these shabby players, truly knew his lines.

"Your Majesty," Azmath spoke when the others had quieted down, "I plead with you, in all respect, for the good of Izmer and us all. This council has voted the issue, and you must bow to *our* wishes this time." Then Azmath dared to look up at the Empress herself. "You . . . you don't understand the consequences of your action if you do not decide to comply?"

"*Decide?* You hear what I have declared, and you dare to say *decide?* If your ears are not full of spiderwebs, you have already heard what I have *decided*, Azmath, you and every other mage here."

Leaning forward on the dais, she gripped the railing until her fingers turned white. Her glacial eyes touched every man there and left them with a touch of frigid northern air.

"Do not patronize me, Azmath. You, or any of you, I pray. I am not, as you would have me be, my father's child, for I am no child at all. I am the Emperor's heiress, who has taken her rightful station. I am Empress of Izmer, *your* Empress, and I shall be revered and obeyed.

"And yes, I violate the law by defying my councilors. And you, mages, have violated *my* laws and your very oaths by your betrayal of me. If I were to give you this scepter, my crime would be graver still, for I would be defying my conscience, my father's will, and the good of all my people."

Once more, the Brotherhood of Mages rose from their seats, each one flailing his arms about, each one babbling louder than the next. Someone not familiar with this august assembly might imagine they were watching an asylum of hooded maniacs.

"*Silence!* You will hear me out! I demand your silence, or I will dissolve this body at once!"

The mages did, indeed, go silent. Each looked at one another with the same thought in mind: Can she do that? We're in control here, are we not?

"I fear you've forgotten this council was created to protect the people of Izmer, not to bend them to your will. What is your purpose here, mages? Concern for your people, or for yourselves?"

This time it was Profion who rose to quiet the others. At his appearance, a powerful and awesome figure in his full, ceremonial wear, the gallery quieted at once. There was not a mage there—despite his conscience, despite what his true beliefs might be—who did not fear the wrath of this man. Few among them had seen the mage's Chapel of Bones, but none were eager to be invited there. It was said to be a room that had a fine entry hall and lacked a way out.

"And Your Majesty believes," Profion said, "that a deadly civil war is in the interest of the people of Izmer? Are these your thoughts, My Lady?"

"So, here he is at last," the Empress said, pointing an accusing finger at the mage. "I expected your voice here sooner, Profion."

"Majesty, I would not deign to interrupt my Empress," Profion said with a clearly mocking bow. "It is not my place to do so, as I'm sure all present here will understand."

"Your manners commend you, mage. . . ."

Savina paused and let her gaze once again sweep across the gallery. "Here, my councilors, is the man who would take the scepter from me and leave the Empire defenseless. Ask yourselves, if you will: Does a man who opposes the right of his people to prosper show *concern* for those people? Take care, my friends, for when he is done with me, you are surely next on his list."

The mages were puzzled, confused. As ever, the last words spoken seemed stronger than the ones that came before.

Profion spread his hands and looked to heaven, as if to say, *I am doing what I can against the powers of this child dressed up to play a queen.*

"Hear her, then. Do. Within days of ascending the throne, she would destroy those things upheld by her own family for generations past. She is not content to break our highest law. Now she would throw us into chaos, disorder, and war!"

"Yes!" the Empress shouted above the crowd. "Yes, it is true Izmer has been ruled one way in the past. That does not mean it has been ruled justly. All citizens, whether commoner or mage, must have an equal chance for prosperity. As your Empress, I have decreed *this* is the kind of Izmer you will see."

Profion gave her a weary grin, as if to tell the others: See my patience, see what a burden I bear for you?

"Pretty words, indeed. Unfortunately, they are the words of a headstrong child. Childhood is a wonderful thing, mages, but children cannot be allowed to run an Empire." He paused and showed the Empress Savina a respectful but clearly mocking bow. "Forgive her, my brothers. She has dressed so prettily today, dressed in grown-up clothes so your eyes might mistake her for a queen."

The Empress flushed, a tide of color heating her face. She stood her ground, hands clamped to her sides. She would not, *could* not let him see her falter, not for an instant would she be anything but his Empress.

Profion said, "Now I must apologize again, for the plain talk of adults has nearly brought our young lady to tears. That, I do greatly regret." Profion hesitated again. "In respect for your father and the good of Izmer, I ask you once more, Empress, to abide by our ruling elders and relinquish your scepter. It is surely a burden to you now."

"I prayed for your wisdom, your awakening to truth," the Empress said, her voice now cold as winter breath. "I do not see that wisdom here. Know that you have not beaten me, mage. I fear you not. And know, all of you, that your Empress will prevail."

For a long moment, she looked out over the gallery, pausing at each and every man there. She saw, as she already knew, that most of these faces, hidden by hooded robes, were lined with age, that the hair on their heads was either silver or no longer there at all.

She felt a great sorrow, a pain in her heart, for she knew that she was indeed a child in their eyes, that nothing she could say or do would change that. They had forgotten whom they'd been. Now, it was inconceivable to them that the young had wisdom, too.

The Empress Savina turned without a word, turned and walked back the way she'd come. The aura of the sun was still there, still a path of gold that led her from the great Council Hall. This time, though, fifteen mages rose and followed in her path.

Profion's blood nearly boiled at the sight of the treachery of his brothers. Still, he would not let the rage within him show. Instead, he smiled and started a round of mocking applause, joined by the mages who had stayed.

"What a fine performance by our Empress. I warned you of her intentions. Now you have seen and heard them for yourselves. If Lord Damodar, our faithful Commander of the Crimson Brigade, were with us this day, he would tell you again how he witnessed the girl's crimes firsthand. Is there anything more I can say? Do we sit back and wait for her to *destroy* Izmer?"

Profion paused. His features fairly glowed with pleasure, and his dark eyes were full of dancing lights.

"Do we rest? Go back to our books? *Or is this indeed the time for us to act?*"

The answer was not in doubt among the mages facing Profion. They rose as one, shook their fists, and cheered their leader, cheered until the very stones of the great hall resounded to their cries.

CHAPTER 28

Even at the height of the day, the deep forest of immense and ancient oaks near mimed the dark of night. Marina and Norda left their mounts and joined Elwood at the hammock strapped to the dwarf's horse, the sling that held the nearly lifeless body of Ridley Freeborn.

"We must do something to help him," Marina said. "If we don't, I think he'll die before the day is gone."

"Don't go talkin' about dying," Elwood told her. "Talkin' death is close enough to bein' there. The dwarves know that, and I expect the elves do as well."

Elwood looked at Norda for a nod, but Norda was kneeling over Ridley, one hand against his brow.

"We'll not rest here," she said softly. "The forest can be a place of peace, and the creatures in it benign. It is not such a place at this time. The elves of the Verdalf clan live not too far from here." She looked at Marina. "The Verdalf have great healing powers. We will take the man there."

No one spoke, but Elwood and Marina clearly agreed. Whether there were truly such things as healing elves, they knew Norda was right about *this* part of the forest. There was something so heavy and oppressive here that neither of the two were anxious to stick around.

Marina rode with the others a while, then let them get ahead—never out of sight, but far enough away to be alone.

There was so much sorrow in her heart that she could scarcely stand the company of her friends. Ridley, perhaps dead, surely dying before they could leave the frightening woods. They had never managed to know one another, never let themselves forget the barriers that stood between them. Now, whatever might have been would likely never be . . .

Ridley near death, Vildan coldly murdered, and the kind and cheery Snails as well.

"I lost them all," she said aloud, her eyes finally filling with tears. "I brought them all here, and nearly all of them have died."

"No, you can't do this, Marina. You cannot take the weight of the world upon your shoulders. No mortal creature is capable of that."

Marina ran a sleeve across her eyes to dry her tears. Norda was suddenly there, riding close beside her.

"We all grieve. You for your love, and me for his kind-hearted friend, but you can't blame the Fates for who they leave and who they take away. They only do what greater powers have set them forth to do."

Marina nodded but couldn't face the elf. She looked away into the darkness of the woods.

"Do you truly believe that? That the Fates, whatever they are—old hags or angels—do you believe that's why we live or die, at the whim of creatures who dwell in the sky?"

"As I said, Marina, a greater power than that. It isn't easy for mortals to comprehend. And—take no offense in this—I should think a student of the magic arts would have more understanding of these things."

"I was obviously not a *good* student," Marina said, "and—no offense, as you put it—you're not a mortal. You're an elf. You live longer than humans, and you don't see death as we do."

Norda lowered her eyes. "I saw death today, child. I have seen it before, and I live with a pain within me, one you cannot see. I was forbidden to interfere with the horrors that occurred back there. I cannot tell you why, for I do not know myself. I know only that there are times when we must let the Fates do as they will. Sometimes a great wrong, a great darkness, must show itself to allow a better thing to occur. We cannot know why this is so."

Marina shook her head. "I cannot understand such things, Norda. I'm sorry. I can't see why good men must die to bring about some better day that they will never see."

"No, nor can I. I only know that sorrow is ever with us, but so is laughter as well. You have a life to live. You're a mage, and you have much to offer others."

"I'm not that certain that I want to be a mage anymore."

"Because others have used those arts for evil?"

"That's one reason, yes."

Norda leaned over her saddle and gently touched Marina's hand. "Don't you see? If there are those who practice the dark ways, there is all the more reason to expand the ranks of those for work for the light."

Marina didn't answer. Elwood, up ahead, turned his mount quickly and trotted back to the pair.

"There's someone out there," he said, gripping the haft of his axe. "Can't tell who, but there's more of them than us."

"Yes, I see." Norda looked past Marina and Elwood, studied the woods a moment, then quickly dismounted. She then took two steps toward the trees and stood perfectly still.

A figure stepped out of green shadow and looked at Norda. Elwood was startled. He was no stranger to the forest, but this particular creature had simply walked out of nothing, as if he were part of the shadow, part of the trees themselves.

He knew this was an elf, but not one of the ordinary breed. This one was clearly a hunter, a slender being with a nut-brown face, dark eyes, and pointy ears, a creature with hard and corded muscle, muscle wound up like a spring. His clothes, like the forest, were a hundred shades of green, and his strong, intelligent features were tattooed with the patterns of vines and leaves, marks that twisted across his brow, down his cheeks, and onto a bare shoulder. His eyes were the color of berries, his hair a shade of brown and ocher lichen that grows on the bark of trees.

Elwood watched, fascinated by this newcomer, who had come close enough to slay them all. The dwarf was even more astonished when seven more hunters appeared, each bearing arms.

"If one of them pesky elves tries to haul you off," the dwarf whispered to Marina, "he'll have to go through me."

The elves, who could hear a mouse sneeze a good mile away, grinned at the dwarf's remark.

"These are friends," Norda said. "Their clanmaster, Hallvarth Fyrlief, has offered us the hospitality of his village."

"We should be most grateful for their help." Marina drew in a breath. "Do you know them well, Norda? I mean, are they always so . . . silent and intense?"

"Scary" was the word she had in mind, but she didn't say that.

"I know them quite well, Marina, and the reason they are, indeed, intense, is because they have sensed the coming of war in the human world. They know that when humans slaughter one another—as they are accustomed to do—that other beings will die as well."

"Yes, I see."

Marina looked at the hunter who stood before Norda. She tried, with a gentle smile, to let him know that she was not one of the humans who wantonly killed each other and anything else in their way. The elf held her glance but showed no expression at all.

* * * * *

Marina would have passed the elven village by, certain there was nothing there to see. Even Elwood, whose folk were as different from humans as elves themselves, sensed the presence of life but saw no dwellings, no paths where the grass was beaten down, no smell of campfires or food.

Marina was sure there came a time when she was somehow *invited* to see what there was to see, for the hidden to be revealed. For in that instant a great elven village appeared in the trees. Lights she would have taken for tiny stars were not stars at all, but lights from dwellings twinkling amidst the thick canopy of leaves. The closer she looked, the more there was to see.

The village was a maze of twisted walkways, ladders, balconies, and stairs, not a one that wouldn't pass to the unschooled eye as a cluster of vines or the gnarled branch of a tree. There was no aspect of elven life that intruded on nature—every home, every window, every bridge, and even the elves themselves— seemed as if they were meant to grow here.

If Marina was awed by this glimpse of a hidden world, she was stricken and dazed by the great, towering oak that stood at the center of the village, a tree Norda said was called the Tree of Life. Marina couldn't imagine its height or believe its massive girth. Standing in silence below, she could see the tree swarmed with life, with beings on every towering branch. If she listened for a while, she could hear a thousand whispered voices, like the rustling of the wind through the leaves.

"It is our heart, our soul," Norda told her. "The Tree is our creator, and we are its children, as surely as its acorns and its leaves."

Even to a student of magic, Norda's words seemed more a fanciful tale than a part of the world Marina knew. It was near impossible to believe such a wondrous place was real.

Still, she thought, maybe this is much closer to reality than the noisome and chaotic world of humankind.

* * * * *

The truth of that thought was brought home to Marina early the next day, high in the branches of the Tree of Life itself. A gentle breeze touched the curtain of green, filling the morning with trembling medallions of light. Ridley lay pale and unmoving on a bed of last year's leaves. It broke Marina's heart to see him like this. He seemed hardly alive, not like the Ridley she'd come to know, but a poor, insubstantial imitation of a man.

If he lives, he carries with him forever the image of how his friend died—as I must always see Vildan, murdered before my eyes . . .

Marina caught herself holding her breath as she watched Hallvarth Fyrlief kneeling at Ridley's side. She was puzzled by the ways of the clanmaster healer, for he never touched Ridley, but silently passed his hand over Ridley's still form. His long fingers seemed to have a life of their own as they wavered above the patient's arms, his legs, or his chest, pausing now and then to give special attention to some particular place.

"I've seen nothing like this before," Marina said quietly to Norda. "Can you tell me what he's doing? I confess I haven't seen him do much of anything except this—" she made a fluttering motion in imitation of the elven healer. "Is he going to give him any medication? Will he use a spell?"

Hallvarth smiled softly without turning her way. "Our folk do not require spells to work their magic, lady. We do not use the ways of humankind. Humans think they need to capture and harness bits and pieces of magic's power."

"Humans *use* magic," Norda added. "The elven folk know what you have forgotten: that life is a part of the magic itself."

Marina frowned, looking from Norda to Hallvarth and back. The healer was small and slender, a creature with fine silver hair that trailed loosely down his back. His eyes were a strange and startling shade of blue, eyes that spoke of an incredible number of years.

"I don't understand this," Marina said. "Using magic is one thing, but being a part of it? That makes little sense to me."

"You are a part of it, though, you and all living creatures—even dragons," the clanmaster added, guessing her thoughts. "Humans see only the dragons' power to destroy, but they are a creative force as well, for they live in perfect harmony with the magic all around them."

Marina shuddered. She glanced up at the canopy of sheltering leaves, at the patterns of golden light. "I'm sorry, but I cannot think of dragons as . . . creative forces of any kind. To me they are horrid, ugly creatures who live to destroy our kind."

"I mean no offense by this," Norda said. "I hope you understand, but many beings of other races feel the same about humans: Large, rude, insensitive, and loud."

Norda's mischievous smile took the edge off her remark. Marina couldn't help but laugh.

"I won't take offense, because I have to say it's true. Only some of us aren't as rude—or as loud—as others, you have to admit."

"Whereas every elf is without the slightest imperfection," Hallvarth said without a smile. "We can be most grateful for that."

"All right," Norda said, "it wasn't a nice thing to say. You have an elf's apology, and *that's* not easily given."

"I accept, though I—" Marina stopped and stared. "Ridley? Oh, Ridley, you're back!"

"Am I?" Ridley blinked his eyes and yawned. "Where am I back from? Where have I been?"

"We are pleased to have you among us again," Hallvarth said, clasping his hands together in a circle over his patient's chest. "You will get better quickly now, my friend. Your energy is flowing in the proper direction now. Singing in just the right key, as it were."

Marina leaned closer and grasped his hand. "I was— That is, *we* were greatly concerned. I thought you were— No, now I didn't say that. I didn't say anything at all."

Ridley smiled. "I feel as if I've been on a long trip somewhere. It wasn't very pleasant."

Hallvarth nodded, as if he knew exactly where Ridley was talking about.

"I was dreaming, dreaming about dragons. I'm almost certain that yesterday I came upon a—"

"—a dragon being born?" Hallvarth finished. He smiled at the expression on Ridley's face. "We sensed her birth, but you, you were privileged to witness this thing."

Marina drew in a breath. "Truly, Ridley? This wasn't part of the dream?"

"Truly, yes. It was a magic thing. Nothing I can ever explain, but something I'll never forget."

"Life withers, as it must," Hallvarth said, "in the ever-changing cycle. But the cycle is a natural thing. It has a rhythm, a pulse of its own, and when it is changed, disrupted by an *unnatural* thing . . ." Hallvarth looked at Ridley with a deep and penetrating gaze. "What do you suppose happens when the balance of nature is disturbed in this manner? What do you think would happen if, for some reason, many, many dragons were suddenly to die?"

Ridley felt a chill. "I don't know the answer to that, but I think you're going to tell me."

"I will tell you this: You and your people are very close to irrevocably shredding the very fabric of nature with this—this rod you seek. The Rod of Savrille is a thing forged by man, a dark and terrible thing that was never intended to be."

Marina looked puzzled. "But how can it be so wrong to use this thing in a righteous cause? If we do not—?"

"Yes, of course." Hallvarth cut her off with a painful smile. "A righteous cause. They are all righteous causes, are they not? And the saddest, most sorrowful thing of all is that as lost and foolish as you are, you humans with your great, natural gifts of knowledge, your infinite curiosity, you have within your power more potential to gain perfect harmony with nature than any other creature."

The healer suddenly looked old and very weary. "Instead of using these gifts to bring you wisdom, you are slaves to your petty needs and fears. There is no cause so righteous that it can intrude without harm on nature's ways. You must learn to live *with* the world, my friends. Turn against it, and it will most surely turn upon you in ways too terrible to imagine."

Hallvarth swept his hand gently over the length of Ridley's body. "Your healing is under way. Rest and a peaceful mind is all you need now. The latter will be harder for you to attain, but it, too, will come to you in time."

It was something Ridley wanted very much to believe, but he wondered, with all that had gone before and all that might come again, if it could ever truly be.

CHAPTER 29

Sleep, as the healer said, worked its special brand of magic, and when Ridley woke at last, he felt as if he'd truly been reborn, that the Ridley who had come so close to death, had perhaps stepped through some nether door, had shed his weary flesh and emerged brand-new again.

Moreover, when he looked at the spot where Damodar's blade had torn a ragged hole through his chest, all he could find was a rough pinkening of the skin. The wound, it seemed, was healing itself. Some force he couldn't name had filled him with new energy and strength, sent a surge of power through his veins.

Elven folk do not require spells to work their magic. You must learn to be a part of the magic itself.

Ridley couldn't remember hearing the words, but he knew they came from the healer, and that they were graven forever on his mind.

Ridley realized he'd slept throughout the day. Only a few dim lights blinked above and below. He rose, stretched his limbs, and stepped out of his quarters to lean on the balcony railing and enjoy the pleasant night air.

"How could we be so different?" he wondered aloud. "Was it always this way, or did humankind and other folk take a different path in some far and distant time?"

"Talking to yourself? I thought you were getting well."

Ridley turned, as Marina appeared across the bridge of twisted vines that linked his quarters to hers. She was dressed in an elven robe, a garment of some strange material that shifted shades of green as she walked.

"I'm glad to see you're up. Feeling better, I hope?"

"Depends upon what kind of better you're talking about, I guess."

"Snails . . . yes. I'm very sorry, Ridley."

"Thank you. I appreciate that."

"I don't suppose it helps to know he died for a worthy cause, for the good of Izmer and—" The look in Ridley's eyes silenced her at once. "No, I don't suppose it does."

"What cause are we talking about, Marina? The Empress's cause against Profion? The fight for control of Izmer? That's not a cause. It's politics. The rich fighting the rich, so one of them can make it up the ladder a notch." Ridley shook his head. "You remember what the healer said about righteous causes? He's right. There aren't any. I'm finished with that, Marina. Snails gave his life away for nothing that did anyone any good—just like my father, tossed out like the daily garbage. Those people in their high towers don't even *know* some of their garbage has a name."

Marina looked away. "That isn't so. He did die for something worthwhile."

Ridley turned on her, fury mixed with sorrow in his eyes.

"You're a mage! You're one of them, Marina. Of course you think it's worthwhile because you live on the other side. Snails didn't want any part of this mess. If I'd listened to him, he'd still be alive."

"Oh, fine, how did I guess I'd hear that?" Marina's anger matched his own. She was so close now, he could see the veins pulsing in her throat. "It's easy, isn't it? Something awful happened to your father, something the mages did. So now, when anything bad happens to you, you can be certain there's a mage behind it somewhere. All dogs bark, and all magicians are as mad as Profion and Damodar. Like Vildan, for instance? Like Pellius of Aston, and Littian the Great, who fought and died to bring Izmer up from a patch of mud huts by a river? You don't know all their names, but I do.

"I'm a mage, Ridley. Am I another Profion to you? Do you really know what Savina's fighting for? For change. To make life better for people—for people like you and Snails."

"I don't need her," Ridley said, "and she's a little late for Snails."

"She's risking her life to change things for all of us. People in those so-called lofty towers and down in Oldtown, too. That's what Snails died for, whether you're too ignorant to see it or not!"

When Marina stopped, an awkward silence lay between them. The intensity of her anger had taken Ridley aback. He couldn't buy her warped sense of reason, her total belief in a cause worth the life of his friend. Still, he didn't want to fight her, didn't feel right about the distance that kept growing between them. He couldn't help but think she didn't want that, either.

Damnation! If only she weren't so stubborn, he was sure she'd see his side of things. The world wasn't the same looking down from Sumdall City, as it was looking up.

Ridley wanted to talk to her, to make her understand, but he didn't know how. He stood at the edge of the great branch, leaned on a railing over the bridge, and peered down into the endless thicket of leaves. Now and then he saw a shadow, a bright flash of green, heard a hint of soft laughter—colors and sounds that turned, for an instant, into an elven form.

"You know, Ridley," Marina said, "when Vildan told me what the Empress was facing, that Profion's demands would bring her down and destroy the Empire as well, I wanted to do what I could to help her. Still, I—I couldn't understand why she wanted commoners to be equal to us. That wasn't the way the world was supposed to be. It had never been that way.

"I didn't want to change, and I didn't want to give what I had to someone else. Now, though, after I've . . . after I've been with you and seen what you truly are, I know that you do believe in the same freedoms Savina wants for her people."

Marina paused, and after a moment Ridley turned to face her.

"Ridley, will you help me? Let me show you that we're not that far apart, that we just might be working for the very same thing?"

Ridley looked at her. She had never stood this close to him before, never so close that he could breathe in the sweet scent of her skin, discover that her hair smelled exactly like rain.

"I . . . think I could manage that," he said, his throat too dry to talk.

"Really talk to each other, Ridley? Learn that we're not too far apart?"

"I think I can guarantee that we're not too far apart."

"Oh." A slight smile wavered on her lips before she pushed it back down. "We're not, are we?"

"We're doing all right. We could do a little better, though."

"Ridley—"

"I know."

She laid her hands against his chest, let them slide up about his neck. "I can't believe this is happening. Not you and me. Not *us.*"

"Me neither. Don't think about it."

"I don't think I will."

Ridley remembered putting his arms about her, tilting her chin, remembered her eyes wide with wonder as her lips touched his. He remembered it was night, remembered they were there, together, in a very big tree, remembered he stopped thinking completely after that. . . .

*   *   *   *   *

Norda sat alone on a very high branch in a thicket of oak leaves. A night bird called. A squirrel turned over in his sleep. Ants paraded over mountains of bark in a dizzy caravan.

If she tried, Norda could hear a great many things that few other beings could. Now though, she had shut out every sound, every tiny rustle nearby or far away. In her present state of being, she could not feel her breath or the beat of her heart.

She was only aware of the glowing crystal in her hand and the image of Savina therein.

"May I hope you have news for me, Norda? Something I long to hear?"

"Majesty, we have reclaimed the map that will lead us to the Rod of Savrille. We will begin our search with the sun."

"That is good to hear, my friend. Norda, I must tell you that I have refused to give the scepter to Profion. A few councilors have supported me, but many more have not. Profion and his followers will move against me now. There is no way we can avoid a civil war, a war that I fear we will lose."

"Lady, you need me there. I'll return to Izmer at once."

"No. There's nothing you can do here. Find the rod if you can. If I fail here, then you're our last hope."

"If I was there, there are things I could do—"

"No. Do not come, Norda. You must finish what I set you out to do."

"I won't fail, Savina. I promise you that."

"I pray that is a promise you can keep."

Savina's image faded. Norda stared out into the night.

"I pray it is, too, my Empress," she whispered. She was glad that Savina was far away, for even an elf can't always hide the fear that wells up from the heart.

CHAPTER 30

He met her at the bridge at first light, marveling in the strange understanding that he had never truly seen her before. Closer, it was clear her thoughts mirrored his. They covered their surprise with a quick and cautious morning kiss. Both, searching each other's eyes for the right message there, the message that said this is fine, this is good. Both glad of heart, keenly aware that such a fragile thing might shatter and come apart with a word, with a look, and simply vanish in the first morning's light.

After a near silent breakfast with the others, trying not to look each other's way—and fooling no one at all—they found their mounts ready at the base of the great tree. Packs, waterskins, and food were checked and checked again, until finally Norda was satisfied. She left them there with a silent farewell and walked back toward the tree. They were all true companions now, and there was little they could say to one another that could not be conveyed with their eyes.

The hunter elves were on hand to bid them farewell. At least two were from the group they'd met on the trail the day before.

"May all the gods watch over you this day," an elf named Derika said, and another named Claferion added, "It is a fine day to travel, but also a day to take a special care."

"Thank you," Ridley said, "and please tell Hallvarth I am ever grateful to him for giving me back my life. Especially now," he added, with a quick glance at Marina.

Claferion showed him a rare elvish grin. "He would be here himself, but he is off somewhere. One says of Hallvarth, 'He is always here; he is always gone.'"

Claferion walked a few steps back to the great tree and returned with a long object wrapped in pale green cloth as fine as a spider's veil. Drawing the veil aside, he handed the object to Ridley.

"This sword Hallvarth would have you carry into whatever awaits you back in the human world. It is elven-made, and it will protect you from harm."

"I thank you, and I thank Hallvarth for his gift."

Derika stepped forward again. "Hallvarth would have me remind you: Let yourself become free of those things within you that bring you fear. Cherish honor and strength. Do this, and you will find your true path, Ridley."

Ridley gazed into the elven hunter's eyes and felt at that instant that the power of the Tree of Life itself was a part of him now, that the wisdom of these folk would be with him, whatever he might face in the days to come.

"I thank you once more. And in answer, I will tell you that your spirit is already in my heart."

*   *   *   *   *

The two elven hunters stood beneath the great tree until Ridley, Elwood, and Marina disappeared in the green shadows of the forest. None of the party would ever know that the bowmen would follow them like a silent, invisible army until they were safely on their way.

"He is not who he was," Claferion said. "The violent colors of his spirit have gentled to more thoughtful hues."

Derika closed his eyes. "Do you think he knows? Does he understand the extraordinary qualities within him?"

"Not yet. All he knows is that he has been changed, that he perceives the world and the people in it in a different way."

"I believe that this human will live to discover who he is."

"If this is so," Derika answered, "our own kind and the others of this world may survive another thousand years. It is as Hallvarth has said: 'The great cycle is a mole within the soil of time. One can easily tell where the mole has been, but even the mole itself cannot imagine where it will be.' "

* * * * *

Those who studied weather in a serious manner watched the day begin in Sumdall City with great trepidation. An immense cloud, black as the parting night itself, held to the rim of the earth, smothering the sun beneath its mass.

For an hour past the dawning, only pale, feeble shafts of light escaped into the sky, and when the sun dared to struggle free, that dreadful cloud refused to let it go. It was no more than a pale and sickly eye, a bloodied orb with veins of gray, a thing that might suddenly swell, bloat and give birth to some horror that would swallow up the earth.

Even common folk, who lacked the vision, the parchment,

and the pen to immortalize their thoughts in proper prose, peered at the sky that day and liked not what they saw. . . .

* * * * *

The Empress Savina, clad in armor of golden scales, stood in silence on the battlements of the royal palace. There was little warmth from the errant sun, and the scepter she held was winter-cold to the touch.

With all the strength and courage she could muster, Savina sought to keep the dreaded instrument from trembling in her hand. The heavy, golden shaft was the Scepter of Dragon Control, an instrument of such great power that no leader of Izmer had even imagined using it before.

Now though, Savina's enemies had forced the issue, pushing her into an action that could save her people or set the world afire.

"How do they dare," she said in a voice that reached only the man at her side. "It is insane to pursue this thing. Don't they know what I do may be the end of *themselves* as well as me?"

"They do, Lady, but greed closes their minds to the truth. Profion has convinced them only he and the mages are fit to rule."

The Empress sighed. General Nitadis spoke truly, of course. "Right" wasn't the issue here, and perhaps, in a way, it seldom was among men.

"What would a victory give him that he does not have now? Why this hunger to rule? It is a burden, Nitadis, one that any person in their senses would gladly forgo."

"Not if you are mad, Highness, and madness is what you face here."

Savina didn't answer. She glanced at her general and the officers who stood behind him, their armor dull in the lifeless sun. So few . . . so pitifully few offered their loyalty to her, knowing that they would almost certainly lose privilege, honor, and even their very lives.

Past the battlements, she could see the rebellious mages and the more than adequate soldiers who waited upon their call. They were gathered far, far below, atop the school of magic. She couldn't see their faces from this distance, but she knew what they were doing at this very moment, that all eyes were upon her, waiting for her to begin the dreadful act, waiting to use that moment to seize control of the Empire themselves, waiting to see if she would, indeed, defy them and loose the power she held tightly in her hand.

"If it is your wish, Empress," Nitadis said softly, "now is the time."

"Yes. Yes it is, General, and I hope the gods will forgive me for what I do."

"What you do is blameless," Nitadis said. "What they do dooms them to a hellish afterlife."

Savina turned to face the others. "I cannot thank you too much for the bravery, the courage, and the loyalty you show me today. My father would be justly proud to lead you if he were here. He gave his life— His life *was taken* from him, for the cause you and I fight for today." She paused a moment and gave them her very best imperial smile. "We will prevail. Believe that. We will prevail."

"We will prevail!" shouted the men around her. "We will prevail for you, Empress!"

"No, not for me. For the people of Izmer."

With a silent prayer, she raised the golden scepter, held it steadily for an instant, then swept it in a fearsome arc across the sky. Once, twice . . .

"May the gods forgive me," she said as she raised the scepter once more, a slash of gold against the faded crimson sun.

In that instant, thunder rolled across the heavens, thunder so mighty, so deep that it shook the very earth, trembling great palaces and shabby huts alike, tumbling stones from the city's high walls, shivering upon the rivers and the sea.

Brave men fell in fright and died. Horses, wide-eyed and crazed, ran until their hearts ceased to beat. The darkness that had smothered the sun now swallowed the sky itself. The Empress, her leaders, and the mages who had sold their very souls to bring the kingdom down watched in awe and sudden fear as the darkness loosed its horrors, and the dread and mighty creatures of an ancient world appeared. . . .

CHAPTER 31

Ridley stood beneath a high pinnacle of stone, the weathered spine of some mountain that had died when the world was very young. The map in his hand showed just such a rare formation, a bleak and arid scene with an "X" fifty paces to the east.

Ridley frowned and stabbed a finger at the mark.

"An X is important. You never see an X on a map unless it's the spot where you're supposed to be."

"Well, this X is different," Elwood grumbled. "This one doesn't mean anything at all."

"It has to. That's what it's for."

"I have to agree with Ridley," Marina said. "Just because we don't *see* anything, doesn't mean it's not there."

Elwood leaned on the haft of his axe. "Spoken like a true mage. I'd be grateful if you kept such observations to yourself. Stuff that doesn't make any sense makes a dwarf dizzy in the head."

Ridley made a face. "What do you have to do to keep one from blabbing for a while?"

"I heard that, boy, and I take offense. We might have to settle our differences right here."

"We might not, too," Marina put in. "Ridley, put your back to that pinnacle again. I'm sure fifty paces is right. Angle to the left a little this time. The map is so incredibly old, east may not have been east at the time."

"Now that's old," Ridley said, shuddering at the thought. Everything else might change, but directions were supposed to stay put. A person ought to be able to count on that.

"You don't walk natural-like," the dwarf said. "You take *big* steps when you're walkin' off a map."

"I'm walking just fine," Ridley said, backing off and starting over again. "Don't talk until I'm through, all right? If you were doing this, we wouldn't be doing fifty steps. More likely, a hundred or so."

"Damnation, that tears it!" Elwood said, hefting his axe in one hand and pulling at his beard with the other.

"Stop it, both of you." Marina looked for help from some phantom in the sky. "Why me? What did I do to deserve the two of you?"

". . . forty-eight, forty-nine, fifty," Ridley finished. He looked down at his feet. "I don't see a thing any different over here."

"It's not supposed to look different," Marina pointed out. "If someone wanted it to be real easy, they'd have painted a sign."

"Absolutely," Elwood muttered. "My thoughts as well."

"We can do without your thoughts just fine." Ridley turned to Marina. "Now what? If there's an X here, it's made for ants to see."

"Do I have to do everything? Honestly, Rid . . ."

Gently pushing him aside, Marina went to her hands and

knees and began to brush aside the dry soil. Ridley glanced at Elwood and shrugged.

"Your sword," Marina said, without looking up.

"What for?"

"Just do it, all right?"

Ridley drew his blade and handed her the hilt. Marina grasped the weapon and began to dig.

Ridley gasped. "That's a weapon, not a shovel! Stop that!"

"You're right. It's a terrible shovel, but it's all we've got. There has to be something here. If there wasn't— Hah!" Marina looked up and grinned. "Come on, don't just stand there. Give me a hand."

Ridley and Elwood bent to the task, widening the small hole Marina had uncovered in the soil. At first, Ridley could see nothing at all, only that Marina had struck rock half a foot down. No big surprise there. That's where rocks are from, down in the ground. This rock though, he had to admit, was unusually smooth and perfectly parallel to the surface itself.

He gave Marina a curious look. Marina, apparently, had the very same thought. She picked up Ridley's sword and tapped the hilt against the stone.

Ridley drew a breath. "Hollow. By the gods, we've found it."

"I've found it," Marina said. "Let's try and remember that."

"Fine, I will. Elwood, don't just stand there and gawk. Give me a hand with this."

The moment the dirt was wiped away, it was clear the stone had been carved by intelligent hands. Elwood peered at the ancient runes etched on the surface. He rolled his eyes and said he hoped they weren't turned into snakes or something worse than that.

The stone came away with surprising ease, and the air that wafted up from below was dry and musty, as if no moisture had penetrated the earth since time itself began. There was another scent as well, one that Ridley found disturbing and vaguely familiar. Elwood smelled it too, and he wrinkled his nose. His glance told Ridley he didn't like it either, but, for once, he kept his opinions to himself.

The drop from the surface was less than five feet. The only light came from the entry itself, and the way ahead was black as a demon's heart.

"Let me go first," Elwood said. "No one knows more about caverns and the like than a warrior of the Oakenshield clan. I was born in a burrow, and— *Ulp!*"

Whatever it was, it struck Elwood hard and knocked him flat. Ridley helped him up. Elwood shook him off, groaned, and rubbed his nose.

"Whoever you are, you've made the worst mistake of your life in striking Elwood Gutworthy."

The dwarf hefted his axe, and attacked the darkness again.

"No! Wait!" Marina stepped in his path. "There's no one there. It's a power of some kind."

Elwood gave her a wary look. "Magic? That's what you're sayin' it is?"

"Stand back over there. You too, Ridley."

"And do what?"

"Something that's very difficult for you both. Don't do anything at all."

Marina drew in a breath, and then she pointed her left hand into the dark.

"*Amaka lavat . . . imisha . . . santir . . .* What magic is hidden here, now reason reveal it . . . make it clear!"

The green gemstone at her wrist began to glow, slowly at first, then quickening into a pulsing light that made Ridley look away. When he glanced back again, the gemstone's power had formed a shimmering circle, a narrow entryway.

"What is it?" he asked.

"It's a wall of force of some kind," Marina replied. "I've never encountered this sort of magic before. There's a way through, as you can see, but I can't get past it."

"You can't? How do you know?"

"I just *know,* all right? The force I'm up against has made that clear." She paused and closed her eyes. "I think we've been through this before. Only the seeker can go from here."

"Don't tell me," Ridley finished. "This is that wraith's doing, isn't it? I'm the one that's got the Dragon's Eye."

"Lucky you," Elwood said.

"Both of you, wait right here. I'll be right back," Ridley said. "I think."

"Be careful, Rid. Please?"

Ridley held her glance for a long moment. He liked very much what he saw there. It almost made him feel it would all work out, that in the end, everything would be fine.

Almost.

* * * * *

The mouth of the tunnel was dry, dark, and deadly silent. A few steps in, however, water seeped from the ceiling and the narrow stone walls. The damp, rocky surface glowed with a faint luminescence—tiny creatures, Ridley guessed, or minerals in the stone. Whatever the source might be, it was not enough to light the way.

As far as he could tell, the path was straight as an arrow. In spite of the constant drip of cold water, the unpleasant scent was still strong—like an old and empty house, full of mold, dead spiders, and mice in the walls. . . .

Ridley stopped. For the first time, the tunnel curved abruptly to the right. Peering cautiously around the curve, he saw that the tunnel continued straight ahead, as it had before.

He took a breath, walked past the curve—

—and into a solid wall.

Not a wall at all, he saw at once—only another illusion, one that seemed perfectly real until you came up against it and flattened your nose.

"I'm glad you're not here, Elwood," he said. "I don't need you crowing over this."

Now what? He knew there was something else, some other way. The map wouldn't lead him this far and then suddenly end.

"All right, I'm here," he said aloud. "Any wraiths listening? Anything here at all?"

Ridley's answer came at once. The ground beneath his feet disappeared. One moment he was standing on solid rock, the next he was falling through darkness, tumbling down a steep and odorous slope with nothing to stop him, nothing to break his fall.

Even flailing helplessly about, Ridley suddenly knew exactly what he smelled. Something was dead. Something had been dead a very, very long time.

CHAPTER 32

The warrior in the blood-red uniform and armor black as night stopped at a respectable distance from his master. He did not dare speak, not until the great mage deigned to notice he was there. The warrior feared his master, as every soldier did.

Still, Algamar was proud to be a member of the Crimson Brigade. For, as he feared his master, so did warriors of lesser degree fear him. It was said, and rightly so, that murder, torture, and the vilest of cruelties was common practice among the members of the Brigade, that the most unspeakable of crimes were only granted to those in favor with the master himself.

Algamar, the warrior who waited now, prayed that the mage would choose him for special duty one day. To that end, he had taken extra care. He had brushed his uniform, cleaned and shined his boots. He had polished his armor until he could see his reflection in its dull iron surface.

That reflection, he noted with pride, showed a man who had already risen to privileged rank within the Crimson Brigade. All of the mage's men wore helmets in the images of the most ferocious of beasts. Algamar had fought through the ranks of Savage Lion, Striking Serpent, and Black Wolverine, and now he wore the coveted helmet of Fearsome Boar.

This image was truly frightful with its ugly snout, sharpened tusks, and even an array of long bristles incised into the iron.

It was also heavy, heavy and hot. Sweat rolled down his features inside the metal mask to sting his eyes, rolled past his neck and into the hollow of his chest. Still, he waited, held himself rigid and moved not an inch until the hooded figure turned and saw him there.

"What is it? What have you to say?"

Algamar hoped he hadn't betrayed himself through any slight movement or gesture. The great Lord Damodar was a man to be feared at any time. Now though, since that writhing horror had come to live in his head, it was all a man could do to look him in the eye. If he did not, if he once looked away . . .

"Lord Damodar, they have found the entry. All three of them have descended into the earth. As you have ordered, sire, they are under careful watch, but no one has approached them."

"You will make certain they do not."

"Sire."

"And you. You are. . . ?"

It was all Algamar could do to keep from looking away. Damodar's eyes seemed to bore a hole through his skull.

"Algamar, Lord, of the Fearsome Boars Second."

"I can see what you are, fool, and I can see that like the swine you mimic, you have slept in a sty. Your uniform is filthy, and your armor smells of dung. Get out of my sight, and do not ever dare to enter my presence in this manner again!"

Somehow, Algamar stood his ground under Damodar's rage. He backed slowly out of the mage's tent, and when he was far enough away, he leaned over in the brush and retched.

* * * * *

Damodar followed the trooper with his eyes until the man disappeared. "A worthy fellow," he muttered to himself. "He does well."

An instant later, the man was forgotten. Damodar looked through the trees at the barren, rocky scene below. He was pleased with the trooper's news. It was all coming together now, coming together exactly as he had planned.

Following the trail of his prey from the encounter at the thieves' den, he had exercised great caution and a mage's power of stealth. The three companions and the interfering elf had led him to the outskirts of the fabled Tree of Life itself. There, he had waited, alone, not daring to bring soldiers of the Brigade any closer.

It had worked, worked in every detail. No one, he knew, could have accomplished what he had done, coming so close to elves without revealing his presence.

Dogging their heels from there was a relatively simple matter. The thief, the dwarf, and the woman, Marina Pretensa, had faithfully followed their map and led him exactly where he wanted to be.

Damodar let a smile twist his hideous features.

"Stay on your quest, little thief," he whispered, "and bring the prize to me. I'll grant you a short but oh so painful death if you succeed."

CHAPTER 33

R idley thought his frightening ride down the dark slope would never end. When it did, he scarcely had time to tuck his head between his knees. He hit hard against yet another stone wall—this one no illusion, this one very real.

Picking himself up, he found that this small stone chamber was somewhat better lit. A myriad of tiny creatures swarmed along the walls, emitting an amber-hued glow.

Once his eyes grew accustomed to the light, he saw the massive and deeply-carved stone emblem on the far wall. Ridley caught his breath, for the emblem looked remarkably like the ruby Dragon's Eye he carried in the pocket of his vest. Drawing the gem out, he walked to the wall and placed the jewel directly over the emblem.

Whatever he expected to happen, didn't. The gem and the emblem were a perfect match. Other than that . . .

He backed away and stared at the wall. What was it the wraith had said? He tried to recall the words.

Only through the Dragon's Eye can one see where the rod does lie. . . .

"I hate riddles," Ridley muttered. "Why can't someone give you a simple answer sometime?"

He held the ruby to his eye and peered at the emblem on the wall. For an instant, he was too startled to move. There were two double doors there that hadn't been visible before. On each door was an exquisitely-carved dragon. And only one of them had an eye.

"Well, even an unschooled thief can figure this one out," Ridley said. He stepped up and placed the ruby in the left-hand dragon's empty socket. The ruby began to glow, and the doors slowly opened. . . .

Ridley stood rigid. His heart nearly stopped. The room beyond was filled, heaped, virtually drowning in treasure: Silver goblets and golden plates, scepters, crowns, bracelets, necklaces and rings, all made of precious metal, each encrusted with diamonds, sapphires, emeralds and milky pearls. Strewn carelessly about the room were great chests spilling over with gems of every sort. There were bags piled high as Ridley's head. Several had split from age and loosed a river of golden coins.

Ridley laughed aloud, pulled a pouch from his belt, and bent to fill it with gems and shiny coins. He paused, then, and stood straight, recalling what the wraith had also said.

Do not be lured by the dragon's treasure, for in it lies great sorrow, not pleasure.

"Now why did I have to think of that?" Ridley was greatly irritated with himself. A good memory was helpful sometimes, and sometimes it was not.

Still, he thought, the words might not even be true. Wraiths didn't know everything, did they? If they did, they'd surely appear as something more substantial. They wouldn't go around looking like *fog* all the time, now would they?

If he just took a handful, no more than that, who'd ever know? Who'd miss a whole ton of treasure from a pile like this? Who'd even care if he—

"Yaaah, get away—from—*me!*"

Ridley backed away, flailing at the horror that dangled before his face. He stumbled and nearly fell into a chest of jeweled crowns. Now he knew what smelled bad in the cavern. The thing hanging there was a long-dead corpse.

There were still bits of dark, mummified flesh clinging to its bones. Its eyes were hollows laced with spiderwebs, and its mouth was open wide, as if it had died with a scream on its shriveled and petrified lips.

Glancing up, Ridley could see the remains of this monstrous creature hung from a rusty iron hook. Wrapped about its skeletal frame were the tattered shreds of a mage's robe, and, clutched in its bony fist, was a dusty and ancient crimson rod.

"Now that's how I like to see a mage," Ridley said. "Doing something useful for a change."

Stepping up to the swinging corpse, he boldly snatched the rod from its bony fist. The corpse promptly reached out and grabbed it back.

"You! Why do you disturb the Keeper of the Rod of Savrille?"

Ridley nearly jumped out of his skin. Something cold ran up his back.

"All right," he said, determined not to pass out on the spot, "what's the deal this time? You know the wraith. You fellows work together, right?"

"Quiet, boy!"

Ridley backed off. He could smell the thing's terrible breath. Still, it was simply *hanging* there. It wasn't likely it could hop down and chase him through the door.

"I need the rod. I'm supposed to get it and save the Empire of Izmer. This wasn't my idea, but I've come this far. I hate to turn back."

"Do you know who I am?"

"No, of course not. I wouldn't have the faintest idea."

"I am Savrille, creator of the rod. I was cursed for attempting to control the red dragons. This is what happens when you push the gods too far. Remember that."

"I think I've already got the idea. Listen, can we get back to my problem? I've got people waiting back there—"

"Do not interrupt me again!"

"Don't *breathe* on me, all right? I can't handle that."

"I am sentenced to this purgatory until someone worthy of the rod's power comes to take it. You are such a man."

Ridley shrugged. "I don't know about worthy, but I will find out."

"Be warned. Anyone who dares to yield to the power of the rod will suffer a horrible fate. The evil the rod creates cannot be undone, not unless its spell is broken."

"And how would you go about that?"

"That . . . *you* must discover."

The dead mage lifted its rotted hand. Ridley reached out carefully, grasped the rod, and stepped back.

The rod began to glow and pulse with an eerie light. It rapidly began to change, shifting from one color to another. For an instant it was a brilliant emerald green, then red as a demon star. It was heavy with dazzling diamonds and rubies, yet cold to the touch. Red dragons, intricately carved by a long-dead master of the arts, twisted and turned about the instrument's shaft.

Ridley felt the awesome power of the thing, felt its energy flow through every cell and every vein. He raised the rod high, filling the chamber with its unworldly light.

Ridley gasped, nearly dropping the thing right there. As the rod's great power filled the room with a brilliance cold as any star, he saw that the wall beyond the hanging corpse was afire with an ancient fresco of dozens of red dragons in flight. It was truly an awesome, breathtaking sight, so real it seemed they might burst out of the painting and fill the treasure chamber with their might.

He couldn't take his eyes off this marvel. It seemed as if he'd been frozen before these magnificent creatures forever, as if a thousand years had passed. . . .

When he looked at the dead man again, its hooded skull had slumped against its hollow chest.

Its purgatory is over, Ridley thought with a shudder. I wonder if mine has just begun?

* * * * *

A shaft of sunlight filled with golden dust motes lit the rocky floor below the entryway. Ridley thought he'd never seen such a glorious sight. He hurried forward then pulled himself up into the blinding light of day.

"Marina! Elwood!" he shouted. "I've got it, I've—"

His words faded, and all his strength drained away. Damodar stood behind Marina, a thin silver blade pressed against her throat. Marina's face was drained of color, and her eyes were bright with fear.

"Good work, little thief." Damodar smiled. "I can't thank you enough, but I know a thousand ways to try."

CHAPTER 34

lwood stood behind Damodar, his face as grim as death. Two uglies from the Crimson Brigade held their blades at his back. One of the guards moved aside, and Ridley was stunned to see Norda there as well.

He knew where we were, knew all along. . . .

"I can see what's in your rather primitive mind," Damodar said. "Do I need to remind you that sticking your nose into other people's affairs got your other friend killed? Don't be responsible for finishing off the ones you have left."

Damodar grinned and slid the dagger across Marina's neck. Marina gasped, and a thin line of red appeared at her throat.

"Oh, I'm terribly sorry. I'm afraid I lost control of myself."

"Don't. Don't hurt her!" Ridley took a step toward the mage, one hand tight around the hilt of his sword.

"You're not that much a fool," Damodar told him. "You know how to finish this business. Give me the rod and we're done."

"And you'll let her go?"

"Of course. Why would I want to harm her? What kind of person do you think I am?"

"Don't," Marina cried. "Don't do it, Ridley!"

Damodar looked pained. "You doubt my word. I'm truly offended, now."

"Your word," Ridley said, "is worth exactly half a mug of spit. Here, and be damned to you."

Ridley tossed the heavy rod and watched it twirl and glitter in the sun. Damodar seized it in the air, grasping it tightly in his metal-clad hand. A smile of sheer pleasure, a near indecent glow of satisfaction crossed his ugly features. For an instant, the demon within him slithered from his ears and his nose and lashed its dark tendrils about, sharing, in its own bizarre way, its host's moment of glory.

"There," Damodar said, thrusting Marina roughly aside. "I said I would set her free, and you doubted my word. I'm very displeased with you, boy."

It was all Ridley could do to hold himself back, to keep from drawing his blade and separating the mage from his head.

"Marina," he said, without taking his eyes off Damodar, "come here beside me."

Damodar laughed and spread his hands. "I said I'd let them go, and I will. *For them!*"

He swept about suddenly, facing his Crimson Brigade. "I've held them back long enough. Now they'll have their day!"

Damodar clutched the precious rod in his fist, then waved it wildly above his head. "Kill them, all of them! Any man who doesn't will answer to me!"

Ridley moved but not quickly enough. Damodar drew a pouch from his belt, grabbed a handful of dust, and tossed it in the air.

"A simple spell, indeed, is it not? Even a student mage can use it well." He grinned at Marina. "A quick wit and a pretty face, for sure, but that's *not* what we're looking for, my dear."

The space around him seemed to slide and melt away like cheap tallow wax. A blue, indistinct circle shimmered in the air, buzzing like a hive of angry bees.

"To Profion," Damodar said. "Take me to him now!"

The mage leaped into the portal and vanished at once.

"Hurry!" Marina called out. "We can get through it, too!"

Kneeling quickly, she mumbled to herself, her eyes staring into the fading circle. For a moment, it held, blinked, and held again. A Crimson warrior shouted, leaped forward, and tossed Marina cruelly aside. Elwood cursed, ducked beneath the swords at his back, and ran at the warrior who had brought Marina down. The guard cried out as Elwood's head rammed him squarely in the gut. The soldier's helmet, the face of an angry swine, clattered across the bare ground.

Ridley leaped over the downed warrior, while Elwood pounded the man with his fists. Four more red-clad guards jumped on him, pummeling the dwarf with the flats of their swords. Elwood howled and sent two of them tumbling head over heels. Ridley faced the rest, his blade slashing the morning air. Three more swordsmen joined their comrades, eager for a kill.

"Anyone care to go one on one?" Ridley asked. "I know you louts don't know the word *fair,* but it's really more fun that way."

All of the warriors disagreed and fell on Ridley at once, forcing him back against the high pinnacle of stone.

"All *right,* it was just an idea. We'll do it your way."

Ridley knew for certain the best way to get to the afterlife fast was to take on five men at once. With no warning at all, he let out a blood-curdling yell and lunged at the pair to his left, slashing out wildly at one and then the next.

The swordsmen did exactly what Ridley expected them to do—they stepped back quickly, raising their blades in the proper defensive stance and leaving a hole between them that gave Ridley room to dart free.

He turned at once, pressing the weakest of the two. The man was tall, but awkward and slow. The open-jawed lion on his helmet was an awesome sight to see, but the man underneath was scarcely frightening at all.

Ridley feinted, lured the man in, and cut him down with a blow to the knees. The soldier cried out and collapsed. Just as the blow was struck, Ridley saw the man's partner dashing in from the right, an enormous blade raised over his shoulder in a two-handed grip designed to neatly part a man from his head. Ridley ducked, let the blade hum by, then thrust his sword in a quick, deadly jab. The warrior grabbed his belly, staggered drunkenly about, then fell and went still.

Two down and three to go, Ridley thought, and none of them friendly as near as I can see. Time for another plan.

Ridley ran. He met another pair head on, side-stepped the two, and ran full out again.

"Ridley!"

Ridley leaped across a small ravine. Marina stood with her back to the shimmering portal, a snake-nosed ugly bearing down on her fast. Ridley knew he couldn't do it, couldn't reach her in time. Desperate, he drew a small dagger from his belt and tossed it swiftly through the air. The weapon clanged against the soldier's helmet and fell to the ground. The warrior stopped, turned, and looked at Ridley.

Norda came out of nowhere, a good-sized rock in her hand, and smashed it soundly against the soldier's iron-clad head. The man turned, mildly annoyed. He looked at Norda and laughed.

"Big mistake," Ridley muttered, and he struck the man with the side of his blade.

The soldier made a pained sound and sank to the ground.

"Ridley, it's fading!" Marina shouted. "Hurry!"

Ridley went quickly to her side, held her close, and watched in dismay as the portal shimmered and died.

Marina closed her eyes. "That was our only chance out of this place. Now what?"

"Now we don't do that. Now we do something else!"

The crimson-clad trooper was nearly upon him before he could parry his blow. Three more crowded behind the first, swords cutting the air. Ridley didn't waste a moment's time. He bent low, lashed out, and slashed the soldier across his thigh.

"Come on! We're out of here!"

Norda stared. "Out to where?"

"I don't have the foggiest idea. Anywhere."

He glanced across the shallow ravine. "First, I'd better help that dwarf, though I'm sure he won't thank me for butting in."

Elwood, his short, powerful legs rooted firmly to the ground, stood in the center of a swarm of crimson warriors. His features were dark, nearly black with rage. His axe was a blur, cutting down hapless warriors with every murderous swing. No one noticed Ridley stalking up from behind. In an instant, two more of Damodar's uglies were writhing on the ground.

A moment later, it was over. A few soldiers moaned and tried to crawl away, but none of them were looking for a fight.

Elwood spat on the broad blade of his axe. "There's none of

'em pretty, but a couple of them could fight. Not that it did 'em any good against Elwood Gutworthy. Did I tell you 'bout the time—"

"No. And don't."

Elwood gave him a menacing frown. "What's got *your* hackles up, lad? You not havin' any fun?"

Ridley didn't answer. Marina was back across the ravine, waving frantically in his direction.

"It's not gone yet!" she said, a look of fierce determination on her face. "Watch this!"

Elwood, Ridley, and Norda stood aside as Marina tossed a handful of dust where the portal had disappeared. A pale blue circle blinked into life then vanished at once.

"Don't look like much to me," Elwood said.

"It's not. It's weak, but it's there. I think it'll work the way it should."

"The way it should?" Ridley looked pained. "What are some of the other ways, Marina? I don't believe you mentioned that."

"That's because you don't want to know, Ridley. What I mean is, it could take us where Damodar went, or possibly somewhere else."

"You folks go on ahead," Elwood said. "A dwarf's got more sense than to step into something like that."

"Elven lore tells us there is an infinite number of planes of existence," Norda said solemnly. "Some of these would be much like our own. Others would be places where we couldn't exist at all, much less comprehend."

"Like I said, I'll see you people sometime. It's been real fun."

"Elwood, get back here right now." Marina set her hands on her hips and glared. "I'll go first," she said. "Ridley?"

"I guess I'd better hold your hand, in case you get in trouble somewhere."

"How nice for you both," Norda said. "We're wasting valuable time."

Without another look at the others, Norda stepped into the portal and disappeared.

Marina looked at Ridley. Ridley nodded back, reached for her hand, and followed Norda somewhere, or nowhere at all.

Elwood stood alone in the shade of the rocky spire. He looked past the scattered bodies, past the thicket of woods, past the stony plain. He hesitated, took another look as if he meant to capture the scene in the event there was nothing else he ever got to see.

"Anyways, if an elf and a couple of humans can do it, it's somethin' a dwarf can do, too. Though I'm double bedamned to figure how I got into this kinda mess at all."

CHAPTER 35

The scent of war was in the air, and war itself not far away. Rage, fear, and dread anticipation were the odors of the day, as men prepared to live or die. Dark clouds gathered in the east, and boiled across the sky, casting bleak shadows on the hapless figures down below.

On the high battlements of the school of magic, the rebellious mages of Izmer waited. They were clad in armor now, their robes of piety cast aside this day, as seers and prophets readied their arsenal of spells and earthly engines of war.

Ballistae, mangonel, and trebuchet appeared, as well as iron pots of liquid fire. Every man was armed with deadly weapons—swords of great value and renown for mage and noble born, pikes, bows, axes, and spears for the hands of lesser men—all sharpened for the kill.

Rigid in their heavy armor were the troops of Damodar, men who hid their features under frightful masks of iron. Far across the city on another height waited the Empress's loyal men. Every man who followed Savina was there, commoner and royal, old and young alike, for her ranks today were most pitifully thin.

For the moment, all was silent across the great city. The air bore down upon the armies from a hot, oppressive sky. Time itself appeared to pause and catch its breath.

Then, against the lowering clouds, with scarcely a warning at all, a clash of thunder rolled across the heavens, a sound of such power that great buildings trembled, men hid their faces, and children cried. Even the soldiers clad in iron, men who had never prayed to any god, pled for mercy now.

Of a sudden, against the blackened skies, a tiny star appeared, a star as bright and pure as liquid gold. One soldier saw it and pointed it out to a friend. The friend told another, and another after that.

A solemn murmur of awe and wonder spread through the gathered crowds. They watched and waited as the star grew closer still. An instant after that, those with a practiced eye drew in a frightful breath as the bright star exploded into a great horde of dragons, massive beasts with wings that ate the air, and hides of golden scales.

Fear, like a swift and deadly plague, like winter wind across a barren plain, touched every man. At that very moment, the tall and daunting figure of Profion appeared, his features a mask of twisted rage, his voice a challenge to the thunder overhead.

"Stop! I command you!" he bellowed against the wind. "Stop and fight, you cowards, or every man of you will perish by my hand this day!"

Profion's eyes flashed fire, and a jeweled finger stabbed into the crowd, settling on one man, then the next, until there were ten. One by one, these warriors shrieked and writhed as their flesh turned to tallow and blood filled their eyes.

"I'll do it again, burn the first man who flees!" Profion warned them. "Now destroy these things, blast them from the sky!"

Stones and balls of iron flew from a hundred trebuchet. Mages spread their arms and loosed fiery spells into the skies. Lancers tossed their weapons, and archers fired their arrows, though none came close to the golden demons overhead.

On the great horde came, one golden dragon, then another, shrieking down on their human foes. One roared and veered away as a fireball singed its wings. The others hurtled down on the army gathered below, so close now that mage and warrior alike could see their ruby eyes, their wicked teeth and claws, the pulsing veins in wings that beat the heated air.

Then, as if from a prophecy of old, rage begat rage, and fire begat fire as tongues of flames roared from the dragons' great jaws to smother the humans below. Men screamed and flailed the air, waving blackened limbs about. The horror was over in seconds, but it seemed to last forever for the hapless soldiers caught in the dragons' charge.

Profion himself loomed over the crew of a ballista, a giant crossbow mounted on a stout oaken frame. Sweating soldiers tightened the twisted skeins. Others moved the heavy weapon, trailing a flight of dragons across the city's heights.

"Fire! Let it go, you fools! Fire!"

A crimson-clad soldier loosed the trigger of the weapon, and a massive bolt shivered through the smoky air.

The dragons, who could sense the hatred of their kind in every human heart, scattered quickly to let the deadly bolt pass. Only one, a dragon nearly past its prime, darted directly into the missile's path.

As the bolt pierced the creature's underbelly, it opened its great maw and screamed, a sound of such agony and pain that every man who heard it carried it forever in his dreams.

The dragon turned and twisted, pounded its wings against the air, struggling in vain to right itself. It plummeted to earth, impaling itself on a lofty city spire. For a long and terrible moment, its death-cry echoed through the heights of Sumdall City, then was quickly gone.

Not far away, the Empress Savina watched in agony as the gold dragon died, then she turned away.

"What have I done, Nitidas? I've killed us all, every one!"

"Lady, you have not," the general told her, resisting the urge to comfort this frightened young woman in his arms, to treat her like a child.

"You have done what is right. It is they who have brought this to us today."

"And so, General?" She looked into his hard gray eyes. "Will fault bring my father back? Will it help the Empire survive? Tell me, my friend, does it matter if Profion is wrong, and I am right?"

General Nitidas never answered, for at that moment, the black clouds boiled and spread their darkness across the sky. Now, there was not the slightest touch of day, only the hellish night.

*　　*　　*　　*　　*

Atop the school of magic, with the smell of burning flesh in the air, the mages looked up, startled at the sudden darkness, a spell that none among them could apply.

"Look," Azmath said, a tremor in his voice. "Look at the skies."

"It's dark," Profion said, eyeing the man with disgust. "Are you afraid of the dark? By the gods, you're not a child. Stop your whimpering, man."

"He's right," Mage Sidaurus said. "It's unnatural, Profion, it's the world turning black."

Profion laughed aloud. "You should take pride in such *blackness*. When we're finished remaking the world the way we want it, nothing will ever be the same. What do you think I've been working for?"

"It isn't right," Azmath muttered, shaking his head. He clasped his hands together, twining his fingers about like restless snakes. "You were wrong, Profion; the Empress was right. This is a madness that can't be stopped. You have no power over this."

Profion glared. "You betrayed the Empress as well as I, you fool. Now you stand there and tell me I'm *wrong?* Now you betray me as well?"

"It is not betrayal. It is common sense, mage. I am not blind, and I can see the darkness you've unleashed on the world. In your pride, you've destroyed us all."

"And you are beginning to bore me. I cannot abide a whiner, especially whiny old men who are useless to anyone."

"Profion—"

Azmath's eyes went wide. He tried to speak, but the words stuck in his throat. Still staring at Profion, he sank to the ground, a dagger buried to the hilt in his chest.

The mage Sidaurus gasped and stepped back. Mendal, a tall and pale-eyed mage, bent over Azmath, started to touch his face, then jerked his hand away.

"You've killed him." Mendal looked up at Profion in disbelief. "He's dead."

"You have truly amazing powers," Profion said. He turned to

face the seers gathered behind him. "Any more complaints, my Brothers? Any more *suggestions*, any more *advice*? Please don't hesitate. We're all professionals here."

The mages were silent. Not a one dared look into Profion's eyes. Each, though, within himself, knew that they had pledged themselves to a cause they might most heartily regret before this day was done.

Before they could ponder any further on this, the gold dragons wheeled about and came at them again. While dragons do not think in the manner of men, they are wise and clever in their cruel and ancient ways. This time, they did not attack in any organized manner but darted down from every height and angle, leaving their foes in fear and disarray. No sooner had the soldiers turned to face a dragon to the east than three rushed down upon them from the south, deadly fire spewing from their gullets, turning men to torches, then cinders, then ash.

Throughout this chaos and disorder, Profion stood calm and unyielding, directing his forces with a leader's strength and skill. Inside, the great mage was seething, boiling with a rage he could scarcely contain. The Empress Savina was winning the day. The power of her scepter was awesome, greater than he had ever imagined. Even the spells of all the Council of Mages combined could not hold the beasts at bay. Profion knew that only the Rod of Savrille could have turned the tide this day, and Damodar, that arrogant fool, had failed him, leaving him to fight the battle alone.

The mage searched his mind for every power, every deadly spell he'd ever known, aware, in his black and ruthless heart, that nothing could defy the Empress now. Her dragons would sweep his forces away, destroy them to a man. Nothing but soot would remain of those who'd defied this stripling, this *child,* who would rule Izmer at the end of this day.

A blast of searing flame struck the parapet directly over Profion's head. The mage went to ground, turned, and wrapped his cloak about his head. He could feel the searing heat, hear the cries of dying men, and when he dared look up again, he could see great slabs of stone melting just above and sizzling down the high wall.

"Merculon! Hankis!" he bellowed. "Get your men from the north! I need them here!"

"Idiots," he muttered. "By the time they get here, there won't be anything left. I have to do everything, everything myself."

Profion staggered, covering his face as a sharp blast of thunder nearly punctured his ears. A blue, shimmering portal appeared before his eyes, and Damodar leaped out, knocking a soldier to the ground before he reached Profion.

"By the dark gods," Damodar said, taking in the smoke and carnage all about, "it appears I'm either sadly late or just in time." He bowed, slightly, a mockery of pleasure on his face. "Here, Lord. I believe you might need this."

Damodar brought the heavy, crimson Rod of Savrille from under his cloak and presented it with a flourish to Profion.

Profion made no effort to hide his pleasure. His eyes went wide as he tore the instrument from Damodar's grasp. At once, he could feel the thing's power, feel it surging through every vein, humming through every cell. He watched in unbelievable joy as sparks of power danced visibly over his shoulder, across his chest, down his arms, and into his gauntleted hands.

Now, now little Empress, now we shall have our day. Now we shall see the old world die, and the new one begin.

CHAPTER 36

"M y, ah, head," Damodar said. "I've done as you asked, and I'd be grateful if you'd get this damned thing out of there. Do you have any idea of the pain, the humiliation—"

"*Enough!*" Profion turned in a fury, raised one hand, and swept it past Damodar's face. "You're fortunate I *leave* you with a head, you prideful fool. Don't interrupt me again."

At once, Damodar's flesh began to writhe, tremble, and stretch in tortured disarray. Sharp tendrils of hellish blue lightning began to whip his body. A terrible cry escaped his lips as the corners of his mouth began to crawl up his cheek, smother his nose and envelop his eyes. The damp, quivering tentacles of the demon in his head snaked out of his ears, his nose, and his mouth, jerking frantically, wildly about as if they sensed their time had come. Damodar sank to his knees, clutching the distorted flesh that quivered atop his head and rolled across his face. The watching mages and soldiers shrank back in horror, each one aware that Profion's wrath could just as easily fall upon them.

Finally, Damodar rose shakily to his feet, lowered his hands, and revealed the handsome, haughty features back in place again.

"What are you looking at?" he scowled at the few onlookers. "I'm myself again, and you louts are as ugly as you were before. More's the same, you're all filthy as—"

Damodar stopped, startled, as a dragon appeared through a cloud of greasy smoke. It swept the dark veil aside with its leathery wings, diving at the crowd with incredible speed.

Damodar jerked a lance from the hand of a soldier, hurled it at the beast, and leaped aside. The dragon, screeching in fury, loosed a searing gobbet of fire at the humans down below. The blast caught a trooper, burning the fellow to a crisp before he could topple to the ground. The fire licked and boiled across the ground, setting two mages aflame as well.

Imperial soldiers and warriors of Damodar's Crimson Brigade loosed bolts and heavy stones from mangonel and trebuchet. Arrows clouded the sooty air, and mages hurled their magic fireballs at the sky—all, it seemed, to no avail. The gold dragons learned quickly and well. With each new attack, they changed their tactics to further confuse and demoralize their foes.

Amid this chaos, Profion stood firm, unmoved, as if he were on another world, some tranquil plane where the cries of burning men could not be heard. Indeed, a narrow smile creased his cruel features as he raised his right arm and thrust the Rod of Savrille at the darkened sky.

Now we try our powers, he thought. Now we challenge the very gods themselves! Now we win or lose the greatest game of all!

A blinding red beam left the mage's rod and laced the skies above. A hot, howling wind arose and filled Profion's cape, making it seem as if a dark demon had suddenly appeared in his place.

At once, the mage saw a shaft of gold arise from the palace towers and cross his bolt of red.

Profion laughed. The Empress had met his challenge with her scepter, and the true war had begun.

The gold dragons, circling high above, turned away at once, wings on edge, and dived straight for the Empress's stronghold.

At the sight of the dragons' retreat, the mages and soldiers on the roof of the magic school cheered and waved their arms about. Some of the troopers tossed their weapons to the ground, certain this was a sign they wouldn't have to tangle with dragons anymore.

"Stop that!" Profion shouted. "You're not done here. Pick up your weapons, or I'll turn you all to serpents and frogs!"

The soldiers and seers went silent. Profion didn't bother to see if they'd obeyed. His eyes were on the far palace tower. He knew, as no other did, what was happening there, what powers the Empress would embrace.

He knew, as well, the force he would bring against her. He sensed, even now, that this dread power was upon him. He could feel their very presence, smell their hunger, see the fury in their eyes. As he turned, facing the cold wind of the north, he saw their awesome image in his mind and knew they were very near.

He looked at the dragons that circled the Empress's keep, forming a dazzling crown of gold. One, whose scales were brighter than the rest, whose wings seemed spun of the sun itself, detached itself from the rest and swooped down to grasp the Empress's balcony in its massive claws. Beating its great wings to keep its balance, it bowed its head before the Empress's gaze.

Once more, Profion clenched his metal glove about the Rod of Savrille and swept it in a blazing arc across the sky.

"Hear me!" he demanded. "I entreat you now to answer my command!"

A bolt of northern lightning ripped the clouds, shaking the city down below.

"Answer! Answer me now. You are close; you are near. You belong to me!"

Still, the things he sought did not appear. They were there, he knew, somewhere up in the dark. "Why are you waiting?" he said. "I have commanded you here!"

A great cry of anguish rose from the masses at his back. Profion turned, waved a veil of smoke aside, and looked up to see the most numbing sight of his life.

The gold dragons were molten streaks against the sky. The awful din of their cries assaulted the senses of every human down below. Profion saw them turn then, one by one, only to come together again in three magnificent flights from the east, the west, and the south. One, which Profion knew was the leader now, began the attack, veering down in a breathtaking dive, a signal to the others to join the fray. Riding boldly astride this great beast's back was the Empress Savina herself.

"Good," Profion said beneath his breath. "You have the heart for it, girl. I'll give you that. Come and get me, if you can. . . ."

The dragons came on, closer, closer . . .

"Fire! Fire now!" he shouted. "Kill them! Kill them all, or you'll not live to see another day!"

The iron weapons of men clouded the skies, followed by the roar of fireballs conjured by the mages' spells. Still, the Empress and her dragons came. Fire and missiles whined past their wings, but none struck home.

Profion knew, even before the attack began, that he was

Savina's target, that her mount was shrieking down straight for him. It came as no surprise when the dragon dipped low and loosed a bellyful of fire directly where the mage stood.

Profion laughed, watching this inferno broil down from the sky. He stood his ground, refused to move an inch, even as he vanished in a roiling cloud of smoke and flame.

Mages and soldiers gasped in disbelief, rushing to see his blackened corpse. As the smoke cleared away, they gazed at one another in wonder, for the mage wasn't there.

The Empress, her mount skimming just above the roof of the magic school, eager to see this horror come to an end, drew in a breath and stared as Profion appeared in a flash of brilliant light far from the spot where the flames had engulfed him scant moments before. Their eyes met for one brief instant, then the Empress and her mount were past and out of sight.

Dragons screamed by, loosing their fearsome breaths of fire. The dazed and dwindling army fought back, hurling iron and magic at the skies.

Profion, untouched, stood alone, seeming no part of the fray at all. While flames burned soldiers all about, roasting poor brutes in armor that could no longer save them, he stood atop a hot and blackened wall, his cape, in the wind, like a bright red flame of its own.

To the mages and soldiers down below, he seemed a giant, a warrior of old, a man near a fearsome god himself.

It was well they could not see the great concern, the doubt, and the fear that burned within his heart, within his darkened soul, for he had sent forth the powers of the Rod of Savrille, he had prayed, he had cursed the distant stars, and still the help he sought had been denied. He could *feel* those awesome forces, sense them in the heavens, knew they were near, lurking out of sight.

"Why do you taunt me? Why do you laugh while my followers die? Come to me, my horrors, for I wield the rod that commands you. I demand, and you obey!"

As his words cracked like thunder, flashing across the fiery sky, he raised the Rod of Savrille once more, shouted ancient words, magic names of demons that had tortured mens' souls, and haunted their every dream for a thousand dreary years.

For an instant, a deep oppressive silence blanketed the city, a silence that struck men with fear, leaving them cold and frozen in their boots. From the north, a great wind began to howl, began to shriek through Sumdall's towers, stripping roofs bare, hurling bricks and stones, tearing ancient trees from the ground, and raising black funnels of dust that churned everything in its path.

As suddenly as it had come, the wind died and disappeared. Profion waited, drawing in a breath until it nearly exploded in his lungs. He could feel the power of the rod come to life, bathing his body in ghastly web of red . . .

Through the pall of smoke, through the foul desecration of the skies, the clouds began to pulse with a horrid crimson shade, with a dark unearthly hue. It was not a color any living man had dreamed before, yet each man who saw it knew it heralded some fierce and alien thing, something no mortal was ever meant to see. The strange color whirled, turned upon itself, twisted in alarming, impossible shapes that couldn't be, shapes that were old when the world itself began.

Not a breath stirred atop the ruined and beleaguered magic school. All eyes were on the skies, and every man saw what he'd never imagined and never hoped to see. Unnatural forms came together, unlikely colors coalesced, and the choking skies were filled with great horrors unbound.

*　*　*　*　*

Damodar had seldom felt fear, but he felt it now. Profion had summoned them, brought them out of nightmares, brought them out of myth—immense, grotesque creatures, creatures of awesome strength and size. A man without a conscience, a man with a heart as black as sin itself, Damodar now shrank from the part he'd played in this fateful event, helping a madman bring his dark dreams to life.

Dragons . . .

They were here . . .

Profion had loosed red dragons on the world.

Profion sensed the man's presence and peered at him a moment with a gleam of triumph in his eyes.

"I have done it, Damodar. No one believed that I could, even you."

"Yes, Lord, you have indeed."

But I brought the bedlam to you, Damodar thought, you didn't go and get it yourself.

"Now," Profion continued, "my day is here. My destiny fulfilled. I've brought true glory back to Izmer, glory to us all."

"So you have, sire."

You've doomed us all with your lunacy—this is what you've done. There is no glory here!

Though none dared say it, every mage there, every common man, seemed to mirror Damodar's thoughts: That Profion had used them cruelly, made them all fools who shared in his terrible crime, bartered their bodies and their souls for a horror that would surely doom them all.

CHAPTER 37

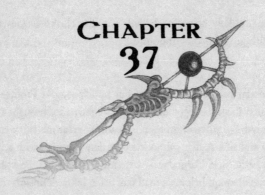

Ridley gasped for breath. For an instant, he felt as if his lungs might explode, then he fell out of nowhere, landing on his shoulder and stumbling to his feet. The world around him was afire. Men screamed and died as dragons howled above, spewing jets of choking flame.

"Marina," Ridley cried, "get down! Don't—"

He stared and gasped in dismay. His hand held empty air. Marina was gone, no longer at his side. Norda, Elwood—all of them gone! Ridley's stomach churned with cold fear. The portal had hurled him to the hellish scene of battle atop the magic school, but it had left the others behind.

Left them where, though? Some world, some star a billion lifetimes away? Or nowhere, nowhere at all . . .

Ridley ducked and threw himself aside as searing flame split the rock wall behind him and sent deadly shards through the dark, oppressive air. A Crimson Guardsman howled as a fiery missile of stone nearly sliced him in half.

Ridley blinked, looked past the hapless soldier, and saw them for an instant as the smoke whisked away: Profion and Damodar! The great mage himself and beside him, the devil who had murdered Snails, killed him and tossed him aside, kicked him off the wall without a thought, like a man tossing garbage to his dogs.

A howl of rage started low in Ridley's chest, started there and grew, rising up the scale to a screech of such fury that all who heard it turned aside, lest this madman strike them down as well.

* * * * *

The Empress Savina, garbed in golden armor and helm, was an awesome sight to see. Those who remembered this day said the Lady and her steed seemed as one, that a strange and mystic union had occurred in the Empire's bloody skies.

Indeed, who could see the young queen astride her golden beast, braving magic from her foes, and doubt they had watched a legend born? Who could forget the holy moment when she led her Golden Furies through the deadly fields of fire?

Glory ever has its time and can just as quickly fade, as it surely did that day. Savina's great fortune was a moment to remember, and it took but a moment to fade away.

The horde of red dragons that answered Profion's call shrieked down upon the golds, tore through their numbers, and scattered the smaller beasts like leaves before the wind.

Dragons collided, dragons died, and dragons fell crippled from the sky. Savina, though startled and dismayed, did not for an instant betray her noble blood. With all the courage she could muster, the scepter of her office gripped tightly in her hand, she rallied her poor depleted golds to fight again.

Profion, battling the Empress with the powerful Rod of

Savrille, laughed at the efforts of the queen he called a child, and he shouted his mighty dragons on:

"Butcher them! Kill them! Let their blood rain from the skies!"

Truly, a more savage, brutal encounter the world had never seen.

* * * * *

Profion shook his deadly talisman at the sky, calling down curses upon the Empress and her dragons screeching above. It was Damodar, therefore, who saw Ridley first—saw him, or sensed him perhaps, but he knew he was there. He stared at Ridley and threw back his head, laughing.

"Well, there's still a thief loose in Sumdall, I see. You keep turning up, and I'm getting weary of that."

"You're looking better," Ridley said. "I told you to see someone about your face."

Damodar teased him with the point of his blade, a habit that irritated Ridley no end.

"You'd best admire me quickly. You don't have a lot of time. I think I'll have more fun with you than I did with your late lamented friend."

Damodar's words were meant to taunt Ridley, to blind him with a rage that would let the mage quickly run him through. Instead, the barb had the opposite effect. Ridley's anger vanished, and cold, unwavering reason took its place. The mage read this in his foe's eyes, in the stiffening of his features. He would have to dispatch this foe at once, or the fellow would surely do the same to him.

Ridley came at the mage, slashing out with calm, effective

blows. Damodar parried his attacks, but Ridley refused to give an inch. Dragons red and gold howled overhead. Gouts of fiery breath struck the frenzied armies on each side below.

Damodar rushed with a burst of savage strength that nearly drove the thief to his knees, but Ridley struck back with a will. He no longer saw the mage as a foe, as the man who'd cruelly slaughtered his friend. He was merely an object now, a thing, a slab of meat and bone, a gross irritation that stood in his way and kept him from Profion.

Damodar knew he was better than this unschooled lout from Oldtown. He knew, as well, that there was nothing more deadly than a man obsessed, and this, surely, was what he was facing now.

"I'm sick of you," he said, the tip of his sword ripping a patch off Ridley's vest. "I find it demeaning to fight a man who lacks all noble blood."

"How do I know *your* blood's noble, mage? I think I'll have to see it first."

Damodar laughed. "I can tell you it's a rich and hearty shade of blue, but you'll not live to see a precious drop, my little thief!"

"Oh? We'll see if I—*don't!*"

Ridley plunged quickly past the mage's defense, a point he'd carelessly left unguarded for a second and a half, a path that led directly to the pale patch of flesh between his helmet and the mail across his chest.

The mage moved, stepped aside so quickly that Ridley knew, too late, he'd walked into a clever trap. The mage struck him on the side of his head, hit him with the flat of his blade, a blow that nearly knocked him senseless, taking his sight away and sending him reeling back.

Ridley struggled to keep his balance. His knees gave way, and he tumbled hopelessly to the ground. His heart pounded hard against his chest. All he wanted to do was retch. He shook his head to get his sight back and slashed out blindly to keep the mage away.

"You're absolutely pathetic, thief, too ridiculous to kill."

Ridley drew a ragged breath. He could see the man now—not just one of him, but three. He blinked, rolled, and came to his knees. Better. Only two Damodars now. The idea was to work it down to one.

"Stop crawling about," Damodar said. "You're annoying me now. Let's get it over with, boy."

Damodar swung his blade with both hands. Ridley cried out, using every bit of strength he had left. He raised his sword, lifted it to meet the mage's blow, and knew in his heart that it was over, finished and done, that he truly had nothing left to give.

He was certain, for an instant, that he saw Marina's face, a vision remembered from a night in the great elven tree. The lovely phantom vanished as quickly as she'd come, and there was no one there but Damodar.

CHAPTER 38

F ar above in the dark embattled skies, the young Empress
stared in terror at the great red dragon looming up behind.
She still could not believe the crimson beasts were so monstrous,
so immense. These ferocious creatures of myth made her gold
dragons look like angry sparrows snapping at an eagle's tail.

From the moment the reds appeared, one thought had held
sway in her mind, a thought she couldn't seem to sweep away—
that she and all her ladies in waiting would scarcely have made a
meal for just one of these beasts. Still, there was nothing to do
but fight on, fight and surely die.

She could almost feel the hot, sickening breath of the creature
that intended to bring her mount down. His scales had a moist,
unhealthy look, as if they were caked in iridescent slime. His great
jaws were open, like a portal into the underworld itself. A veil of
dark smoke dragged at the corners of his mouth, streaming from
his hideous nose. His enormous wings swept the strongest wind
aside, and his talons were as long as a soldier's iron lance.

How many ways to die! Crushed between those teeth! Roasted by its breath! Father, Father, I hope the gods don't let you see me now. . . !

The Empress turned away from the monster at her back. She swore at herself in one of the three foul words she knew.

She could feel the red's leather wings slapping the smoky air. If she dared look back, she knew she would see the beast's swollen belly heave, see its ugly nostrils flare, see the first spout of deadly fire. . . .

"No, not this time," she said aloud. "I'm not ready to be your supper now."

Raising her scepter, she waved it in a perfect circle above her head. Almost at once, her gold dragon shrieked, swept into a high, punishing loop, and Savina gasped at a world suddenly up instead of down. The red's fiery blast came so close that she could feel its heat upon her skin, smell it singe her hair.

"All right," she shouted, "our turn now!"

Her dragon came out of the loop so quickly that Savina, for an instant, felt as if she weighed hardly anything at all.

"He's yours! He's yours! Take him now, my friend!"

The red, suddenly ahead and below, tried frantically to veer and break away. Half a second later, it found itself engulfed in a shroud of deadly fire. It screamed and began to tumble, its wings tucked tight against its sides. For a moment, Savina watched it plummet to the earth, then she abruptly turned away.

"Yes," she whispered, tapping the scepter lightly against the dragon's neck. "Hurry to the others. They badly need us there."

One quick glance at the choking skies told her what she dreaded, told her what she knew: That the heavens were nearly empty of her golds, that she could count precious few.

CHAPTER 39

Old warriors over cups of sour ale said a man's whole life passed before him in the instant that he died. Ridley was certain they were liars, for he saw nothing at all except the blur of a great, enormous blade intent on slicing off his head.

One thought, and one alone flashed through his head: What an awful thing to happen. I would rather do most anything than this.

Then, with an awesome sound that cut through the din of battle, Damodar's blade struck the elven sword and cracked, splintered, and shattered like shards of broken glass. The mage backed away, stunned, but scarcely more so than his opponent. Ridley stared at his sword, the gift of Hallvarth, and saw it at once for the wonder that it was, a blade that shamed the gross metal of iron, a shimmering silver thing entwined with thick and twisted vines, with the lush green tendrils of the great Tree of Life.

"Elven magic, is it?" Damodar's features curled in disgust. "You've tainted yourself with forest trash."

"And you, sir, seem to have lost your sword."

Ridley was on his feet in an instant, lashing at the mage with bloody intent.

"Hold, boy!" Damodar stepped back and spread his empty hands. "Damn you, I'm unarmed!"

"You're the gentleman, remember? I'm the common lout."

Damodar cursed, and raised a heavy gauntlet to block Ridley's blow. Ridley's blade rang again and again on the mailed and armored gloves. The mage stepped aside and made a peculiar motion with his wrists. At once, three hooked iron blades whirred into place on each hand.

"Try these," Damodar grinned. "You'll need more than an elven spell."

Ridley drew a ragged breath. Though he held the sword of Hallvarth, his arms were the arms of a man, and his strength was waning fast. He'd seen these wicked blades before, the day of Snails's death, and he knew the horror they could bring.

Damodar caught his foe's hesitation at once, knew Ridley was tiring, and knew that a mage had staying power denied to ordinary men.

"Almost over, thief. Merely hold, and I can put a blessed end to this and send you quickly to your friend."

The mage sprang at Ridley in a fury of motion, his bladed hands moving in a blur.

Ridley stepped back, his lungs afire. His body had turned to lead, and this arrogant brute was fresh as a new spring flower.

He slid along the battlement, fending the mage off. Something felt different at his back. Metal, now, not stone—a railing on the edge of the building itself. He didn't dare look, but he sensed there was nothing down below.

Damodar lashed out with both hands. A blade stung Ridley's

cheek. He stepped away from the blow. Metal shrieked, and Ridley felt the railing shudder, give way, saw the sudden smile of triumph on Damodar's face as he lashed out for a killing blow.

Ridley let it come, stepped into the deadly fist, and moved deftly aside as the gauntlet brushed his cheek. He leaped then, leaped toward nothing at all, slammed his boots against the shaky rail, felt it give, felt it shudder, and caught a single glimpse at the street far below. Kicking one foot into empty space, he twisted and saw the startled look on Damodar's face as he turned to face his foe.

Ridley's blade sliced through the silver mail, through the mage's chest, cleanly to the hilt. Damodar tried to speak. A pale red froth bubbled at the corner of his mouth.

"Help me, thief. I can . . . be of great help to you!"

"Ask Snails."

"Wh— Who?"

"See, I knew you'd forget."

Ridley lashed out at Damodar with his boot. The railing shrieked and gave way. The mage loosed a ragged cry and flailed his arms. Ridley watched him fall. He turned, looked up, and saw red and gold dragons lurching crazily through the thick veil of smoke above. Flames lashed the top of the magic school. Warriors scattered and shook their weapons at the sky.

A howl went up to Ridley's right. He turned, saw a horde of Crimson Guards, heard the clash of arms, a scream, and then a more familiar sound: the terrible ring of a mighty axe crushing an iron helm, slicing through armor like a knife through fresh bread.

Ridley laughed aloud. It couldn't be anyone but Elwood Gutworthy, wreaking havoc to every living creature in sight.

Ridley wanted to shout, but he knew his voice would never be heard above the din.

If Elwood made it somehow, then Marina and Norda were here as well. They had to be! And they would stay close to Elwood if they could.

Ridley climbed atop a fallen battlement to get a better look. The rooftop was half obscured in a yellow, poisonous veil of choking fumes. He searched the chaos below but couldn't spot his friends. It was clear the tide had turned for the worse since his fight with Damodar. The gold dragons were now reduced to a pitiful few. With the stronger, larger reds in control, Profion's forces had turned their attention from the skies to another foe: the green-clad troops still loyal to the Empress, who had joined the field, pouring onto the rooftop and throwing themselves into the fray.

It was clear from Ridley's perch that the Empress's soldiers were badly outnumbered but fought with a fury born of dedication to their cause.

Straining to see through the sulfurous air, he saw, beyond the green and crimson hordes, the great mage himself, sweeping the Rod of Savrille across the bloody sky.

Ridley watched him for a moment then quickly turned away. Profion was wrapped in a spell, an aura of red that made Ridley queasy and burned like acid in his eyes.

Climbing off the heights, he sprinted along the crumbling battlement, keeping as low as he could to avoid the swarms of the Crimson Brigade. He could her the dwarf's roar, the ring of his axe, the screams of pain when his weapon brought another victim to the ground.

Dodging from one bit of cover to the next, Ridley ran smack into a crimson-clad ugly, knocking them both to the ground. Scrambling to his feet, Ridley hefted his sword, but the trooper was faster still. His blade came down in a blur, straight for Ridley's chest. Ridley rolled away, and his foe's weapon sparked stone where he'd been.

"Now, what are you hiding under that lovely snout?" Ridley said, warding off another blow. "Might be the handsomest man in your squad, and we'll never get to know."

"You get to be dead's what you get!"

"Is that all you people think about? Don't you have a hobby or something? You like to play cards?"

The soldier's curse was lost behind his heavy helm. He came in low, slicing the air above Ridley's knees. He was a big man, broad in the shoulders, broad in the neck—broad, Ridley decided, nearly everywhere else—a man very possibly descended from a tree. His attack seemed confined to those areas from the waist down. This made Ridley very nervous, and he wished the brute would stop.

"Up here!" Ridley said. "I've got other parts, you know."

The soldier answered with a vicious swipe at Ridley's knees. Ridley faked to the right and slashed in from the left. The soldier roared, startled, and found himself backed against a wall.

"Mardo! Sidus! To me!"

"Hey!" Ridley said. "It's already crowded in here."

He saw the man's eyes shift beneath the iron mask, risked a quick look to the left, and saw the ugly's companions bearing down fast.

"Great. Now I'm getting irritated, friend."

Ridley came in low, borrowing the fellow's tricks and slashing at armored legs thick as stumps. His enemy tried to dance away. Ridley's blade caught him on his unprotected ankle, and he rushed in to slam his boot hard on the warrior's foot.

The soldier cried out. Ridley didn't have time to watch him fall. The new pair were on him, blades whipping in from both sides. Ridley parried the first, driving him back, then quickly leaped away.

"Who's Mardo and who's Sidus? You look the same to me."

"Huh?" The second man looked startled. Ridley rushed in and struck his armored face with the flat of his blade. The man staggered back, dizzy from the bells that were ringing in his head. Ridley ducked as he felt the other soldier's weapon whistle past his head. The man held his hilt in both hands, winding up for another blow.

"Huuulf!"

The soldier went rigid, dropped like a stone. Ridley stared, then turned and laughed aloud. Marina stood there with a foolish grin, a wicked looking club grasped in her hand. She came to him, falling into his arms.

"Great gods, what happened to you? I thought you were lost!"

"We were just a bit late," Marina said soberly. "Magic isn't perfect, you know. You don't always go where or *when* you want to be."

"I'll try to remember that," he said.

"Please do."

"I'm very glad to see you," Ridley said.

"And I'm . . . quite pleased to see you."

"You've got a little soot on your nose."

"You've got a lot."

"And I'm going to be the only one standing here alive," said a familiar voice at his back, "if you two don't stop doing that."

Ridley reluctantly freed himself and grinned. "I'd be willing to hug an elf. Are you people into that?"

Norda nocked an arrow into her bow. "Not with humans, no." She raised one hand to her chin and gave him a curious look. "What happened? Something happened to you, but I can't tell what."

"I've been busy. There's a war on, you know."

"Yes, I do, but—" Norda's eyes went wide. "Damodar! It's Damodar, isn't it?"

"What?" Marina looked confused.

"We had a little quarrel. Well, a big quarrel, I guess. I won, he lost."

Marina's mouth dropped open. "You— Are you all right? Ridley—"

"He's all right," Norda said, looking at him in a way she had never quite looked at him before. "If you're going after Profion, my friend, you're going to need some help."

Ridley didn't waste time asking just how she knew that.

"I'm going to need more than I've got," he admitted. "If we could pull Elwood away from his friends . . ."

"Oh, I can do that."

Ridley and Marina exchanged a look. Norda couldn't see Elwood from where she stood, but she didn't seem concerned about that. An arrow left her bow, sailed in a high, silent arc, then dropped out of sight.

Ridley heard a great bellow, a string of dwarf curses, another bellow and a roar.

Marina looked appalled. "You *shot* him, Norda?"

"Of course I didn't shoot him. I got his attention is all."

Ridley turned as a shout, a scream, half a dozen shrieks, and a yell erupted from the crimson-clad troops. An instant later, Elwood emerged from the rapidly dwindling crowd, swinging his great axe through the air.

"I should've known!" the dwarf raged, turning his bloodshot eyes on Norda. "My old daddy, Black Hackwater, told me once if he tol' me a thousand times, don't *ever* turn your back on an elf. You do, and you'll live to regret it, only more'n likely you *won't.*"

"My father told me the very same thing about dwarves," Norda said.

"Huh! Look at that," Elwood said, holding up his axe. "If

your arrow hadn't struck the haft, it'd be stuck in *me.*"

"If I'd aimed at you, dwarf, we wouldn't be having this conversation."

"All right, enough," Ridley said. "We'd better shut up and get out of here. Those louts have got their hands full with the Empress's troops, but that isn't going to last long, not if those red monsters keep setting everybody on fire."

Marina gave him a hard, penetrating glance. He'd seen that challenge in her eyes before.

"We are not going to lose, Ridley. We simply can't, all right?"

"All right, then we won't."

"I agree," Norda said.

"I got nothing else to do," Elwood said, "except I'd like to find lunch somewhere."

"Hang around," Ridley said, "and lunch'll find you."

It seemed, for a moment, that indeed the crimson uglies had turned away, their harsh cries of victory a terrible din as they rushed to finish the Empress's harried men. Then, as if the mage himself had sensed the thoughts of Ridley and his friends, a horde of soldiers in armor and garish red appeared to block the way.

Ridley's heart sank. There were too many of them, no way to stop them all. His sword was too heavy, his hands so numb he could scarcely grasp the hilt.

"We can," Marina whispered. "We can."

"We can surely try," Norda said.

"What we can do is stand and die," Elwood said.

Ridley didn't answer. He drew a ragged breath of the thick and choking air, looked at Marina, and decided he would very much miss that lovely mouth and those river-blue eyes.

Here we go, Snails. Let's do it, friend.

CHAPTER 40

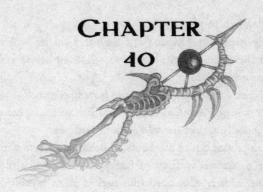

One was all right. Two, Ridley didn't mind. Three, four, five at a time . . . that didn't seem fair.

Clearly, the crimson uglies didn't care. They came in swinging, iron blades flashing, a wall of red armor, hard-bossed leather, breastplates, helms, and brazen shields.

Ridley took the left, Elwood the right. Norda stood behind the pair, her bow dropping foes on either side. If a soldier got careless and tried to come in from behind, Marina downed them with her club.

Ridley was no longer aware of the dying, of the smell of blood. It seemed as if he wasn't even there, as if some mare of the night had snatched him up and cast him down into a dreadful afterlife.

There was always a face there before him—a hideous smile and merciless eyes, always there, always past the next man in line, a tall and powerful mage with a scarlet cape that billowed in his wake, that alien instrument clutched in his metal-gloved hand, drawing red death from the skies. . . .

"Ridley, lad! To your left!"

Ridley turned at Elwood's cry, slashed a soldier across his armored chest and brought him down—but not before a blade sliced down his thigh.

"Stop that!" Marina shouted. "You leave him alone!"

With that, she knocked Ridley's assailant senseless, her club ringing soundly against the soldier's iron-clad head.

A man jabbed a pike at Elwood and earned an arrow in the eye. The dwarf was in front of Ridley now, clearing a bloody path. The soldiers who faced him backed away, making little effort to bring him down. They had joined the Crimson Brigade to kill tamer foes, not sawed-off madmen like this.

Ridley heard her scream. He turned, saw her, and his belly tightened up. A lion-helmed soldier had Marina and was tugging her by the hair, dragging her off toward the building's edge. Norda was down on her hands and knees, clutching her bow in her hand.

"Get to the lass!" Elwood bellowed. "I'll keep 'em here!"

Ridley wasted an agonizing moment till the dwarf backed up and Norda was safely in his care.

When he looked at Marina, his heart nearly stopped. There were three of them now, two covering the man who had her. A dagger was in the lion-helmed man's hand, pressed against her heart. Ridley met the first one, felt the heavy blade meet his own, drove him quickly back, let the other come, and cut him in the shins.

The man went down, cursing Ridley and grabbing at his legs. Ridley moved, half a second late. The second man's blade painted a bloody line across his arm from elbow to wrist. Ridley dropped his sword and staggered back to retrieve it with his other hand. The soldier laughed, raised his blade, and brought it swiftly down at Ridley's head—

The swordsman stopped, loosed a frightful howl, and Ridley stared as an arrow pierced the warrior's brow.

Marina's captor had a second and a half to stand and gawk, the color draining from his face. He dropped the dagger, tossed Marina from him, turned, and ran. The arrow caught him in the bare, unprotected spot between his throat and his chin.

Ridley glanced back at Norda. She was on her knees now. She waved her bow and showed him a weary smile.

Ridley clutched his bleeding arm and stumbled to Marina's side. The wound in his thigh hadn't bothered him before, but it burned like fire now.

"Are you all right," Marina asked. "Are you badly hurt?"

Ridley forced a painful grin. "You're always asking me that. No, I think I'm just fine. How about you?"

"Absolutely scared out of my wits."

"To him now," Ridley said. "Profion. That's what I came for. I'm not finished here yet."

"But you can't. You're hurt."

"Everybody up here's hurt or dead, Marina. Elwood, over here!"

The dwarf was backing toward him, Norda slung limply over his shoulder. A pair of uglies watched him but decided they wanted to make it through the day. Sheathing their swords, they turned and ran.

"Norda—is she all right?" Marina bent down anxiously over her friend. Elwood had let her down easily behind a rubble wall, out of sight of soldiers fighting the Empress's gallant men.

"I figured an elf'd be light as a butterfly. This one's a whole lot heavier than you'd think."

"I am not." Norda opened her eyes and smiled at the dwarf.

"Thank you, Elwood. That was a very brave thing to do."

"It was, truly," Marina said.

"Just don't tell anybody I was carryin' an elf around. If my friends was to ever find out . . ."

"Your secret's safe with me." Norda sat up, her keen senses tuned to the chaos just beyond the wall. "We're losing, I'm afraid. It's not going well."

Marina squinted at the sky. "The Empress is still alive," she said. "As long as she's here, there's hope, Norda."

Norda glanced past her at the sight far above. The sky was alive with red dragons. There were few golds left at all, and the Empress was nowhere in sight. Norda looked back at Marina, then turned to Ridley again.

"There's time," Norda said. "It's not over yet."

"*Elf* time, maybe," Elwood said. "Dwarves don't live forever, you know. We can't squat and chant up in a tree."

"It wouldn't hurt you to try."

"All right," Ridley said, "cut it. We don't have time for a lot of talk."

For the moment, he decided, they were nearly out of sight behind the scattered rubble. He spotted Profion on the far edge of the roof, surrounded by crimson uniforms, shouting and waving his magic rod about.

The rod, Ridley thought, the one that snake-face lackey of yours stole from me. If there's anything I can't stand, it's a thief without a speck of honor, a plain amateur with no respect for his craft at all.

"There's not much happening on the east side of the roof," he told the others. "If I can get close to the battlements there, I think I can get to Profion before those red-clad louts know I'm there."

"You and what army?" Elwood looked pained. "What am I supposed to do, while you're out playing hero, friend?"

"I thought perhaps you'd distract them for a while."

"Uh-huh? Doin' what?"

"What dwarves do. You know, sort of run amok."

"Act like I'm crazy? Scream and rush about? Maybe foam a little at the mouth?"

"You've got it."

"All right." Elwood gave a feral smile. "I can handle that."

"Good. I knew I could count on you."

Norda nocked an arrow in her bow. "I'll do some real damage while Elwood gives himself a stroke."

The dwarf's smile turned nasty. "Why don't the rest of us sit back and wait, lest we get in your way?"

Ridley risked a look over the top of the rubble. "Marina, you have a couple of spells left in that pretty bracelet of yours?"

"It's not a bracelet, Ridley. I've told you that before. A bracelet is ornamental jewelry. This is an accumulator. It gathers power from the infinite source."

"And where might that be?"

Marina sniffed. "That's a really foolish question. Where do you think it might be?"

"You're the magician. You tell me."

"If you folks are done," Elwood said, "I'll start runnin' amok. It takes a while to get all worked up."

"All right. What I'd like you to do is—"

Ridley's words were lost as the dwarf filled his lungs and loosed a ragged war cry that shook the stone beneath them. His face turned an apoplectic red, his gaudy horned helmet trembled on his head. Ridley ducked as the sawed-off warrior swung his axe in a wide, killing arc, leaped atop the rubble, and raced like a madman toward the fray.

Ridley let out a breath. "I didn't tell him about my plan."

"He's a dwarf," Norda said. "A dwarf won't listen to a plan. It muddles their heads."

"Yeah, well . . ." Ridley drew his weapon and ran his finger across the blade. He was amazed to find the elven blade was no more dulled from use than if it had never met steel.

"Spread out," he said, "and follow me."

"Great plan," Marina said. "Sorry the dwarf missed that."

CHAPTER 41

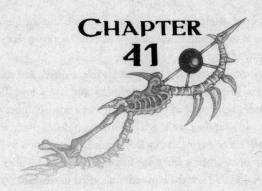

Ridley had little time to curse Elwood. The dwarf's berserker charge was anything but a distraction. Instead, it drew crimson uglies like flies to dead meat. Everyone in armor with a snout or a muzzle on their helm rushed in to hack Elwood down, and, since the dwarf had run directly *toward* the big battlement instead of the other way, Ridley and the others were right in the thick of it again.

"Thanks a lot!" he shouted, slashing his way through two husky soldiers with faces like rabid iron pigs. "Just what I needed!"

"You're as welcome as you can be!" Elwood yelled back, certain Ridley was tossing a compliment. "Any time, friend!"

For a moment, Ridley could see the blur of Elwood's axe as he cut down defenders like a scythe through a field of bloody wheat. Then, Crimson Brigade uglies cut him off, and he fought to stay alive.

One man down, then another after that. The third, a man twice as big as the other two, came a hair from separating Ridley from his head. Ridley stumbled, caught himself, and the big warrior came at him again. It was clear he had the energy to slash and hack about all day.

Ridley took the flat of a blade on his hilt, twisted, and turned it away. His foe stepped aside, feinted high, and struck low. Ridley sucked in his belly, stepped back, and fell over enemy number two.

He could hear the man laugh beneath his hideous mask. Bracing himself on one arm, Ridley lashed out in desperation to keep the fellow off, but the soldier was still on his feet, and Ridley was on the ground. He saw the blow coming, tried to scoot away, and knew he didn't have a chance. The blade was a blur coming right at his face, and he could see the pale eyes of his foe behind the iron mask.

The first arrow struck the man directly in his ear, the barb going through the thick armor and out the other side. The soldier turned drunkenly, the blade still clutched in his hand. The second arrow found its mark in his throat, the third in his heart. Ridley could have sworn that all three arrows arrived at once.

Ridley rolled and came up on his feet. A pair of warriors spotted him at once. Before the two could blink, each wore an arrow through the eye. Ridley couldn't see the elf through the raging crowd, but he knew she was there. None but an elven arrow could pierce a steel helm as if it were a paper hat. From the corner of his eye, he caught a brief flash of green light, and he knew Marina's accumulator was taking an enemy down.

Ridley hacked and slashed his way forward, each downed warrior bringing him closer to Profion. A soldier fell before his blade. Another cried out, grabbed his arm, and staggered away.

He felt as if he were not in his body anymore, that he was watching from somewhere safe and apart, away from the blood

and the chaos and the pain, away from the men with iron blades
and cruel helms.

After a while, he no longer saw the crimson-clad warriors as
men, but only as phantoms that stood in his way, creatures that
kept him from his goal.

Red dragons screamed overhead, rival armies clashed on every
side, brave men and cowards met and died . . .

And, of a sudden, there the mage stood, a madman driven by
his pride—Profion, looming bigger than life, casting ancient
spells, raving at the sky.

Armored men blocked his path, but Ridley slashed through
them, sent them fleeing, sent the dying to the ground—another,
and another after that, until not one stood in his way.

Ridley could scarcely see—every breath was a blade that
pierced his lungs, every step the last that he could bear. He leaped
a burning catapult, stumbled, fell, and stared in a dead man's
eyes. Ridley picked himself up and threw himself at the vague,
indistinct figure, the shadow-black creature framed against the
greater dark.

"You can run, your ladyship," Profion was shouting to the
skies, "but you'll never run far enough from me!"

His great, hollow voice seemed to shake the very earth itself.
He raised the great Rod of Savrille and swept it across the thick-
ened clouds above.

"Let the gold dragons die! Let their blood rain from the sky!"

In that instant, Ridley came in low, thrust his shoulder into
the seer and drove him to the ground, reaching for the rod
clutched tightly in the mage's hand. Profion shouted in pain and
surprise. The mage glared at his foe, swept him roughly aside,
and knocked the weapon from his grasp. Ridley drew a painful

breath, came to his feet, and searched for his sword, which had vanished.

Profion rose quickly, swinging his staff about. He stared in disbelief then threw back his head and laughed.

"By all the dark gods, I'm sick to death of common trash. Your presence is offensive to me, boy. You'll pay dearly for that!"

Ridley struggled to find his weapon, tried to wipe the sweat from his eyes. "You don't know how—" he gasped, struggling for breath— "how mean we commoners can be . . . once you get us . . . stirred up."

"Really?" Profion raised a brow. "Are you truly so deluded to think you can take what is mine, steal what the Fates have destined for me? I've got a new destiny for you, thief, a destiny full of pain and new senses to feel it with!"

"Not if I . . . not if I kill you first, mage."

"And how do you even *imagine* you might accomplish that?"

"Same question snake-face asked. Come and find out."

For an instant, Profion looked surprised, then he laughed aloud and came at Ridley in a blur, in a motion so swift Ridley was sure there was magic as well as power behind the mage's charge.

"This will be a real pleasure," Profion whispered as he slashed relentlessly at Ridley, driving him back with every thrust.

Ridley stumbled away, searching for his sword. His strength was draining quickly. Without a weapon, there was little he could do. All the mage had to do was take a step or two and finish him off.

"Let it be," Profion said, easily reading his thoughts. "Simply let it be, boy. That's your fate. You surely know it now."

Ridley didn't answer. Backing against the edge of the battlement, he stumbled over a dead warrior and stepped quickly aside to keep his balance. Something rang out against his boot. Without looking down, he bent quickly and clasped his hand around the hilt of the dead soldier's sword.

"You must have gotten the wrong message," Ridley said, grinning at the mage. "It looks as if Fate's not finished with me, friend."

The mage laughed, clenched his metal-clad fists, and spat out a harsh and deadly spell. A stout wooden staff appeared in midair. Profion seized it and shook it in Ridley's face.

"I don't have time for this, thief. This ends now."

Ridley came at him, but Profion easily deflected the blow with his staff. Ridley stepped back, slashing desperately at the swiftly moving foe. As if he were fighting a child, the mage swung his staff in a wide arc and lifted the blade from Ridley's hand.

Ridley stumbled back. The blows didn't stop. Profion struck him soundly, again and again. Ridley cried out, held up his arm to ward the blows away, felt his arm crack and hand go numb as he fell to the ground.

Profion tossed the staff aside. Now, he clutched only the deadly Rod of Savrille. He stalked toward his downed foe, looked up, and laughed at the skies. Directly overhead, two giant red dragons pounced on a smaller, golden beast, tore it to shreds with their talons, and sent it tumbling to the ground. Now, Profion saw, there were few of the Empress's dragons left, only a pitiful few, and their death shrieks filled the air even as he watched.

Ridley tried to stand, tried to drag himself to his knees.

"Don't bother," Profion told him. "It's too late, thief. But don't think I haven't enjoyed our little chat. It's time for you to leave, but I do want you to enjoy a little pain before you die."

Profion aimed a gloved finger at his downed foe, and Ridley cried out. Blue sparks danced on his chest. He doubled up and screamed as his skin began to bubble and burn.

"You should last a while," Profion said quietly. "Long enough to remember me well."

The mage looked away, as if some small and insignificant creature had disturbed his afternoon.

Ridley could scarcely see. Profion was distant and indistinct. The pain was more than he could bear, like white fire burning inside. He knew, now, what Profion had done. The mage had wrenched him out of time. It didn't matter now how long his death took, it would go on forever in his mind.

"I see you understand your punishment, boy. I'm very pleased. The eternal death spell is a favorite of mine. It scarcely lasts forever—but what's the difference if it feels that way?"

Profion paused then smiled. "You did a great favor to me, boy, in killing Damodar. What a clever lad you are! If you cared to live, I might let you take his place." Profion bent down close to Ridley's face. "There. See what a glorious life you could live."

Lightning flashed, and Ridley saw who he was, who he could be . . . A mage in a glorious robe of red and blue, a garment heavy with precious jewels, a beautiful sword at his side. Everything was his. Nothing would be denied.

He glanced down then, and saw himself in a pool of clear water. His body was misshapen, hideously deformed. His face was studded with warts and open sores. The image changed again, and his features belonged to a swine, an ugly, snouted creature covered with bristles and filth.

"Choose," Profion said. "Choose what you wish to be. I'll even be generous. I'll give you the girl as your personal toy." The terrible image vanished. At once, Ridley was back within his true self, the pain so intense he couldn't scream out. "I take it that's a no? I'm not awfully surprised. Oh, and I never keep my promises, you know. Now die, and suffer as well. I'm sending you where pain was born!"

Ridley drew in a breath—knowing, for certain, it was his last.

Profion began to chant. His hands came together and stabbed at Ridley like a knife. The mage's shadow seemed to grow, as if he might blot out the sky. He pointed at Ridley, again and again. Each time, the pain arched his back and lifted him off the ground.

"That's the beginning!" Profion shouted. "That's the *start*, boy! That's—!"

"Huh?" Profion blinked, staggered back, as pain struck the side of his head. The Rod of Savrille dropped from his hand and rattled across the stone floor. The mage turned, staring in disbelief. A young girl stood in his path, clutching the staff he had cast aside. Profion shook his head in disgust and shoved Marina roughly to the floor.

An unearthly howl shook the air. Elwood came at Profion, leaping over Marina, his great axe whirling in a deadly arc overhead.

Profion laughed, flicked his wrist, and froze the dwarf in his tracks. Elwood's eyes went wide. Profion circled two fingers in the air, and the dwarf went tumbling across the floor.

"It is not finished, mage. You have much to pay for, in the this world and the next."

Profion turned, surprised for an instant at the sight of the elven archer standing before him with an arrow nocked in her bow.

"Ah, well, my little elven tracker. And what would you be up to now? Wait, let me guess—"

The arrow left Norda's bow, streaking in a blur toward the mage's chest. A bare inch away it stopped, quivered an instant, then clattered to the ground. Profion merely nodded at Norda. The elf gasped and fell to her knees.

"Enough then, all of you? Is everyone finished with their pitiful efforts to steal destiny from my hands?"

"I don't think so," Ridley said. "Not yet, Profion."

Profion turned. For an instant, he stared at Ridley, standing before him with the Rod of Savrille in his hand. He threw back his head and loosed a great burst of laughter.

"Oh, come now! Do you really think you could *use* that, my little burglar?"

"It's in my hand, mage. Have you noticed?"

"Ridley—"

"The girl wants to tell you that thing is useless to you. It wasn't meant for your sort."

"And it was made for yours? I can't believe that, mage. I don't believe that at all."

Ridley turned his gaze to the skies. He felt the power, felt the crackling webs of energy, the great span of blood-red stars that spread across the dark universe. The confident smile melted from Profion's face.

"No," Profion muttered. "Put it down. It doesn't belong to you!"

Far overhead, the great red dragons began to come together, circling low and bending to the rod's indomitable will. Lower they came, and lower still, their shadows now dark against the roof of the magic school.

"Impossible," Profion said. "It can't be!"

Ridley smiled, feeling the power of the great rod coursing through his body, the awesome strength and knowledge that awaited him there.

"Ridley," Norda said gently, "believe in yourself, no one else. Be what you must be."

"I can . . . I can have it all—anything, everything, for the power dwells in me."

The red dragons waited, hovering above, listening for his command.

"Ridley," Marina said. "Ridley, look at me. Look at me now."

Ridley blinked. Whatever cold and alien thing had huddled there and whispered in his head was gone, gone and left him as he'd been, as he'd ever wanted to be.

"You don't even know, do you?" he said, looking straight into the mage's eyes. "You don't control this damnable thing; that's not it's nature. *It controls you.* A wraith and a dead magician tried to tell me that. I guess I listened better than I imagined at the time." Ridley shook his head. "I don't think I'd care to be a slave to this thing, and I'm double-damned if I want to be like you."

Ridley retrieved his elven sword and gripped the Rod of Savrille firmly in his hand. He tossed the staff to the floor.

"No! You can't!"

"You can't, mage. I can."

Ridley loosed a great and joyous cry from the depth of lungs, picked up the elven sword, and smashed the rod lying at his feet.

Profion came at him in a rage. Ridley swung his blade and forced him back. Profion moaned, clawing at his face as if a sudden madness had possessed his dark soul.

"One thing more," Ridley said, "and it's done." Reaching into his tattered jacket he drew out the Dragon's Eye. Hefting it in his palm, he gave the gem one last look and hurled it into the rubble at his feet. Now, both the great instruments of power were no more than scattered shards.

"Lad, look there." Elwood pointed a stubby finger at the sky.

Ridley followed his glance. The red dragons had vanished, gone as quickly as they'd come, leaving a rumble of earth-shaking thunder in their wake. Then, out of a suddenly cloudless sky, great heads held high, scales shining like a thousand tiny suns, five gold dragons shrieked down upon the roof of the magic school. Riding the lead dragon was the Empress Savina, her battle-dress as brilliant as the dragons themselves.

The golden steed landed gently on the roof of the magic school. As the Empress slid off the beast's back, enemy warriors and loyal troopers alike bent to their knees.

Profion stared, trembling as Savina approached.

"Your Majesty," he said with a sweeping bow, suddenly adopting the role of the most humble subject in the land. "It is a pleasure to see you looking well. I hope you do not in any way feel the issues between us were personal. I assure you they were not."

"It's over, Profion. Now." The Empress's voice was as cold as glacial ice. None who heard her could mistake her meaning in any way.

"The battle, as you say," Profion said gently, "is over, Majesty. But not the war!"

A hundred men surged toward her, but the mage was too swift for them. He raised his iron-gloved hands and loosed an unearthly howl. Power welled within him, and a form born of a thousand nightmares, ghostly and pale, emerged from the mage's trembling body. Misshapen and skeletal, the spirit lashed about with its tail, striking the young empress full in the chest. Savina cried out and sank to her knees as the tail enveloped her.

Ridley and all others about him looked on in horror, frozen in the mage's powerful spell. Profion closed his eyes and raised his head to the skies. A terrible chant left his lips, and those who heard his ancient words remembered them in nightmares the rest of their lives.

The Empress struggled, all the color drained from her face. Profion's voice rose to a fever pitch. His words cut like daggers, touching every person there with their unworldly pain.

Reaching deep within herself, gathering all the strength she could find, the Empress fought the razored spell that cut, sliced, gnawed at the very fiber of her soul. Savina cried out, fighting the horror within. She tried, again and again, clutching her golden scepter till the jeweled hilt cut into her flesh.

Nothing. Her hand fell useless, rose, fell again, and with a last, hopeless effort, she struggled to bring the heavy instrument to bear, to lift it an inch, and then an inch again. . . .

Profion paused, frowning. He started his deadly chant again. Something wasn't right. Something was very wrong—

He turned swiftly, a cry of pure terror dying in his throat. There was no sky above, nothing but the bright, ruby throat, the curve of ivory teeth, the horrid maw of a gold dragon, the stench of its unearthly breath. In an instant, but surely not quickly enough, those golden jaws snapped shut. The mage's head disappeared, then his shoulders and his chest.

Some said they heard a terrible cry from the creature's gullet, while others claimed they heard nothing at all.

Dragon wings churned the air, and the beast took flight.

No one spoke as it vanished over the ruined towers of Sumdall, the charred, crumbling remains of this grand and ancient city.

Izmer's great center of wealth and power had seen many a wonder in its day, but none to equal this. Over countless cups of ale, for many years to come, there were none who would pray that such a day might ever come again.

CHAPTER 42

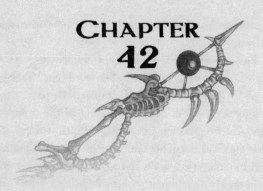

Though little time had passed, a stranger passing through the city gates would never have dreamed this Empire's great citadel had, not so many weeks ago, been a place of fear and dread, a city caught in the darker side of magic, tangled in a web of evil spells.

Along the cobbled avenues, doors stood open, and windows let in laughter from the streets. The market square was full of goods and the heady scents of spice and baking bread. Here, people greeted one another as they wandered freely about.

One saw a soldier now and then, dressed in the Empress's colors of silver and pristine white. These men wore handsome golden helms with a plume of willow green upon the crest. Gone, and gratefully forgotten, were the red-clad thugs of the Crimson Brigade. No more wolfish muzzles, no more piggish snouts.

Oldtown, once a grim and shameful blemish beneath the city's walls, its people poor and foully oppressed, had flourished under the Empress Savina's gentle rule. Even the Council of

Mages—those still left and untainted by Profion's rule—had come to terms with Savina's new and shocking belief that the least of her citizens had rights along with all the rest.

On this spring day, Sumdall City, and in the outlands of the Empire as well, every street was bright with rainbow banners, and the Empire's proud new flag: a Golden Dragon wreathed in oaken leaves, rampant on bright squares of silver and white.

In a tower high above the city, the sun slanted through high windows, brightened the Royal Hall, and shone upon the people gathered there. Cheers resounded as the Empress greeted her loyal subjects, counselors, officers, and ladies of the court. For the first time in Izmer's history, men and women were present from every guild and trade—merchants, warriors, common seamen, people of every sort, and dwarves and elves as well.

"I'm not real sure about this," Elwood said. "Dwarves don't like to be around a lot of other folk."

"A lot of people don't like to be around dwarves," Ridley said, "so it works out even, I'd say."

Elwood muttered under his breath. "See, that's what I'm talkin' about. You got to watch your back all the time, make sure no one's shovin' a frog-sticker in."

"Hush, both of you." Marina frowned, then stifled a smile. "If you two embarrass me when we meet the Empress . . ."

"What?" Ridley looked pained. "I'm surprised at you. How could you even think such a thing?"

"Yeah, that really hurts," the dwarf said.

"If they do get out of line," Norda said, "please turn them into snakes, or better still, mice. I shall look the other way."

"She's not that good," Ridley said. "She's just a student mage. She doesn't even have a robe yet."

"That's true, isn't it?" Elwood blinked in alarm. "You're not, are you? I mean, if you were, I'd like to say I've been an admirer of yours from the start—"

The dwarf nearly jumped out of his skin as a hundred golden trumpets blared at once, announcing the royal presence in the hall.

"Well, that's a couple of dozen dwarf years down the drain," Elwood said, pulling himself together again, "not that anyone cares."

"Mice," Norda said under her breath, "definitely mice."

The Empress was breathtaking in golden dress armor and golden helm. Her royal officers, ladies, and counselors stood slightly behind her and apart. Mixed among them were commoners and nobles of the realm, all in dazzling attire.

The high, clear notes of royal trumpets had scarcely died away before the High Speaker stepped forward and tapped his staff loudly, a sound that echoed off the marble floors and walls.

"Marina of Pretensa, daughter of the Ninth Level Mage, Farnoff, and Nalrid of the House of Staverid! Norda, Master Archer and Tracker to the Royal House, Eminent Maiden of the Ancient and Royal Clan of Trepidantes, The Tree of Life! Ridley Freeborn, son of Maskalades, Renowned Inventor of Mechanical Devices That Fly, and Estalena, his ever-patient and most resourceful wife! Elwood Gutworthy, Warrior First Class and Master of Arms of the Ancient and Revered Oakenshield Clan! These four will step forward and present themselves to Her Royal Highness, Savina, Empress of Izmer!"

Marina, concerned the moment before about Ridley and the dwarf, was suddenly somewhat worried about herself.

"What'll I do, what'll I say? What if she looks right at *me?*"

"Look right back," Ridley whispered. "She seems like a decent sort to me."

Marina felt the color rise to her face, for she hadn't imagined she'd spoken aloud.

The crowd that packed the Great Hall studied the small group as they approached the Empress's throne. "What a peculiar bunch," some murmured to themselves. All were finely dressed, yet somewhat simply, certainly not as grand as some.

Marina Pretensa, quite lovely in a sea-blue gown with gold piping, her brown tresses cascading about her bare shoulders, approached her Empress with a demure yet dignified smile.

The freeman, Ridley, dashing in tight-fitting black trousers, black jacket with buttons of gold, black boots, and jaunty black cap to match was straight-lipped, but his eyes glowed with a wonder and joy most often seen in children at play.

Norda, the elf, was elegant and slim in quiet shades of green that mirrored every leaf, every blade of grass, every shadow of her forest homeland. She walked with a quiet grace that spoke of something altogether otherworldly.

The dwarf, now—the dwarf was something else to see. His trousers, boots, jacket and wide leather belt were of every possible color and hue, and some that very few had seen before. His horned, fluted, ivory and gem-encrusted helmet of gold was an awesome, even frightening thing to behold.

Who were they, then, this diverse and fascinating band? And what were they doing here, standing before the Empress's throne?

"People of the Empire, I present to you the Champions of Izmer. From this day forward, they will each and all be known as Defenders of the Throne and Champions of the People, for the deeds they have done have truly earned the gratitude of us all."

The Empress paused, then raised her royal scepter high above her head. The crowd drew in a collective breath.

"I have waited long for such a day as this. Now that day is here, and I do declare that from this moment forward, each of you is equal in rights to the other, that each shall have the chance to rise to their talents, to the true and honest strength of head and heart, noble and commoner alike."

Once more, Savina hesitated, and let her gaze touch one and all.

"I, your Empress, shall be the first to abide by this declaration, for I relinquish, at my pleasure, as my heartfelt wish, this scepter, this symbol of a power I have no desire to use. If I am indeed fit to rule, then I shall rule gladly through the will of my people and not by the ruinous magic that resides in *this!*"

With that, the Empress brought her hand down with the strength, the courage, and the will that would symbolize her reign for many years to come. The rod that could bring the wrath of dragons shattered into a thousand pieces on the hard stone floor beneath her feet.

CHAPTER 43

There were few people left in the Great Hall. The Empress and her court were long gone, and most of the many invited guests. Elwood and Norda had left, with Norda's solemn promise that she would buy the dwarf a mug of ale, or possibly two.

Now why would she do that, Marina wondered, when she really cared little for dwarves, and never, ever consumed wine or beer or ale?

Marina, as well as Ridley, was quite aware—though neither would admit it to the other—that they had found some reason to linger until the others had gone. For some time, they hardly spoke at all, but only stood and watched the evening begin to dim the sky beyond the empty throne.

"You and I need to talk, I feel," Marina said, finally breaking the silence. "I think we have . . . things that we should say."

"You do?"

"Yes, I truly do."

"I think so as well."

"Really?" Marina looked up, and saw he was closer than she'd thought.

"Does that surprise you, then, to know that I would have such thoughts as well?"

"Not—truly so, no. It does not." Marina met his eyes, and gently touched a gold button on his chest. "That is a really fine-looking coat. It fits you quite well."

"Thank you. I, uh, feel that your clothing is most attractive, too."

"I don't usually dress up in such finery as this."

"I *never* do. Not until now. And never dreamed I would."

"This is a very special day."

"It is. In many ways."

"What sort of ways, Ridley? I'd like to know just what you mean."

Ridley reached out and gently took her hands. His heart beat loudly against his chest, for she made no effort to get away.

"I'm a commoner, Marina. I have done very little in my life except steal. I'd be willing, though, to try some other trade or craft. I never thought I'd say that, but I will."

"I think there are a number of things you could do quite well."

"Perhaps. Though I wonder what they'd be. I suppose I could— By the way, I want to thank you for what the Empress said about my mother and father. I know that came from you."

"Well, I thought it was certainly proper that they both be recognized."

"One thing I could do," Ridley said, "and I think I might do it well, is follow in my father's footsteps. I have some ideas for things that have never been seen before, things such as flying machines, craft that would float upon the air—"

"Ridley . . ." Marina touched a finger to his lips and came gently into his arms. "We can talk about your career at some later time. I really don't think that time is now."

"You have a very good point," Ridley agreed, drawing in the flowery scent of her hair, praying that his knees wouldn't suddenly give way. "A excellent point indeed."

He held her there, awed that such a thing could truly be, that all the things that had happened so quickly could be real, and most especially this.

As he held her, as he dreamed of tomorrows he'd never dreamed before, a shadow fell across the evening, blocking out the light from the balcony door. Ridley drew in a breath and held it, staring past Marina's shoulder, scarcely able to believe what was revealed.

The gold dragon flapped her great wings then gripped the stone rail in her strong and massive claws. Ridley knew at once it was the Empress's royal steed, for it wore Savina's banner in its fine array of dragon horns.

He knew, though, there was much more to this moment, more than simply a dragon and a man, for the dragon looked at him with her strange and alien eyes, and the thought came to Ridley's mind unbidden, as clear as if the creature had whispered in his ear. . . .

I know you, human. You and I have looked upon one another before.

"And I know you. I know you as well!"

As he spoke the words aloud, Ridley felt a great and wondrous joy in his heart, for there was no anger in the creature's thoughts, only a moment shared, only two beings met for an instant again.

Marina drew away and gave him a questioning look. "What's this now, talking to yourself? There is much I need to learn about you."

"Me? Talking to myself? Why, how could you imagine such a thing?"

He took her in his arms and held her there as the evening closed in, and there was nothing past the balcony now, nothing there at all.

CHAPTER 44

In the gray morning light, he alone stood in the silent grove, yet not truly alone at all, for he felt at that moment that his friend was truly there, not beneath the earth, cold beneath a plain stone marker he had placed upon the grave, but there in another way that he could neither fathom nor explain. No more than he could explain the wonder that had passed between himself and the golden dragon. That was real, too, he believed. A different kind of real, but real all the same.

"It's not going to be the same, Snails, not without you. You're a part of my life that's gone forever, but it's a part I'll always treasure, something I won't forget.

"You made a lot of difference in the way things worked out here. I never thought you and I would do something like that, but there's no denying it. We did.

"I wish you could see this real nice jacket I got. It's better than anything we ever stole, but you'd like it just the same.

"Well, I guess I'd better get going, or I'll miss my own knighting ceremony. 'Ridley the Savior.' Can you believe that? Don't laugh. Wherever you are."

Ridley paused, trying to think of something more. He wished he could talk to someone like Norda's friend Hallvarth again. The healer always had the right words to say.

Don't mourn for your friend, boy. Friends leave us for a while, but they always come back in another guise when we need them again.

Ridley liked the thought and was greatly surprised that such wise words would come from him. Truly, it was exactly what Snails would likely do: Show up when least expected, looking for someone to pay for lunch.

THE END

The tales that started it all…

New editions from DRAGONLANCE creators
Margaret Weis & Tracy Hickman

The great modern fantasy epic – now available in paperback!

THE ANNOTATED CHRONICLES

Margaret Weis & Tracy Hickman
return to the Chronicles,
adding notes and commentary
in this annotated edition of the
three books that began
the epic saga.

SEPTEMBER 2001

THE LEGENDS TRILOGY

Now with stunning cover art by award-winning fantasy artist Matt Stawicki,
these new versions of the beloved trilogy will be treasured for years to come.

Time of the Twins · War of the Twins · Test of the Twins

FEBRUARY 2001

The War of Souls

THE NEW EPIC SAGA FROM
MARGARET WEIS & TRACY HICKMAN

**The New York Times bestseller
—now available in paperback!**

Dragons of a Fallen Sun
The War of Souls • Volume I

Out of the tumult of a destructive
magical storm appears a mysterious
young woman, proclaiming the
coming of the One True God.
Her words and deeds erupt into
a war that will transform
the fate of Krynn.

Dragons of a Lost Star
THE WAR OF SOULS • VOLUME II

The war rages on...
A triumphant army of evil Knights
sweeps across Krynn and marches
against Silvanesti. Against the dark
tide stands a strange group of heroes:
a tortured Knight, an agonized mage,
an aging woman, and a small,
lighthearted kender in whose hands
rests the fate of all the world.

April 2001

FORGOTTEN REALMS

**COLLECT THE ADVENTURES OF
DRIZZT DO'URDEN AS WRITTEN BY**

BEST-SELLING AUTHOR

R.A. SALVATORE

**FOR THE FIRST TIME
IN ONE VOLUME!**

Legacy of the Drow
Collector's Edition

Now together in an attractive
hardcover edition, follow Drizzt's
battles against the drow through
the four-volume collection of

**THE LEGACY, STARLESS NIGHT,
SIEGE OF DARKNESS,**
and
PASSAGE TO DAWN.

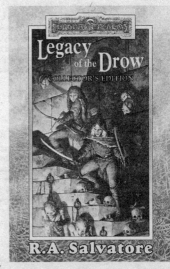

The Icewind Dale Trilogy
Collector's Edition

Read the tales that introduced
the world to Drizzt Do'Urden
in this collector's edition
containing *The Crystal Shard,
Streams of Silver,* and
The Halfling's Gem.

**NOW AVAILABLE
IN PAPERBACK!**

The Dark Elf Trilogy
Collector's Edition

Learn the story of Drizzt's
tortured beginnings in the
evil city of Menzoberranzan
in the best-selling novels *Homeland,
Exile,* and *Sojourn.*

Enter the magical world of the
DUNGEONS & DRAGONS®
setting in these novels based on
classic D&D adventures!

THE TEMPLE OF ELEMENTAL EVIL
Thomas M. Reid

Years ago, the foul Temple of Elemental Evil was cleansed of the evil that dwelled there. Or was it? The Temple has brooded in quiet decay as the seasons passed, but once again, dark forces are stirring in the land. In a quest to avenge his slain master, a tormented elven wizard must lead a band of rugged heroes into the very heart of evil itself.

May 2001

KEEP ON THE BORDERLANDS
Ru Emerson

In recent days, the Keep has been increasingly hassled by elusive bandits and vicious monsters, but the Castellan can't spare any guards to deal with the problem. An odd mix of heroes-for-hire ventures outside the Keep to deal with the troubles, but they find more than they bargained for—and maybe more than any of them can handle—when they venture into the dreaded Caves of Chaos.

September 2001

QUEEN OF THE DEMONWEB PITS
Paul Kidd

For one man, fighting in the Greyhawk Wars wasn't hell.
It was practice.

When Lolth, Demon Queen of Spiders, seeks revenge against the Justicar and his companions, it may well be the last mistake she ever makes.

November 2001